The Case of the Missing Milk Money

A Richard Sherlock Whodunit

By

Jim Stevens

ISBN: 978-1-942424-04-8

For Marian

The Richard Sherlock Whodunit Series

The Case of the Not-So-Fair Trader

The Case of Moomah's Moolah

The Case of Tiffany's Epiphany

The Case of Mr. Wonderful

The Case of the Woebegone Widow

Also by Jim Stevens:

WHUPPED

Hell No, We Won't Go,
A Novel of Peace, Love, War, and Football

And Coming Soon:

WHUPPED TOO

Certain instances in this novel are based on actual events, the remainder are totally made up.

I'm on a roll.

I've never played most of these games, but I can't seem to do anything wrong. On the roulette table, instead of playing red or black like most of the players, I put my chips on the intersection of four numbers, and in three successive spins, one of my four numbers comes up each time. Better yet, I let each bet ride, and when I do my money piles up faster than drifting snow in a Chicago blizzard. When I pull my winnings off the green felt, I have a pile of chips, which dwarfs the other players'.

At the blackjack table, I hit twenty-one three times in the first five deals. And during one hand, some guy behind me shows me how to double down, and I make two blackjacks instead of one. I'm not only rolling, I'm steamrolling. While the others at the table are getting dealt sixes, sevens, and eights, aces are coming my way like manna from heaven.

"Are you counting cards?" the lady on my left asks, obviously amazed at my good luck.

"The only cards I'm counting are those adding up to twenty-one," I tell her.

"You should do this for a living," she tells me as I beat the dealer's sixteen with a pair of queens.

"Maybe I should," I tell her. "If there is one person in the world who needs a new career, it's me."

I hit another blackjack with the next hand. Ring that jackpot bell!

I can't remember having so much fun.

The hundred bucks I paid to get into the *casino* has been the best money I've spent in years. Not only did I get two drinks, dinner, and a chance at some yearly grand prize, I got a bag of chips to play any game I want. I could care less about the tacky decorations, the cheap linoleum floor, or the dealers wearing silly visors. I'm having a blast. I realize my fellow gamblers aren't real gamblers, and are here for an entirely different reason, but if you're gambling, you're a gambler, and in this group, there's no doubt that I'm the best.

I'm winning so often, the croupier keeps exchanging my white chips for reds and my red chips for blues. They even give me a plastic tray to hold my winnings. Yes, my cup hath overflowed. I don't bother counting or figuring out what my stash may be worth. When you're on a streak like this, you got to play it out, keep it hot, and let the good times roll.

Now it's time for the big Kahuna, Mohammed to climb the mountain, and gentlemen to start their engines. I'm heading for the craps table. This is where the real gamblers play, where you win it or lose it all, where you break the bank or the bank breaks you. There's no room for the weak-kneed, half-hearted, namby-pamby, or dithering decision-maker. This is the craps table where men do, boys lose, and cowards watch. If luck is riding with you at the craps table, get ready for the ride of your life.

It's crowded. I have to squeeze in between two players, whose faces tell me they're not happy campers. The guy with the dice throws a three and the entire table explodes in painful anguish. There is a short explanation of the game posted behind the guy running the table and I take a quick read of the rules. I understand about a third of it. I watch a couple of tosses. The guy with the dice places bets on the pass line, throws a six, and adds a number of bets on the table. Others do the same. The table is filling up with chips. The guy throws an eight. "Ohh's" and "Ahh's" from the crowd. The guy throws a nine, and the tension and expectation rise. More bets go down. I'm getting the hang of it. The guy throws a six, and the people explode. The croupier stacks chips all around the winning numbers. Everyone is ecstatic, except the guy who had his money on the Don't Pass line.

It's time for me to get in the game. I put my tray of chips on the edge in front of me. Players immediately notice as I stack four piles: two blue, one red, and one white. I make sure each of my stacks is taller than any others on the table. I want everyone to know I've arrived, I'm here to play, and I'm here to win.

I can feel it. The wind is at my back, four-leaf clovers are sprouting, rabbit's feet are dancing, and lady luck in is my corner, smiling down on me like a proud mom watching her baby's first steps.

The guy who made the pass tosses again and snake eyes come up. The stick comes out and bets are swept into the house. It goes to show just how fast luck can change. The dice passes to a woman. I can tell she has no clue what's she's doing. She thinks it's funny to give the dice a quick kiss before she tosses. She rolls a two. Nobody wins. When I roll, the last thing I'd do is kiss the dice, especially during the cold and flu season.

There's only two other players before the dice are in my hands. I can't wait. I can feel it. It's gonna happen. I'm going to go all out. The guy rolls. Boxcars come up. The board is cleared. The dice pass. A three is thrown. The table is now cold as ice.

The dice comes to me. I look up to see the players imploring me with their eyes to turn up the heat. I place a stack of blues on the pass line, the biggest bet on the table. Other money goes down. People can feel my good vibes. I give the dice a few shakes and send them cascading down the table. A four. I can feel it. I double my pass line bet with another stack of blues right behind my first. Other gamblers do the same. A few guys put their money on the numbers. I give 'em a shake, toss, and the dice bounce off the back wall before coming up... a six. Cheers all around. More people gather to watch a real pro in action. They're all rooting for me. I can see it in their eyes, "Beat the house. Beat the house." I play a stack on the numbers, and an even bigger stack on the hard way four at the end of the table. A few people gasp as I make the bet. More money goes on the table. The dealer calls for "all bets down," and pushes the dice to me.

I pause, increasing the tension, give a short shake, and let the dice fly. A six! I did it again. I'm still in the game and the table is so hot now, you could fry an egg on it.

People are laughing, backs are being slapped, and high-fives go all around. This is what gambling is all about. I'm feeling unbeatable. Nothing can stop me. No one can touch the master. I'm invincible!

I'm gonna go for it. I only have to roll a four, and if I roll it the hard way, they'll have to go into their vault to get enough chips to pay me. I lay down every bet I can. I have stacks so high on the table, it looks like I'm designing skyscrapers. There must be ten people deep behind the players crowded around the edge of the table. They want to see me win as much as I want to blow the whole casino into bankruptcy. This is what it's all about. I'm in, almost every chip I have is bet somewhere on the table.

"All bets down."

I take the dice, rub them together a few times, give them one shake, and just as I am about to throw, I hear words I have come to detest more than any words in the English Language.

"Oh, Mr. Sherlock."

I stop dead in my roll.

"What are you doing here?" she asks as she wedges herself between my new fans at the edge of the table.

"Tiffany?"

"Daddy's got a case for us to investigate."

"Now?"

"Yes. We got to go."

"Can't you see I'm busy?"

"No."

The crowd is getting restless. "Come on, roll," a number of gamblers implore me.

"We gotta go."

"Forget it, Tiffany. I'm taking this one last toss, and if I win, maybe I won't have to go with you at all."

"Oh come on. Who are you kidding, Mr. Sherlock?"

"I'm serious."

"Mr. Sherlock, you know when Daddy calls, you got to drop what you're doing and hop right on top of it."

I know she's right, but I can't leave now. I got my whole life sitting on the craps table. My fate has been cast to the wind and only I can make it blow.

"Mr. Sherlock, we got to go."

No way. I rub the dice in my hands, look down the table, concentrate, and hear, "Drop 'em, Mr. Sherlock."

Instead of tossing the dice down the green felt to bounce off the back wall, come up a four, and relieve me of my wretched life, the dice fumble through my fingers and plop onto the table like a couple of spilled beans off a fork. They land as unceremoniously as a pair of shot-gunned mallards into a mucky duck blind pond.

There are three dots on one die, four on the other. Seven.

I crap out.

***

My name is Richard Sherlock. I spent nineteen years in the Chicago Police Department, sixteen as a detective. I got kicked off the force due to a very uncharacteristic temper tantrum. I took a swing at my superior's face and made a solid connection. I lost my position and my pension, and couldn't find another job. I ended up as an on-call investigator for the Richmond Insurance Company where I'm forced to investigate settlement frauds, suspected frauds, or any settlement that can be proven fraudulent.

I hate my job.

I'm also a divorced dad of two girls, twelve and fourteen going on twenty. I have a bad back, no savings, and an ex-wife who hates me. I live in a crummy one-bedroom apartment. I'm a lousy dresser, can't find a steady girlfriend, and drive a 1992 Toyota Tercel.

Am I a loser? I'm certainly one tonight.

A major portion of my job with the insurance agency is mentoring (aka babysitting) the twenty-something, spoiled heiress of the Richmond fortune, Tiffany Richmond. On the surface Tiffany is a vapid, spoiled-rotten, rich, self-centered, egotistical girl who will never experience an "I can't afford it" moment in her life. Deep down Tiffany is a vapid, spoiled-rotten, rich, self-centered, egotistical girl with a good heart. I've found in life if you have one of those, all other frailties diminish. Plus, my kids think the world of her. I suspect they like her more than they like me. I really can't blame them. I like her more than me.

***

The dice pass to the next unlucky sucker.

"Tiffany, how do you always seem to find me?"

"Oh, Mr. Sherlock, I have ways."

"Are you going to tell me what they are?"

"No."

I leave the few chips I still have on the table as a gift for the next shooter. I hope he appreciates it.

As I make my way away from the table and through the throng of people who did cheer me on, I do get a couple of slaps on the back, two "better luck next time" comments, and one melodious, "You got to know when to walk away, know when to run."

Gee thanks.

"If you want to waste all your money gambling, Mr. Sherlock, why didn't you go to a real casino?" Tiffany asks. "This place is about as tacky as a trunk show at Target."

"It's a fundraiser for Care and Kelly's school."

We pass by the stainless steel food service line where the *hot lunch* kids scoop up wilted ptomaine Romaine, veggie vittles, and the mystery meat of the day; and the *bring their own lunch* kids, like mine, buy whole, two-percent, or chocolate milk to wash down the delicacies their parents, like me, have so lovingly brown-bagged for their culinary convenience.

"Isn't it kinda dumb, Mr. Sherlock, that a school would have a fundraiser that does something that's against the law to do?" Every so often but not often enough, Tiffany does come up with a salient point.

"The next fundraiser will probably be a marijuana tasting party."

We head for the outside door.

"Tiffany, what possibly could have been so important that you had to show up tonight?"

"People are trying to rip off our insurance company, and you know how Daddy just hates that."

I know, and I know it all too well.

"Do we have to start on the case now?" I ask. "It's almost ten o'clock at night."

"A lot of my days don't start until ten o'clock at night, Mr. Sherlock."

I know that all too well, too.

"And there's no time like right now for getting a present."

I don't think she got that right.

We are just about out of the cafeteria casino when we are interrupted by a booming male voice on the school's PA System. "Richard Sherlock, please report to the principal's office."

Tiffany stops dead in her tracks and peers up at me like I'm the devil in disguise. "Did you get caught cheating, ditching classes, or wearing a skirt that doesn't hit the ground when you kneel down?" Tiffany accuses more than asks.

"No."

The PA voice repeats with a little more boom, "Richard Sherlock, please report to the principal's office immediately."

"We better get in there, Mr. Sherlock. I can't wait to see you get expelled."

CHAPTER 2

I'm not saying that I didn't spend a fair amount of time in the principal's office during my formative years, but it has been quite a while since I've made a visit. Seems a bit nostalgic, in a bad way, opening the door labeled *Principal Eldin Puddle*.

"Hi, I'm Principal Puddle. I'm sorry to take you away from the festivities," the man says, meeting us in the outer office of his office.

"That's okay, I already lost all my money." We shake hands. "This is Tiffany Richmond."

"Hello."

"Tiffany is my assistant," I explain, so Eldin doesn't get the wrong impression and put me on a list that doesn't allow me to be less than two hundred yards from the school grounds.

"What did Mr. Sherlock do?" Tiffany asks. "Was he cheating, passing notes, or get caught smoking in the bathroom?"

"No. I didn't call Mr. Sherlock for those reasons."

"So he did something worse than what I did?"

Eldin smiles. "I have a favor to ask... a favor, shall we say, of a sensitive nature."

"You want me to leave?" Tiffany asks and explains, "Because I don't do favors."

"That would be up to Mr. Sherlock," Eldin says.

"What can I do for you?" I acquiesce to his offer.

"Please come into my office."

Principal Eldin Puddle looks like a principled principal. He's about fifty-something, wears a well-worn, tweed, three-piece suit, and shoes that need a good buffing. His eyeglasses make him look distinguished and professorial. He moves slowly but with conviction. He's a big man, well over six feet, heavy in spots but not overly overweight. It's obvious the only time he spends at the gym is at his own school's gym for an assembly or sporting event. Any kid, five to fourteen, walking into his office would be intimidated by Principal Eldin Puddle.

"I understand you are a Chicago police detective?" He

phrases this more as a statement of fact than a question.

"Was."

"He got kicked off the force," Tiffany fills in for him.

"I didn't know that," Eldin says.

"He punched his boss in the face." Tiffany is a wealth of information all of a sudden. "And he did it on TV during a press conference. The clip went viral and had over a million hits the week after it happened."

"Really?"

"Yep," Tiffany acknowledges, and demonstrates the action. "Wham. Right in the kisser."

Eldin looks down at me like he's about to impose a sentence of after school detention for the rest of my life.

"That's why he works for my dad now." Tiffany just can't seem to stop talking.

"You still investigate?"

"Only when I have to," I answer.

"Is that often?"

"Way too often for my blood," I admit.

Eldin sits back in his big chair, lets his stomach relax outward, and says, "I need help."

I should verbally agree with him, but instead I say, "What can I do for you?"

"Somebody is stealing our money and I can't figure out who."

"Do you have an ex-wife?" I ask.

"No."

"I always like to start with the obvious," I explain.

Eldin shifts in his seat. "This may sound trite and a bit silly to you, but the problem is a lot bigger than I would have ever imagined."

"Where is the money being stolen from?" I ask.

"The cafeteria, I think."

"Why do you think that?" He's making an assumption and my first rule of life is never assume anything.

"It's the only place where there's cash," Eldin says. "Kids either pay for hot lunch or for their milk."

"Do they get like a nickel at a time?" Tiffany asks.

"With five hundred kids attending Pat Nixon Grammar School and another four-fifty at Ann Margaret Middle, almost all are enrolled in our Healthy Bones Project, where we offer cut-rate milk for sale. Each student pays either two dollars a week or fifty cents a day."

"In cash?" I ask.

"Quarters and small bills," he explains.

"Easy to pilfer," I say.

"Have you looked for kids who may have consistently, bulging pockets?" Tiffany asks.

"Only in passing," Eldin answers.

"Have you considered bringing the TSA in with one of their metal detectors?"

"Not yet."

"Have you seen any kids flashing a wad around or totally blinged out with a lot of fresh tattoos?" Tiffany continues.

"No."

"How much are we talking here?" I ask, wondering how much a small hand could pull out with one grip.

"Accounting is hardly my forte, but I think it's been as high as two-hundred a week."

"Missing?" I'm amazed.

"At least."

"Ouch."

"How much in total do you think is gone?" I ask.

"Fifteen hundred to two thousand," he says sheepishly.

"That's a lot of spilled milk," Tiffany says.

"I'm embarrassed even to admit this," Eldin says. "That's why I'd really appreciate you keeping this under your hats."

"We're not wearing hats," Tiffany informs him.

Eldin looks at my assistant as if she is one whom the American educational system has failed miserably.

"Tell me how the milk program works," I say to Eldin.

"Pretty simple. At the end of the cafeteria line, students can show a weekly milk pass or pay in cash."

"Who takes the money?"

"The PTA, who initiated the program at the beginning of the school year."

"Where does the money end up after lunch?"

"In a lock box in our Assistant Principal's office."

"What exactly do you want me to do?" I ask.

Tiffany answers for Eldin, "Find the crook and get him into the principal's office. Duh." She turns to Eldin. "Then you can take out a big stick and whup his butt."

"No, there will be no physical punishment administered. I just need to know who is doing the stealing and stop it." Eldin pauses. "And you should be as discreet as possible. The last thing my schools need is negative publicity."

The CPS, the Chicago Public School System, has had to endure some pretty choppy water in the past years. Due to budget cuts across the board and declining enrollment, which is due to the declining city population, a number of schools have closed or have been combined with other schools. Some schools have gone the charter route with the immediate community taking more control. And other schools have become specialty schools by upping the areas of learning of a specific subject; i.e. math, science, and arts academies. The teacher's union has not only been dead set against many of these changes but wants more money for what they do and have no problem vocalizing their opinions. Throw in the declining test scores, a frightening truancy rate, a few guns brought to school in back packs, and you have enough daily fodder for a TV News Exclusive titled, *The Continuing Crisis in our Schools*. The last thing Principal Puddle wants is to see is Pat Nixon or Ann Margaret in the latest Breaking News on WLS TV.

"You have to realize it is difficult for me to do my job without being noticed," I mention to the man.

"I know."

"Maybe you could go in undercover, Mr. Sherlock?" Tiffany suggests. "You could wear pants that hang beneath your butt crack, ride a skateboard, or tell everybody you're a foreign exchange student from Mongolia."

"I'm not sure that would work, Tiffany."

"Don't they ride skateboards in Mongolia?"

"No. Yaks."

"Oh, you could get around the yak thing by telling people you only speak Mongolian."

"Why don't we work on a Plan B?" I suggest.

"Luckily, I've never had to take one of those." Tiffany offers up too much information.

"You could possibly find some reason to be here and snoop around without letting anyone know you're snooping around?" Eldin suggests.

"Let me work on that angle."

"Could you hurry? We have only a few weeks of the school

year remaining, and I sure would like to get to the bottom of this before summer school starts," Eldin says.

"Mr. Sherlock, don't forget you have other fish to sauté," Tiffany reminds me.

"I realize that, Tiffany, and I assure you and your daddy that my work here will not compromise my Richmond duties."

"Good because I hate compromising as much as I hate favors."

Eldin rises to show us out. "Thank you very much, Mr. Sherlock. I appreciate your help."

"I'll do what I can."

"Good luck back on the tables," he says, bidding us goodbye as we head for the cafeteria casino.

"My luck pretty much ran dry before it even started to trickle," I tell him on my way out his door.

As we stroll through the locker-lined hallway, I ask Tiffany, "You know, you never told me why you needed me so soon."

"I didn't?"

"No. What's so important?"

"Oh, yeah. One guy is suing Daddy because his expensive cigars burned up in a fire, and another guy is writing too many prescriptions to cure people who have cancer."

"Aren't cigars supposed to burn and people who have cancer take a lot of drugs?" I ask.

"Maybe they do, but my daddy sure doesn't want to pay out for 'em."

We reach the cafeteria to find a break in the gaming action. All the gaming tables are empty and the crowd is on the far side of the room standing in front of the raised platform where two women are beside a cylindrical, mesh-metal roller, spinning the slips of paper contents inside, mixing it up like lottery balls before the weekly drawing.

As we skirt the crowd, I hear one of the woman on stage announce, "Hi, I'm Sue Ellen Muldoon, chairwoman of tonight's event, and this is the moment you have all been waiting for... but first, all the members of the PTA would like to thank everyone for all their support, donations, and hard work to make this year the most successful the school has ever had." There is a big round of applause. "And to pick the winner of this year's grand prize drawing is the president of our PTA, Ms. Winky Torelli."

The second of the two women on stage, Winky, steps forward. She is the antithesis of blonde and bubbly Sue Ellen Muldoon. Winky's a bit on the sour side, as if it is her money she's giving away.

There is a huge round of applause as the metal drum quits spinning. Sue Ellen opens a small hatch on the side of the container and Winky's long arm reaches inside and pulls out one slip from the thousands in the bucket. Winky eyes the name on the ticket, winces, and hands the slip to Sue Ellen.

"And the winner is... Richard Sherlock."

I stop. I freeze. I'm stunned.

"Mr. Sherlock, that must be you," Tiffany informs me, yanking on my sleeve.

"Is Richard Sherlock here?" Sue Ellen bellows into the microphone.

"Unless you have a twin, Mr. Sherlock, you won," Tiffany informs me.

"Richard Sherlock? Where are you Richard Sherlock?" Sue Ellen asks, rechecking the slip of paper in her hand.

The crowd looks every which way and finally sees me. "Here he is," a number of voices ring out.

"Well, come on down, Richard Sherlock," Mrs. Sue Ellen Muldoon shrieks like a game show emcee.

Before I realize what's happening, I find myself on the stage. President Winky is reluctantly shaking my right hand and Sue Ellen, the emcee of the event, is holding my left hand upward as if I just knocked out Muhammed Ali. I'm still pretty much in shock, but an odd odor in the air snaps me out of it like a whiff of smelling salts.

"And the amount of your jackpot, which represents ten percent of the total cash raised this school year, is...." Sue Ellen pauses to ask, "Are you ready, Mr. Sherlock?"

I don't speak. Why bother?

"Four thousand seven hundred ninety-four dollars and sixty-seven cents!"

The crowd applauds as a six-foot check, possibly borrowed from the Publisher's Clearing House, appears, and Sue Ellen writes my name with a magic marker on the payee line. She hands the pen to the PTA president, who puts her John Hancock on, and I'm back on a roll.

CHAPTER 3

"I thought you said there was a fire?"
"That's what the guy put down on his claim form."
"Well, they were awful quick to rebuild because his house sure doesn't look too charred to me."

Tiffany and I sit in her Lexus 450 on Melody Avenue, across the street from the four-bedroom, three-bath, and two-and-a-half car garage Bollingbrook home of Don Diego Fumadoro. I wonder if the half-car garage is half the car lengthwise or half the car widthwise? Plus, who would ever buy half a car to put inside?

"Did Richmond have the fire insurance policy on the house or just on some of the contents?"

"The guy's like a big collector."

"Of what?"

"He has policies on art and cigars," Tiffany tells me.

"I would think a Tiparillo and a Picasso would make for strange bedfellows."

"You'd be surprised who sleeps with who these days, Mr. Sherlock."

"Did any of the other stuff get destroyed besides the cigars?" I ask.

"He didn't claim anything else."

"And how much does he want?"

"One hundred fifty grand."

"That's some heavy duty cancer sticks," I say. "And where did the fire take place?"

"Didn't say. Outside, I'd guess."

"His outdoor grill explode?"

"Maybe."

"Drive around the block," I suggest. "Let's see if we can get a good look into his yard. Maybe there's the remains of an oak tree."

Tiffany puts the car in gear and squeals out of the spot like Jimmie Johnson at Daytona. So much for traveling under the radar.

Suburban houses might be roomy and spacious inside, but

they build these tract houses so close together, I'm sure when you hit the lever, the flush can be heard next door. I can't see much of Don Diego's back yard, but if there was a fire, it didn't touch the house itself. "Drive back around the front, Tiffany. Let's go chat with Mister Fumodoro."

"Sí, sí, señor."

Tiffany parks in the guy's driveway. We get out and make our way to the front door. I ring the bell. We hear a short rendition of "Guantanamera". We wait. I push the bell again. "Guantanamera" double play. "Let's go, Mr. Sherlock."

"Why?"

"I hate that song."

We get back in the car. "Where to next?" I ask.

"We got to go see a ho doctor in Chinatown."

I don't bother to ask.

Tiffany gets back on the Stephenson and breaks the speed limit immediately. We slow to a crawl as we get into the city. Even on a Saturday morning, traffic on Chicago expressways can be brutal. "What are you going to do with all that money you won last night, Mr. Sherlock?"

"Pay off my credit card."

"That's boring. Why don't you blow it on having some fun?"

"Because it's no fun having an overdue credit card, Tiffany."

"I wouldn't know," she says.

As if I ever wondered.

"You're not going to have any left over?"

"Maybe."

"How much?"

"None of your business, Tiffany."

"Are you going to tell your kids?"

"No, and you're not, either."

"Why not?"

"Because it's none of their business."

"If I were them, I'd make it my business."

"Tiffany, you have to promise you won't mention it to Care and especially not Kelly."

"Why?"

"Because Kelly will hound me until the cows come home and won't let up until she gets some new purse or pair of designer flip-flops."

"I wouldn't worry about that, Mr. Sherlock. Cows could never climb up all those stairs at your place."

"Promise me, Tiffany." I am quite emphatic in my request.

"Oh, all right. I promise, but I hate promising and I'm not very good at it."

We take the Cermak exit off the Stephenson and wind our way into Chicago's Chinatown. "You in the mood for dim sum?" I ask.

"No, and I'm not in the mood for some dim, either," she tells me.

"You know where you're going?"

"This Ho doctor's office is around here somewhere."

It's time to ask, "A 'Ho' doctor?"

"That's what it says." Tiffany hands the sheet of paper to me.

I read, "His name is Ho Lee Dong?"

"Yep, and I don't think the Ho-lee has anything to do with religion."

I check the address. I've never heard of 23rd Court. "Go right, Tiffany." We cruise down 23rd where the restaurants and shops are, and finally find what looks like an alley but is actually a street. "Go left."

At the end on the street, there is a one-story building with a sign, which looks to me like a bad Shanghai art project. Luckily, under the Asian symbols, there is small lettering in English, reading: *One Stop Cancer Clinic.*

"The place looks like it has cancer," she comments.

Tiffany parks in a handicapped space and we make our way into the dilapidated building. "It's Saturday, you sure they're open?"

"I'm not even sure it's Saturday," Tiffany says.

Two steps after we walk in, we hit the counter, which no one is currently manning. There are numerous signs posted, all of which are in Mandarin or whatever the customers understand. Tiffany dings one of those silver, circular hotel desk bells resting on a sign in Chinese that hopefully translates to, "Ring for Service," but for all I know could translate to "Every time a bell rings an angel gets his wings."

A Chinese woman comes out of the door behind the counter. She is dressed in hospital scrubs. Seeing her, Tiffany bows. The woman stares as if to say, "What?" and hesitantly bows back.

Tiffany speaks very slowly and deliberately. "We come to see Doc...tor Ho." Tiffany bows again, obviously assuming the custom of the immediate surroundings.

"Oh...kay," the woman says in a voice slower than Tiffany's.

Tiffany's voice and inflection doesn't change, "We come from in---sure...ance come...pannn...eee."

"Which one?" the woman asks.

"Rich...mond."

"Why?"

"Too many tick...eees for too many sick...eees."

"Really?" the woman asks with a definite south side twang in her voice.

"Doc...tor Ho in?" Tiffany continues.

"He's in the back."

"See him now?"

Interrupting before Tiffany utters another syllable, I say, "She speaks English, Tiffany."

"You...do?"

"Ah.... Yeah."

I pick up the conversation, saying, "We're here to see Doctor Ho Lee Dong."

"Who should I say is calling?"

"Richard Sherlock." I pause, and politely say, "Is Doctor Dong available?"

"He's with a patient."

"How long do you think he will be?"

"Matters how patient he is," the woman says.

I hand over one of the cheap business cards Mr. Richmond supplied for my use in these situations. The woman disappears back through the door from which she came.

"How did you know she spoke English, Mr. Sherlock?"

"Because she was answering your questions in English."

"Oh, I wasn't expecting that."

There are two metal folding chairs up against the far wall. We sit. "I've heard a lot about this Oriental medicine, Mr. Sherlock."

"Like what, Tiffany?"

"They puncture you with big needles, inject you with rattlesnake poison, and rub ground-up chicken feet on your skin to get rid of warts and stuff."

"And where did you hear these accusations?"

"They're all over the Internet, so they must be true."

"Well, if they are, we're done here because I doubt if your daddy covers chicken beaks on his prescription list."

A man emerges from the same door as the lady. He wears pressed slacks, a starched shirt, striped tie, and a white lab coat with the name Dr. Ho Lee Dong sewed in script over his heart. He looks like an American doctor who's Chinese, not a Chinese doctor in a rice paddy. "May I help you?"

We stand. "My name is Sherlock—"

"Do you live at 221B Baker Street?" the doc interrupts me.

"No."

"Darn." He pauses before asking, "What can I do for you?"

"We're from the Richmond Insurance--" Tiffany answers but is cut off.

"Yes, I deduced that," he says, flipping my business card in his fingers. "Is there a problem?"

"No...maybe...could be," Tiffany tries to explain.

"What was your first clue?" Doctor Ho asks.

"We've been seeing a lot of activity in your account—"

"And that's a problem?" He asks, cutting her off again.

"You've been filing a number of claims."

"Isn't that what I'm supposed to do?"

"Well, yes, but we'd like to know why."

"Because our business has grown and with it the number of claims." He speaks in a tone, which is a far cry from a kindly bedside manner. "Is there some problem with that?"

I don't like this guy.

"No," Tiffany says.

"Then your mystery is solved," he says sarcastically.

I step in. "In situations where there is a noticeable spike in activity, we always review the caregiver. It's standard practice for any major insurance carrier." The last point isn't necessarily true, but I say it because it sounds good.

Ho Lee Dong gives me a competitive stare, a sneer, and motions with his index finger to follow him.

We go behind the counter, through the door, and find ourselves in a large room with at least twelve tilt-back chairs, all of which have small, attached tables on one side. Each lounge chair is occupied by an elderly Asian patient watching an Asian TV show on the HDTV on the far wall, while an IV bag, hanging from a pole, slowly empties its fluid into a tube, which runs into a vein in the crook of his or her arm.

"Asian people get cancer just like Caucasian people, Detective Sherlock."

I should probably respond with a "Touché," but instead I say. "Thanks for the tour."

"Any time," he says. "And since you are here, may I ask if your company will adhere to their ninety-day payment policy? It seems one-fifty is more the norm."

"I'll see what I can do."

"There isn't anything fowl in any of those medicines, is there?" Tiffany asks, pointing at the bags of chemo on the poles.

"Foul?" Doctor Dong asks.

"F-O-W-L." I'm surprised Tiffany can spell fowl.

"Not that I know of."

If I had a tail, it would've been between my legs as I walk out of Dong's clinic.

In the tiny lobby area, Tiffany gives the lady a bow, for what reason I have no idea. The bow isn't returned, but a comment is made. "You've got to be kidding."

Outside, when we are no longer in earshot, I say to Tiffany, "You got me off the craps table for this?"

"I didn't know."

"And why did you bow when we were leaving?"

"When in Rome you do as the Chinese do, Mr. Sherlock."

CHAPTER 4

It is not my kid weekend. The girls are off riding their horse in the wilds of suburban Chicago with their mother. On the way back to my apartment, I have Tiffany stop at a Chase Bank branch in Lincoln Park, so I can deposit my winnings from last evening before some horrendous financial tragedy befalls the school system and a hold is put on the check.

One thing I don't understand about banks these days is why they are building and opening so many new branches? At least in good neighborhoods, there seems to be a new branch on every corner. It doesn't make any sense, because for the last five years, banks have conditioned their customers not to come in and use the bank. Instead, they want their customers to go to an ATM for cash, use a debit card to make purchases, make deposits by taking a picture of the check with their cell phone, and use a computer to set up automatic payments for every bill they receive from their daily newspaper to their dog groomer. The bank teller was destined to become as extinct as the brontosaurus, but they are multiplying inside new banks faster than crooked bankers.

Go figure.

Back in my apartment that afternoon, I change the sheets, do the laundry, clean the kitchen, vacuum, dust, and take out the trash; a houseperson's work is never done. Next, I sit at my dining room table, open my checkbook, remove the bills outstanding, and write a check for each one. I save the Visa bill for last and get a particular prickly sensation when I put an X in the *outstanding balance* square, add my check, stuff the envelope, stamp it, and seal it up tight. Getting out of debt has been a long time in coming.

Manned with a calculator I got as a gift at a Living Trust seminar I attended to get a free lunch, I subtract all the monies going out from the additions and balance that I had going in, and come out with a little over $3,400 in the plus column. Positive cash flow has been a much longer time in coming.

I haven't felt this financially sound since the morning I found a quarter under my pillow, left in exchange for a useless tooth.

***

"And the classroom helper of the day will be Mr. Sherlock."
Care almost falls out of her desk chair. "Dad?"
I wave to my youngest, as her teacher, Lori Lozana,
introduces me to her fourth period pre-pre-algebra class.
"Mr. Sherlock will be in the room today for anyone who
may need a little help."
I make my way to the back of the room, wishing and hoping
that no child in the class asks me for help.
Miss Lozana begins the class, saying, "Open your textbooks
to chapter four."
For the next thirty minutes, she might as well be speaking
Ubeakestanni because I have no clue what she is talking about.
"If X equals four over two, and two equals the square root of Y
minus seven, how many Xs and Os will it take to play Tic-Tac-
Toe during the rain delay of a Cub game?"
This is what they study to learn how to balance their
checkbooks?
During the *work time* in the class, one cute kid asks me,
"Mr. Sherlock, could you help me?"
"Probably not, but I'll give it a go," I tell her honestly.
"The question is," she says. "If X equals two and Y equals
four, what does X plus Y equal?"
"I'm pretty sure two and four still add up to six," I tell her.
"Duh," she says. "That's not what I want to know."
"What then?"
"I want to know why there isn't an X and Y on my
calculator?" She holds up a fancy device with all kinds of crazy
symbols on it. "How am I supposed to get the answer if I can't
use my calculator?"
"I think the point here is for you to figure out the problem
without the use of a machine," I tell her.
"Why would anybody ever want to do that?"
I'm saved by the ringing school bell. Fifth period is lunch.
Time to eat.
Care escorts me and a few of her friends to the cafeteria.
The place is a bustle of activity as we enter. About half of the
Pat Nixon kids and half of the Ann Margaret kids crowd the

room. There are two lunch periods at the schools, fourth and fifth. Care and her friends sit with the other grammar schoolers on the far side of the room, well removed from the older middle school kids, who sit closer to the food service area. Segregation in this large room would give a post civil war Southern town a run for its money. The girls sit with girls, boys with boys, blacks with blacks, Asians with Asians, and whites with whites. Social castes are also evident, the better dressed kids hang together, athletes with athletes, musicians with musicians, and nerds with nerds, who sit with laptops fired up in front of them. The only similar aspect distinguishing every student as a student, is each kid has their own cell phone and is staring into its screen.

From where Care and her friends sit, I can't see much of the cafeteria operation. I need to get closer to the action. I bid good-bye to Care's friends and head toward where the food is being dished out.

"Oh my God."

I sit down right next to my first child. "Nice to see you too, Kelly."

"What are you doing here?"

"I was in the neighborhood and thought I'd drop in and say 'hello.'"

"Dad, this is like totally weird."

"What? I can't have lunch with my daughter?"

"No, not at school."

"Why not?"

"Do you see any other parents sitting with their kids?"

"No, because they don't have such a special daughter like I do."

"Oh, my God, this is like so uncool."

I introduce myself to the other girls at the table, who seem to get a kick out of me being there, or a kick out of seeing Kelly beside herself in absolute befuddled embarrassment.

I announce to the group, "Since I'm here, I wonder if you girls need any advice about boys?"

Kelly almost melts into her chair.

I laugh. The girls laugh. Kelly turns bright red.

As I chat up the kids, I get a pretty good idea of the ebb and flow of the cafeteria in action. Students line up in one of two lines; one for hot lunch, and one for milk only. There are four female servers, who spoon portions of food groups onto plates.

The second line, which is milk only, is self-serve. I pay particular attention to where payments are made for the culinary delights of the day. The kids slide their full trays down lane one to where a food service employee sits. She either rings up money for a sale or checks for the "Daily Lunch Pass" kids carry. Behind her, is the other line, which another lady, not dressed in worker attire, sits with a small cash tray; she's the milk lady. For either two quarters or the flash of a red weekly receipt, each student gets a carton of regular, chocolate, or low-fat milk. Each line is doing a land office business.

There is something wrong about the operation. The kids who get a hot lunch have to stand in the milk line first before they load up on food, or let their hot lunch get cold as they wait in line to get milk. The cafeteria could use a Food Service Engineer, if such a person exists.

I watch for a few moments and notice one boy, about Kelly's age, darting in and around the end of the line. "Who's that?" I ask my group.

"Terrible Teddy," one of Kelly's buddies says.

"Who?"

"Terrible Teddy Tulleners."

"He was voted most likely to do jail time before he gets his driver's license," another girl informs me.

"They got a cell reserved for him in juvie."

"He buys and sells switchblades on eBay."

"I heard he's getting a tattoo for a graduation present."

"I hope none of you consider him dating material," I comment.

Kelly turns another shade of red.

I follow Teddy 's movements closely. The kid gravitates to money like a bee to a budding flower. He watches dollars and change go into the cafeteria coffers and the milk lady's box as if he's a starving restaurant critic salivating over a prime cut filet at the opening of a five-star steakhouse.

Kelly eyes me as I watch Teddy. "You didn't come here to visit, did you, Dad?"

"Why else would I come here, Kelly?"

"I don't know, but I'm going to find out."

The food service cashier and the milk lady close up shop after the last kid goes through the line. The cafeteria employee, who sports a beehive hairdo right out of a James Dean movie, finds a cloth bag in the drawer under the register, takes it out, and stuffs every bit of legal tender inside. Next, she places a small key into the cash register, twists to the left, and holds two keys down on the top row, causing a long printed slip of paper to roll out of the receipt slot. She tears off the paper, carefully makes three folds, and adds it to the cloth bag. She leaves the cash register drawer open, reaches below to open a cabinet. I see her twist the dial of a built-in safe. Once open, she inserts the cloth bag, shuts the safe's door, and spins the dial. She gets up, heads for a door behind the food service area, and disappears. In contrast, the milk money lady takes her tray to a small table in the back of the service area, sits down, and carefully counts out every bill, quarter, dime, and nickel. She writes on a piece of paper, what I will assume, are the totals for the day, although, my first rule of life is *never assume anything*. She then puts the money back into the cash tray, stands up, and carries it all right past where I'm sitting.

I follow.

"Dad, where are you going?" Kelly yells out at me.

"I'm leaving to save you any more embarrassment, Kelly."

"No," she says. "I don't buy it. You're onto something. What?"

"You're at school, Kelly. Go learn something."

"I want to learn what you're doing."

"I'm here to find better ways of embarrassing you."

"Besides that, Dad."

As I follow the milk monitor into the school hallway, I realize Teddy disappeared the same time the beehive cashier did, but I can't be concerned with him now. The woman heads for the administration office, opens the door, and goes inside. This is where I leave her.

I hustle back into the cafeteria. All the kids, except the nerdy lap-toppers, are gone. The nerds sit without speaking, peering at their computer screens as if the answer to "How to be a computer geek and cool at the same time?" is about to come up in fancy script. I go into the doorway where the cashier disappeared, and run head-on into Teddy Tulleners on his way out. Our eyes lock. His peepers are as guilty as a burglar's who gets busted inside a bedroom closet with a pillowcase of silverware in hand.

"What are you doing here?" I ask.

"Not much," he says. "What are you doing here?"

"Looking for rats," I tell him.

"You from the Health Department?"

"No."

"I think I saw one over there." He points.

I sense he's about to bolt, so I hold his arm. "Let's take a walk, Teddy."

"How do you know my name?"

"Your reputation precedes you."

The bell rings for the period to end and kids to return to class.

"I got to go, I don't want to miss P.E. It's my best subject," he says.

"We'll take a walk instead. It should be enough exercise for now." We head down the hallway.

"For all I know, you're some kind of a pervert," Teddy tells me.

"Maybe you should tell the principal."

"Maybe I will."

We walk a little farther.

"Well, now's your chance."

We enter the principal's outer office, and the lady behind the desk immediately says, "Hi, Teddy, back so soon?"

"Hello, Mrs. Chumley," Teddy says.

"Are you having a smiley face day today, Teddy?" the overly sweet older woman asks the boy.

"Not right now," Teddy answers.

"Is Eldin in?" I ask.

"Who should I say is calling?" she asks me.

"Richard Sherlock."

"Kelly and Care's dad?"

"Yes."

"You can go right in," she says.

Teddy and I enter Principal Puddle's office.

"I think I may have found your problem, Principal Puddle."

Eldin stands up, and peers down at Teddy.

"I didn't do it," Teddy immediately says.

"Didn't do what?"

"Whatever he's going to say I did."

"Stealing a little cafeteria cash," I fill in.

"Teddy…" Eldin sighs.

"I didn't steal any money."

"How much did you get?"

"Nothing. I'm innocent."

"What were you doing in the back room then?" I ask.

"I told you, I was chasing a rat."

"Empty out your pockets, Teddy," Puddle orders.

"Fine." Eddie pulls out his jeans pockets. They're as empty as the playground during a blizzard. "See?"

"Shoes off Teddy."

"Shoes, why?"

"Because I said so."

"But school areas are known to have horrible foot funguses. I could catch one and lose a toe."

"Take 'em off, Teddy."

"Do I have to?"

"Yes."

Off comes the left shoe. Eldin examines, finds bupkis.

Teddy pirouettes as if trying to hide his next move.

"Teddy...."

The right shoe comes off and a ten spot floats to the floor.

"That's my after school money. I keep it there in case I get mugged on the way home."

"Teddy, what am I going to do with you?"

"I swear, Principal Puddle, I didn't steal a dime from the cafeteria cash."

"Teddy—"

"You have to believe me, Principal Puddle. This time I'm innocent. I found the money, I swear."

"I'll deal with you later. Go back to class."

The boy leaves the office.

"The funny thing about Teddy," Eldin says to me. "He's not a bad kid."

Back in the 1930s in Omaha, Nebraska, a Catholic Priest named Father Flanagan believed "there is no such thing as a bad boy." He founded Boys Town on that belief and it has helped thousands of wayward boys over the years. But I have to wonder what Father Flanagan would say if he were to meet Terrible Teddy Tulleners.

"Mystery solved, Principal Puddle. I'm glad I could be of service."

I stand, waiting for either a "Thank You," or "Great job,

Sherlock." Instead, I get, "How about the other one hundred ninety dollars? Did you find that?"

Back to the scene of the crime.

By the time I return to the cafeteria, the service lane is pretty well cleaned up. The mystery meat is gone and the stainless steel wiped spotless. I go into the rear area where the food is prepared and see one worker mashing up the hamburgers, which didn't sell today, probably to make chili, which won't sell tomorrow. The remaining green beans, corn, and peas are being deposited into the same container to be the special veggie medley on Wednesday or soup on Thursday. They're freezing the leftover spaghetti sauce, which may become a new gelato flavor on Friday.

Miss Beehive is nowhere to be seen. She may have already hung up her hair net for the day. I search the entire area, ask the other workers, and come up with bupkis on where she may be. For lack of a better idea, I open the door to the outside and see my woman of interest across the playground in an area used for a community vegetable garden. Her beehive is taking a beating in the wind. It looks like she is wearing the Leaning Tower of Pisa on her head. I watch her closely as she walks near the sprouting plants. She carries a small shovel. This is odd. She is either finished with what gardening she may have been doing, or decided not to dig today, because she exits the garden, walks to the shed used to keep the playground equipment, drops off the shovel, and makes her way off the grassy area towards the parking lot. She climbs into one of those monster SUVs, which seem bigger than most school buses. In seconds she is out of the parking lot burning up premium gasoline at a rate of five miles per gallon.

I return to the room where I busted Teddy. It's a storage room. On the bigger set of shelves, there are over-sized cans of ketchup and mustard and sacks of flour and sugar. Smaller shelves are filled with everything from bullion to yeast. I search around half-heartedly for something amiss or that doesn't fit, see nothing strange, and leave the room.

I find it especially interesting that no cafeteria employee asks who I am or what I'm doing in the cafeteria storeroom.

Bouncing back to the trail of the pilfered milk money, I find the door, which the milk lady entered with her stash of cash. The stencil on the door reads: *Administration* and below are the words: *Assistant Principal Ms. F. Mossy.*

I enter. "Excuse me," I say to the middle-aged woman at the desk. "My name is Richard Sherlock."

"Kelly's father?"

"Yes."

"Nice girl, excellent dresser."

"Thank you. But she didn't get the fashion thing from her father."

"I can see that."

I should tell this woman, "I don't follow the trends, I set them." Instead, I ask, "Did Principal Puddle mention why I might be here?"

"Matter of fact, he did." She stands and puts out her hand to shake. "I'm Assistant Principal Mossy, but you can call me Fern when no students are around."

I scan the small office before I shake her hand, and say, "Nice to meet you, Fern."

"What can I do for you?"

"This is where the milk lady drops off her money every day?"

"Yes."

"Can I see where it ends up?"

Fern unlocks the biggest drawer in her desk, slides it all the way open, and reveals a metal cash box in the rear. "You want to see the actual cash?"

"Sure."

From the same set of keys, she unlocks the gray box, flips up the top, and shows me the cash. "The money for the kids who get weekly passes comes in on Monday."

"And the daily totals are they in here, too?"

"No, there is a file on top of the cabinet over there." Fern points to a file cabinet to her left with a full file divider on its top. "It's the one marked *HB PTA.*"

"Is it the same person collecting milk money every day?" I ask.

"They rotate. Although, Ms. Torelli always works the Friday shift."

"Why?"

"She does the final weekly accounting."

I find the file, open to the one page inside, and see a primitive daily accounting scribbled onto the page. "Do you count the money, too?"

"Yes."

"And how does it get to the bank?"

"Ms. Torelli."

"The PTA president?"

"Yes. Winky."

"Does she have a key?"

"Yes."

"How about the money from the cafeteria food?"

"A service picks it up. We never see that."

"Who is the lady with the beehive?" I ask.

"Esther Stiffarm, cafeteria manager, and she refers to it as a white afro."

"Do you trust her?" I ask a bit promptly.

"Implicitly. Esther has been with us for over eleven years. And because of her, we have the longest tenured cafeteria staff of any school on the north side."

"Thank you."

"You're welcome."

I return to Principal Puddle's office.

"You figure out who did it?"

"Not yet."

"Soon?"

"I'm working on it."

I have a few minutes before I get in my car and get in line to pick up the kids. I take a walk out to the garden where I saw Esther Stiffarm visit before she left in her SUV.

Being early in the season, there's no actual fruit or veggies, but the plants are sprouting. Soon, there will be radishes, beans, peppers, tomatoes, and a few foodstuffs I don't recognize. There is no evidence of any recent digging, although some of the dirt around the plant rows has been chomped up a bit. The garden is good for kids. Planting seeds in the ground, watching them grow, and finally eating the fruit or vegetable produced is a valuable learning experience.

While I am sitting in the car waiting for the final bell to ring, Tiffany calls. I give her a brief rundown of what I did at the school. She tells me, "My dad's really mad at you, Mr. Sherlock."

Yet another bit of great news. "Why?"

"Because you're not trying hard enough, Mr. Sherlock."

"I just started today. What does he expect?"

"You should be busy smoking out that cigar guy."

"I don't smoke."

"Well, it's a good time to start."

Ten minutes later, Care hops in the front seat of the car. "It was so cool having you as the classroom mom, Dad."

"Thank you, Care," I tell her as we move toward the middle school where Kelly is in the center of a gaggle of girls.

"Now, can we stop at McDonald's on the way home?"

"No."

I have to honk the horn to get Kelly's attention. It doesn't work, so I yell, "Kelly, let's go. You're holding up the traffic line."

Kelly, reluctant as a first day first grader, finally climbs into the back seat. "That was embarrassing, and like so totally bogus, you showing up at school today, Dad."

"He was there to help out in my math class," Care informs her sister.

"You really think that they'd want someone who can't help you with your homework to help other kids in the class?" Care contemplates the question. Instead of defending my math skills, Kelly says, "You were there for something else, weren't you, Dad?"

"Not necessarily." I skirt the question since I make it a point never to lie to my kids.

"You're lying."

"No, I'm not. I ran into Principal Puddle at the fundraiser and he wanted me to drop by the school to see how it all works."

"I don't buy it," Kelly says.

"He asked me for my thoughts on how to make things run more efficiently." I might be stretching the truth just a bit. "And I told him I'd help out any way that I could."

"Now I really don't buy it."

"Well, Kelly," I tell her, "that's my story and I'm sticking to it."

"You know, Dad," Care says. "You never do help me with my math homework."

"That's because I know you're smart enough to figure it out yourself, Care. And that's how you learn."

"The only thing she learned was not to bother asking you for help," Kelly says.

We're getting close to our apartment, thank God. I change the subject, "Did either of you learn anything new today at school?"

As usual, Care says, "No."

Kelly says, "I learned something bogus is going on at school and I can't wait to find out what it is."

"Well, good luck with that, Kelly, but you won't be hearing anything from me."

We ride the rest of the way in silence.

Someone waits for us at our apartment.

"Hey, look, Tiffany's here!"

As I park, Tiffany approaches the Toyota, waving and yelling like a game show contestant, "Hello there, little dudettes."

"Hi, Tiffany."

"What are you doing here?" I ask.

"I already told you, Daddy's really mad," Tiffany says.

In anger or has Tiffany finally driven him off the edge?

"Now he's getting sued."

There's a big surprise.

"And it's all your fault, Mr. Sherlock."

"Mine?"

"Yes, yours."

"Way to go, Dad," Kelly fills in.

We go upstairs into the apartment. As the girls get settled, I start on dinner in the kitchen. Tiffany can't wait to let loose with her complaint, "We should've waited around all day for the guy to come home," she says.

"Who?"

"The cigar guy, Mr. Humidoro."

"I thought his name was Fumadoro?"

"Fumo, humo—what's the difference? He's suing Daddy for a buck-and-a-half, plus interest," Tiffany says as the girls join us in the kitchen.

"Insurance companies get sued all the time, Tiffany. It's part of the business."

"Well, this case is different."

"What's so different?"

"I don't know, that's why Daddy has you."

"What are we having for dinner?" Care asks, breaking up the conversation.

"Chicken."

"Fried?"

"No, we never have fried chicken. Fried foods are bad for you. How many times have I told you that, Care?"

"You fry eggs and make us eat those," Care retorts.

"Dad's being really evasive, Tiffany," Kelly says. "He hasn't given us a straight answer about the real reason he was at school today at lunchtime."

"He was there because somebody is stealing the milk money," Tiffany says, as if in passing.

"Tiffany!"

"What?"

"I knew it," Kelly says. "I knew there was no way you were there to help out in the classroom."

"Tiffany, you promised not to say a word about this."

"No, Mr. Sherlock, I promised not to say a word about the money you won at casino night at the school."

"Tiffany!"

"Money?" Kelly shrieks. "How much did you win?"

"A lot," Tiffany says.

"That money is none of anyone's business, except mine," I try to lay down the law.

"It's spring, and there's hundreds of new outfits I need," Kelly says.

"I want a puppy," Care says.

"Forget it."

"I'll take care of the little furball. I promise." Care promises as if I need any more promises.

"I think you should get a new car," Tiffany says.

"You won enough money to buy a car, Dad?" Kelly asks. "And you won't even buy me a couple of new outfits? What kind of a father are you?"

"I'm trying to be a good one," I say.

"Well, try harder."

"I tell you what, if you let me get a puppy, I'll let you name it."

"Enough. Stop. There will be no more discussions about money this evening."

"How about the missing milk money, Dad?"

"That is not a topic for discussion."

"That's because your dad has no clue who took it," Tiffany

explains.

"Tell us about the case, Dad."

"No. Forget it."

"Somebody is stealing the money and the only suspects so far are this crummy kid—"

"Terrible Teddy Tulleners?" Kelly shouts out.

"Yes."

"I knew it."

"And this lady who works in the cafeteria who has this totally retro hairdo."

"If you don't shut up, Tiffany, I'm never letting you in on another case again."

"The lady who takes the money?" Care asks.

"She probably stashes the money in her hair, and it can't fall out because it sticks 'cuz of all the hairspray she uses," Kelly adds.

"This is not a topic of conversation. Do you understand me?"

"He saw her outside with a shovel in the garden," Tiffany continues.

"She burying the money outside like buried treasure?" Kelly blurts out.

"I didn't think of that," Tiffany says. "There could be hundreds of dollars buried out there."

"Cool," Care says.

"Stop, people, just stop."

"No, Dad, I think we're onto something."

"We are not onto anything because there is no *we* here. You two are not involved in this case."

"We should start tacking up cards on *The Original Carlo*," Care says.

"Forget it."

"We can help, Dad, we really can," Care says.

"We can be your eyes and ears inside the walls of the school," Kelly adds.

"No. And you two have to promise not to say a word to anyone at your school."

"How about after school?" Care asks.

"No comments anytime, anywhere, or with anybody." I pause, "Now, promise."

"I wouldn't promise if I were you," Tiffany tells the girls.

"You walk down that road, you'll never find your way back."

"Tell us more, Dad."

"No."

"We can help you on the case," Care says.

"We can go undercover," Kelly says.

"Forget it."

"Mr. Sherlock, what are we going to do about Mr. Cigaradoro?"

"I don't know, Tiffany." I raise my voice even higher, and add, "I'll deal with him tomorrow!"

"Gee, you don't have to snap at me," Tiffany says.

"Yeah, Dad. You can't snap at her like you snap at us," Kelly informs me.

I have reached the end of my short rope. "That's it. Not another word about money, milk money, new cars, or going undercover as a cocker spaniel. You two get in there and do your homework. Tiffany, you're welcome to stay for dinner, but you have to learn how to keep your promises."

"Okay, I'll stay for dinner," Tiffany says. "And I promise I won't eat any of your crummy food."

The three sulk off out of the kitchen. Care returns in a few seconds. "Hey, Dad, can you help me with my math homework?"

Oh jeesh.

CHAPTER 5

Don Diego Fumadoro is an older gentleman, dressed in a white suit, and smoking a cigar thicker than a bathroom soil pipe.

"My lawyer told me not to speak with you."

"But you have to speak with us," Tiffany tells him.

"Why?"

"To tell us you're not speaking with us."

I try to stay downwind of the effluent emanating from the cigar. "We would like to clear this claim up without going to court, Mr. Fumadoro."

"Call me Don Diego."

"Tell us what was lost?"

"Over three hundred classic cigars from my collection." Don Diego pays about as much attention to his lawyer as Tiffany does to me.

"And how were they destroyed?"

"Fire."

"When?"

"Not too long ago."

"Where?"

"In my house."

"You had a fire in your house?"

"Yes."

I'm sitting in the living room and it doesn't look baked to me. "Where in the house?"

Don Diego takes a big puff, blows the smoke in our faces, and says, "In the den."

We walk into the den, a real man-cave with massive HDTV, stereo, wet bar, and beer tap. I should be so lucky, although I seldom drink.

"Place looks pretty spotless to me," I tell him.

"Did another insurance company pay off for the fire damage?" I ask.

"Not yet."

"Why not?"

"Listen," Don Diego says. "Richmond wrote the policy on my cigars. Fire protection was covered. I listed every item that went up in smoke, so pay up."

"Those are awful expensive cigars," I say.

"I only smoke the best."

"Smoking isn't good for you," Tiffany informs him.

"Nor is getting stiffed by your insurance company," he tells her.

"Nobody is trying to stiff anybody," I tell him.

"Then why haven't you paid me?"

He's got me there.

"I filled out every form, submitted receipts for the items that burned up, so you people quit stalling and pay up."

"We need some additional information before we can issue payment," I tell him, although I have no clue if this is true.

"No, you don't."

He's right. I hate people who read their policies.

"You got 'til Monday," he says. "Pay up or I'll see you in court."

"Can we negotiate?"

"No, why would I?"

If this keeps up, the tail between my legs is going to become permanent.

We're outside. Tiffany hurries away from the house as if she's afraid of hearing "Guantanamera" again.

"Wait, Tiffany."

She stops on her way to her car, "What for, Mr. Sherlock?"

"I want to go next door."

"You want to compare floor plans?"

Tiffany catches up to me as I ring the doorbell of 424 Melody Lane, the house immediately east of Fumadoro's.

The chimes ring out a rendition of "On the Sunny Side of the Street."

"Excuse me," I say to the lady who answers the door.

"The sign says 'No Soliciting.'"

"I know, I'd just like to ask you one question."

"No surveys, either."

"It's not a survey."

"Are you Mormon?" she asks.

"No, he's pretty smart," Tiffany tells her.

"You're not dressed like a Mormon. Are you a Mormon in disguise?" the lady asks me.

"No. All I need to know is if the house next door has had a fire recently." I point to the Fumadoro residence.

"Is this a trick question?"

"No. I just need to know if there has been any fire activity there in the last six months or so."

"Yes, plenty."

"Was it a big fire?"

"No, it's those awful cigars he smokes. We have to keep our windows closed on that side of the house."

"I can feel your pain." Why this comment pops out of my mouth, I have no clue.

"You should move to a high-rise," Tiffany tells her.

"Thanks for your time," I tell her as we leave her porch.

"I really did like that play about Mormons. It was really funny."

***

We are sitting across the street from Dr. Ho Lee Dong's One Stop Cancer Cure clinic. I've counted nineteen people going in during the time span of an hour and a half.

"This is boring."

"Let me apologize for putting you through such pain and suffering, Tiffany."

"Apologies are only as good as the guilt they're written on, Mr. Sherlock."

I don't think she got that right, but she does make an interesting point.

"The guy's doing a booming business," I comment on the foot traffic.

"I'd say he's making a real killing."

"Bad choice of words for a cancer clinic, Tiffany."

Two more Asian senior citizens walk into the clinic.

"Can we go now?"

"Sure."

Tiffany fires up the Lexus. "Where to?"

I have to make a return trip out to see Principal Puddle, but I really don't want to take the *L* home, walk to my apartment, pick up the car, and drive out to the school. So, I say, "Well,

Tiffany, I could use your help in finding the missing milk money."

"Really? How?"

I didn't expect a return question. "Ah...because you're able to think so much more like a teenager than I can."

"Yes, yet another of my amazing qualities."

We don't arrive at the school until fifth period lunch is over, which is not a bad thing. We head for the cafeteria.

"Excuse me, Miss Stiffarm."

"Yes?"

"My name is Sherlock and I'd like to ask you a few questions."

The staff has the food packed up and stored for use as future menu items and the trays are cleaned and put away for tomorrow. The counters are so clean, you could eat off them, which you wouldn't, but you could.

"My name's Tiffany and I think your hair is really retro."

"Are you from the health department?" she asks.

"No, we're working with Principal Puddle on better efficiencies in the school systems."

"We are?" Tiffany asks.

"Yes," I answer before Tiffany repeats what she told Kelly last night.

Esther Stiffarm is more than happy to give us a *soup to nuts* tour of the cafeteria operation. She is undeniably proud of her own and the work of her staff. "The people who run the schools could learn a lot from the way we do our jobs around here," she tells us. She explains how the food arrives, is prepared, served, and how so little is wasted. "We even have a garden out back," she says.

During the tour, Tiffany asks, "How much of the fruit is organic?" "What do you think of kale?" and "Do you have power shakes for sale?"

Her answers are: "Don't know," "Hate it," and "No."

My last question to her is, "And you're in charge of the money?"

"Yes."

She shows me with no hesitation how she totals out the cash register, places the money in a canvas bag, and locks it in the cabinet safe. "A driver comes every afternoon to exchange safes in the cabinet."

"Quite a system you got working there, Esther," I compliment her.

"You betcha."

"Thank you for your time."

"You're welcome."

"Mark my menu," Tiffany tells her. "The kale power shake is the next super food."

We go upstairs.

"I need to talk to Teddy Tulleners," I tell Principal Puddle.

Eldin calls out to his assistant, "Mrs. Chumley, please go fetch Teddy."

As we wait, he asks, "Any closer to finding out who did it?"

"Not really."

"If you do figure it out, don't say anything until next week. Friday is a big day around here."

Since George Bush passed his No Child Left Behind revamp of the American school system, the system has been is constant disarray. The problem is many of the school districts have refused to abide by the new national testing standards, teacher unions have complained, and money has been reassigned; overall it has been a difficult transition. One of the offshoots of the program has been a shift of certain high schools becoming specialized in certain areas of study. In Chicago, there are math, science, and art academies as well as specialized college preparatory schools. For a student to gain admittance to one of these elite institutions, they must have a superior grade average, apply in advance, and take the Selective School Admissions test between October and January of their eighth grade year. The competition for admittance to these special high schools is fierce.

In my case, this isn't much of an issue. Kelly, who will be going to high school next year, is much more interested in fashion and boys than getting As in all her subjects. She didn't even bother to take the test. Thankfully, the high school in her neighborhood, Hannibal Hamlin High, is one of the better high schools on the north side without being labeled a magnet school or academy.

For many parents, getting their kids into one of these specialized schools has become an obsession. They hire tutors, pick certain classes where they know their child will flourish, and don't hesitate to put pressure on teachers who they don't feel are good enough to teach their child or give their child anything less than an A-plus. There is a special magnet prep class taught at Ann Margaret, but the most popular method of preparation is to have their kids attend a series of private tutoring sessions, which will prepare them for the specialized test. I am told that these sessions, taught often by middle and high school teachers, are grueling experiences way more stressful than anything the child has ever experienced with the exception of their parents' constant demands of perfection from them.

"What happens on Friday?" I ask Eldin, wondering if it is Abondanza Pizza Day in the cafeteria.

"It is the day they announce the placements into the specialized and magnet high schools."

"Doesn't that usually come much sooner?" I ask.

"The school board was too busy arguing, and the date had to be pushed back this year."

Mrs. Chumley brings Teddy into the office.

"Thanks for getting me out of class, Principal Puddle. I hate geography."

"These people need to ask you more questions, Teddy."

Teddy turns and sees Tiffany. "Wow, you da bomb."

"I know," Tiffany says.

"You go for younger men?" Teddy asks.

"Sometimes," Tiffany answers.

Teddy gives her a big smile.

"Younger, not jailbait," Tiffany adds for Teddy's benefit.

Teddy gives her a bigger smile and hikes his package.

"Let's take a walk, Teddy."

"And whatever Mr. Sherlock asks, you tell him the truth, Teddy," Principal Puddle orders as we leave the office.

"And the truth will set me free," Teddy says.

By the time we hit the hallway, Teddy takes Tiffany's hand into his. Tiffany whips her hand away, "What are you doing, you little creep?"

"I want us to start feeling close."

"You try one more feel, kid, the only thing you're going to feel is pain," Tiffany tells him.

"Hurt me," Teddy pleads. "Go ahead, hurt me. I'll love it. "

I walk between the two of them the rest of the way to the cafeteria. When we arrive, Esther Stiffarm is gone and only one worker remains. I ask her to unlock the storeroom; she does and the three of us enter.

"Show me where you found the money, Teddy."

"Over there."

"Over there, *where*?"

Teddy goes to the shelf lined with large cans of tomato sauce. He boosts himself up, and tips one can to its side. "It was under here."

I look. There is nothing under the can.

"Let me get this straight," I say. "One day you just happened to wander into this room, go to this side, climb up, search underneath one can of tomato sauce, amidst fifty-or-so other cans, and find ten bucks?"

"Yep."

"A little hard to believe, Teddy."

Teddy doesn't hesitate. "I got like a sixth sense when it comes to money."

"You do?"

"You ever see one of those guys who finds water by walking around pointing a couple of sticks to the ground?"

"The guy who fixes the sprinklers?" Tiffany asks.

Teddy gives Tiffany a big smile. "Hey, you can work on my watering system anytime, babe."

"A water diviner?" I ask.

"Yeah, that's the guy. I can do that, too, but I find money."

"Really?"

"I'm gifted." Teddy gives Tiffany another big smile.

"You ever find any more money around here?"

"Not a dime."

"You're lying, Teddy."

"No, I'm not."

"Teddy, if you want to become a criminal when you grow up, you have to learn to become a better liar."

"Gee, thanks for the tip."

"How much did you find and how often did you find it?"

"Come on, Sherlock. I find a lousy ten bucks, the school district goes gaga, and brings in a private dick to investigate? No wonder kids can't read."

"Come clean, Teddy."

"Ten bucks. It was a lousy ten bucks."

We drop Teddy back in the Eldin's office. He asks Tiffany for her "digits," but she refuses.

I take Tiffany back to the cafeteria storeroom. "Start looking under every can on the shelf, I have a feeling there's gold in them thar hills."

"Jewelry?"

It takes about twenty minutes. I find a twenty under a can of lima beans and Tiffany finds fifteen dollars under a box of tortillas. "Ole'," she remarks.

The interesting point here is that our two finds are on opposite ends of the room.

"Do I get to keep the money, Mr. Sherlock?"

"No."

"Why not?"

"It's evidence."

"But finders keepers, losers are losers."

We go back upstairs to Fern Mossy's office.

"Back so soon?"

"Explain to me how the accounting works in this place?" I ask.

"Sure." She sits back in her chair. "The district is very careful with their pocketbook, Mr. Sherlock. All major fixed expenses, payroll, heat, trash, water, and insurance are paid directly from the district's accounting office. I do get a copy of each month's expenditures. For payments specific to this school, such as special projects, building maintenance, supplies, tech fixes, and field trips, expenditures must be signed off by myself or Principal Puddle."

"And how do those get paid?"

"Once the bills come in, Mrs. Chumley sorts them, puts them on a spreadsheet, fills out a requisition payment form for each, and passes them along to Principal Puddle, and then to me."

"And you pay them?"

"Yes and no. I do a master monthly payment form, which I send to the district office and they cut the checks or make payments to suppliers who service more than one school and whose bills repeat month after month."

"What's the 'no' part?" I ask.

"The school does have its own checking account, which we use for emergency payments, special projects, additional instructors, and whatever else may come up."

"You write those checks?"

"As a rule. Principal Puddle and I are the only signers on the account."

"And the cafeteria?"

"Totally separate. Matter of fact," Fern says, "food service is so large, it's removed from the district budget and operates on its own."

"So the only real money anyone touches around here is the milk money?" I half-ask.

"Yes."

"And the PTA is in charge of that?"

"Yes and no. Since the district food service has to order the milk, we use our in-house account and pay food service directly. The money the PTA collects goes into their account, and at the end of the month, they write us a check for the amount of milk from food service, and we transfer the amount."

"Sounds complicated," I surmise.

"Not really," Fern explains. "It's all set up so no one can steal any money."

Except somebody did.

"Why doesn't the PTA pay food service directly?"

"Because there is some profit and they want to account for that on their books, so they can show the parents what a great job they're doing," Fern says.

"So, even with all the checks and balances, one day Eldin sees a lot more money going out for milk than was coming in?"

"No."

"Who discovered the theft?"

"Eldin said he did, but it was Mrs. Chumley."

"How do you know that?"

"Because she showed me, and I showed Eldin."

I conclude, "Eldin admitted to not being much of an accountant."

"He wasn't lying."

"Thanks for your time."

"You're welcome," Fern says. "Anything else I can help you with, please let me know."

We leave her office. Once out in the hallway, Tiffany says, "That was even more boring than sitting outside that cancer clinic."

"Let me again apologize for making your life so unbearable, Tiffany."

"I don't know how I make it through some days, Mr. Sherlock."

CHAPTER 6

Over the next couple of days, I feel pretty rotten about the cases I'm working, but I feel fantastic knowing I have money in the bank.

Being in constant debt is like having a terminal case of psoriasis. The disease never leaves you alone. You constantly itch until one day you itch away all your skin in one spot, the blood spurts out of your body like a ruptured oil pipeline, and you deflate faster than a blown tire on the expressway.

After all the years I've been in debt, you'd think I would have gotten used to the feeling but no. Being in debt is no fun. I hate it. But now I'm in the chips and it feels wonderful. I make the decision to use my windfall to improve my life and not do anything rash, stupid, or impulsive with the money. I have many choices on how to best spend the money but can afford only one. In no particular order, here's my top five: 1. I could pay down the money Richmond loaned me to pay off my divorce. I would then be that much closer to freeing myself from being shackled to the company store. 2. Deposit the money in my retirement 401K, which is so low now, it's more like a 001K. 3. Put a down payment on a new used car. My Toyota isn't going to run forever no matter how much oil I keep in it. 4. Rent a bigger apartment. With two teenagers my one bedroom place is getting so small we don't have room to make attitude adjustments. 5. Go to a casino, put it all on red or black, and let the wheel spin. Win, I double the number of choices I can make. Lose, I'm back bailing out the same sinking boat, which I've already had an enormous amount of practice bailing out.

We'll see.

Tiffany calls late Wednesday morning, and asks what she should be doing. I tell her there are a number of good movies playing. "That might be fun."

"No, Mr. Sherlock, on the case. What do you want me to do on the case?"

"Well, you could go stake out the Ho Lee Dong clinic and see if anything fishy is going on."

"No, I did that once and it was totally boring," Tiffany says. "Plus, that's not a place anyone should be eating sushi."

"You could find out if other insurance companies are being bombarded by claims from his clinic."

"How do I do that?"

"You call the companies up, tell them who you are, and ask."

"I could handle that."

"Go for it."

Tiffany calls me back four hours later.

"What did you find out?"

"Let me tell you, Mr. Sherlock," she says. "I call up, they answer right away, and the voice gives you six choices. I punch #3, I'm put on hold, and wait while listening to awful music. Another voice comes on, gives me pretty much the same instructions. This time I punch #2, am put on hold, and wait while listening to more awful music, but with a new voice popping in telling me that they're sorry for the delay. Then another voice comes on, and tells me to 'state the purpose of your call.' I say about nineteen different purposes, none of which register a response. I get put on hold again, this time I hear over and over 'you're calling in our peak times, you might want to consider calling after midnight or on Saturday.' Finally a different voice comes on, and asks, 'What can I do for you?' I don't realize it's a real person at first. When I do, it's too late and I'm put on hold again. Later, I hear another voice, I quickly tell him what I want, and he transfers me to the right department because he says I've been in the wrong department. The 'right' department answers after about thirty rings, but it's another machine and I get put on hold again. I wait, but this time there is no music, instead they play commercials telling me how I can apply for new HMO they are forming for people with fungal infections. Finally, a guy comes on the line, says, 'I'll be right with you,' and puts me on hold, and this time there's no music or commercials. When he gets back on the line, he asks, 'Who got you to me?' I tell him and he tells me that guy 'does this to me all the time' and that he's a total jerk. He transfers me to another department, where a voice tells me to 'punch in the number of the department I want to speak—"

"Tiffany, let me stop you here for a second."

"Are you going to put me on hold?"

"No. What did you find out about the claims from the clinic?"

"I'm trying to tell you."

"Continue."

Tiffany basically repeats what she went on and on about before.

After another twenty minutes of listening patiently to her phone-a-log, I break in again, "Excuse me, Tiffany."

"What?"

"What happened at the end of your phone call?"

"It buzzed."

"What buzzed?"

"The phone."

"Did you find out if they were getting Ho Lee Dong's claims?"

"No."

"Why not?"

"I never talked to anybody."

"You've been on hold for the past four hours?"

"At least until the last recorded message thanked me for calling and hung up."

Insurance companies have their phone system down to an art.

"Mr. Sherlock, what do you want me to do now?"

"Go see a movie."

"I can do that."

***

It's my kid weekend.

Care waits patiently on the school sidewalk. I pull up, she tosses her backpack into the back seat, and hops into the front.

"Hi, Dad."

"Did you learn anything new in school today?"

"No. Can we stop at Burger King on the way home?"

"No."

A hundred yards up the pick-up lane, I see Kelly. She is even more animated than usual in the middle of a troop of chattering monkeys. I honk, stop, get out of the car, and yell, "Kelly, let's go."

All the cars behind me honk and I hear voices yelling,

"Come on, buddy, you're holding up the line."

Tell me something I don't know.

Kelly finally plops into the back seat. I'm about to yell at her but decide it wouldn't do any good. "You won't believe what happened today, Dad."

"You learned to be cordial, polite, and listen to your father?"

"No. Arleta Torelli got into Dick Buttkick. Nobody could believe it. This chick is like so dumb, she can't get both her brain cells to work together. One time the teacher asked, 'Why are big cities usually cooler than farm towns?' and Arleta answered, 'Because the big buildings provide a lot more shade.' And one time in American History, she asked, 'why didn't George Washington take the same bus I took to cross the Delaware?' The chick is an ignoramus idiot." Kelly has to stop to take a breath.

"What's Dick Buttkick?" I ask.

"It's that college prep school downtown."

"Dick Butkis, like the football player?"

"They call it Dick Buttkick cause it's so hard."

"Dad, can we stop at Taco Bell?" Care cuts in. "I'm really hungry."

"No."

"I tell you Dad, Arleta Torelli is so dumb special needs kids make fun of her. No one in the school could believe it."

"So, how'd she get in if she's so mentally challenged?" I ask.

"Her mother's like the head of the PTA and always hanging around school like a bad smell."

"That's not very nice, Kelly."

"You hang with Smelly Torelli and see what you think, Dad."

"Did a lot of kids get into magnet schools?"

"Millions. The brainiacs and the Asian kids, and this one twerpy, Hispanic kid, who most of us didn't think could speak English got into the Science Academy."

"Dad, are we going to have any fun this weekend?" Care asks, remaining oblivious to Kelly and my conversation.

"Probably not," I answer.

"Why not?"

"You make your own good time, Care."

"No, you don't. That's why they invented Disneyland, Dad."

"Did you figure out who is stealing the milk money, yet?" Kelly asks.

"No."

"Can we help you do that?"

"I doubt it."

"Why not?" they both ask, putting us all in the same conversation for the first time.

"Because if I don't know what to do next, I doubt if you do."

"We have to think outside the cafeteria line, Dad."

I hate to admit it, but Kelly has a good point.

***

On Saturday morning I get up early and clean the apartment. After the girls crawl out of bed, and I get at least some breakfast into them, we go on chore duty, which means we get in the car, go to the market, dry cleaners, gas station, drug store, and wherever else is on the list. They complain at each stop, play with their cell phones, and give me suggestions on what to buy.

"Dad, there is a lot of protein in a fruit loop, we should stock up since they're on sale. Think of how much you'll save."

"I'll save a lot more if I don't buy any."

On the way home from the last errand, Kelly asks, "When are we going to get to spend some of the money Tiffany said you won?"

"Never."

"Why not?"

"Because the money is going to be spent to make our lives better," I tell the two.

"Yeah, like new clothes."

"Or taking us to Six Flags."

"No."

"That's not fair."

"It's not that much money, anyway," If I compare my money to Warren Buffet's, this is true.

"Well, if it's not that much money, just give it to us," Kelly says.

"Forget it."

Tiffany stops by in the afternoon.

"Hello there, little dudettes."

"Tiffany, what are you doing here?"

"I was bored, so I decided I'd come over here. You being so totally boring, Mr. Sherlock, always makes me feel less bored when I'm around you."

"It's very reassuring to know, Tiffany, that my miserable life makes your life so much more rewarding."

"You're welcome."

I go into the kitchen to see what's in the fridge for dinner, leaving the three girls in front of the TV watching a show about some rich family in Beverly Hills. I only hear snippets of dialogue from the program, but they're enough to send me in to check on how their minds are being destroyed by the media.

One step into the room, Care asks, "Dad, what's the difference between gay and transgendered?"

Although I hate when people answer a question with a question, I ask, "What are you watching?"

"This husband of a family is becoming a woman because he doesn't want to be a guy anymore."

"Turn it off."

"No, Dad," Kelly says. "This is really educational."

"Turn it off."

"What's the difference, Dad?" Care repeats.

"Gay people like other gay people. Transgender people change their style and equipment."

"What equipment?" Care asks.

This is when I hate being a parent.

"Duh," Kelly says to her sister while pointing her finger to where the change will take place.

"Gross."

"Certainly not my idea of a fun-filled weekend," Tiffany says.

"How do they do that?"

"With cutting edge technology, I would hope," I add.

"Here's what I don't get," Tiffany says.

I clench my jaw, waiting for what's coming.

"If a gay guy went for a gay woman, would that would make him straight?" Tiffany asks.

"I would doubt it."

"If a straight guy went for a transgendered woman, would he still be straight?" Tiffany continues.

"You got me," I say.

"If a woman was gay and got transgendered, then hooked up with another woman would she be straight?"

"It would matter on the other woman, I think."

"If two straight guys both got transgendered into women, and then hooked up with each other, what would they be?"

"An interesting couple."

"Dad, gay guys go for gay guys and gay women go for gay women. Duh."

"Thank you, Kelly, for clearing that up for everyone."

"I'm only here to help, Dad."

"You want to help with dinner?" I ask her.

"Not that kind of help, Dad. I'm more into intellectual help."

"I have another question, Mr. Sherlock," Tiffany says, pointing at the TV. "After this guy becomes a woman, he'd still be married to his wife, who is already a woman, but if gay marriage is illegal, wouldn't they be breaking the law and have to go to prison?"

"If they did, it would certainly make for a difficult cell block decision."

"Dad, if this guy becomes a woman," Care asks, "do you think he'd want to date a guy like the guy he used to be?"

"He shouldn't date," Tiffany answers.

"Why not?" I ask.

"Because he's still married to his wife," Tiffany answers. "And I don't think they let you date while you're in prison."

I can't take any more of this. "Let's all go out and have some fun. I'll even buy dinner."

"Oh, great, where, Dad?"

"Chinatown."

"Do they have a McDonald's in Chinatown?"

***

Chicago's Chinatown pales in comparison to the Chinatowns in San Francisco and Seattle. It's really only a few streets with scattered pagodas, almost all of which are Chinese restaurants. There are shops where you can buy stuffed panda bears, coolie hats, Chinese tchotchkes, and kimonos, although kimonos are Japanese, not Chinese. The merchants selling the items don't differentiate and could care less as long as you buy one. I do notice a number of stores and offices in the area concerned with health care. There are acupuncturists, health food emporiums, and Chinese herb stores. Dr. Ho Lee Dong has picked a good area to do business. Chinatown has become a one-stop destination for all that ails you.

The four of us walk up and down 23rd Street and the surrounding blocks, sightseeing, going into stores, window shopping, and wondering who would want to buy a duck with its head and flippers still attached.

"Let's eat here." I stop at one of the more authentic, i.e. small, rundown, and questionably clean eateries on the street. Its sign reads: Yu RiRi Fatt Chinese Restaurant.

"This place?" Tiffany doesn't notice the eatery is directly in front of Dr. Dong's clinic, and I'm sure she didn't notice there was an entrance door in the alley across from the clinic the day we visited. "Why?"

"Yeah, Dad, you're always telling us Chinese food is bad for you."

"I have a coupon."

As we walk into the RiRi Fatt place, I see a *Help Wanted* sign stating they are in need of a busboy. I wonder if I applied for the job and wasn't hired, I could sue the place for discrimination and make some easy money?

We are seated at one of the two tables for four. We are the only Caucasians in the place, which I consider a good sign. The waitress hands each of us a menu.

"I can't read this," Tiffany says.

"Flip it over. The other side is in English."

"How do we know it's the same food?" Care asks.

"Sometimes you just have to trust people, Care."

"Well, I'm ordering off this side," Tiffany says, pointing to the Mandarin symbols, "because I prefer traditional Chinese, not Americanized Chinese."

The waitress returns. "Ready order?"

"I'll have this one," Tiffany points at set of symbols.

"Me, too," Kelly says.

"Me, too, too," Care follows suit.

"I'll have the cashew chicken." I break the chain.

"One cashew chicken, three whole Peking duck."

I immediately see flashbacks in three faces to the dead ducks previously seen in the window. "Make those three chop suey," I tell the waitress.

"Chop suey, three. Cashew chicken, one"

"By the way," I ask our waitress. "Do you get a lot of business from the clinic behind you in the alley?"

"Lots cancer people eat here."

"What do they order?" Tiffany asks.

"Whole Peking duck."

"How do you know they're from the clinic?" I ask.

"Use bathroom. All use bathroom, over, over, over."

"Before, after, or during the meal?" I ask.

"All time."

This seems odd. I decide not to press the issue in fear of an answer I might receive and ruin my appetite. "Thanks."

"What drink?"

My girls order Cokes. Tiffany asks, "Do you have an odd-year Savignon Blanc?"

I tell the waitress, "We'll all have tea." It comes with the meal.

As we wait for the food to arrive, I get up and wander to the back of the restaurant. I see out the window that the clinic is as busy as ever. Asian people are walking in and walking out; a bit odd to think a Saturday evening would be a prime time for administering chemo, maybe he has non-prime specials available. The Dong clientele is heavily female, senior, and on foot.

I return to our table as the soup arrives.

"What's this, Dad?"

"Egg drop soup."

"Where'd they drop the egg?" Kelly asks peering into the liquid as if waiting to see if a Chinese dragon pops out.

"What kind of egg?" Care asks.

"Regular old egg, I assume." Although, my first rule of life is to never assume anything.

"They drop it on purpose or by accident?" Kelly asks.

"Be careful you don't eat any shell," Tiffany warns. "You could choke to death."

You can dress them up, but ya can't take 'em out.

CHAPTER 7

Sunday morning before I have a chance to argue with the girls about attending church, the phone rings. It's Fern Mossy. She's in a panic.

"What?"

I can't believe what I'm hearing.

I hang up the phone. "Get dressed. We're leaving," I hurriedly say to my kids.

"Why?"

"Where are we going?"

"Hurry!"

If my Toyota could break speed limits, I would have. We arrive at Pat Nixon/Ann Margaret and pull around to the back playground and athletic fields. I can't believe what I'm witnessing. It's a mad, mad, mad, mad world out there.

There must be a hundred people scattered over wherever there's dirt, each has a shovel, and is furiously digging like body snatchers on speed. The athletic field looks like gopher heaven. People are fighting for positions, jousting like knights for what they must think is a prime spot, and ripping up sod faster than a lousy golfer using a Big Bertha.

"I can't stop them," Fern screams as she runs up to us.

"What are they doing?"

"Somebody said, 'there's money buried out here,'" Fern explains.

"Who?"

"I don't know. You have to stop them, Mr. Sherlock."

I run into the middle of the melee. I'm screaming like a banshee while waving my arms like a shipwrecked sailor seeing a plane. "Stop. Everybody stop. There's no money out here. It's all a mistake. There's not a dime to be found."

This, of course, does absolutely no good. The dirt keeps flying like trailer parts in a tornado. This is an Easter egg hunt gone horribly wrong. A fanatical frenzy for free money.

One guy at the edge of the garden screams out, "Eureka!" Other shovelers hear the call and run to the garden where he digs. They plunge their spades in and obliterate any seed from ever growing there again. The guy who "Eureka'd" tries to fight off the interlopers, "This is my claim. I staked it."

"Stop them, Mr. Sherlock, stop them." Fern shows no sign of un-panicking.

"Why'd you call me?" I have to ask.

"You're a cop."

"No, he's not," Kelly informs her. "He got fired."

The guy who "Eureka'd" finds a big rock.

I have no other choice. I run as fast as I can towards the school. When I reach the buildings, I search frantically for the little red box. It takes me about a minute to find the box, five seconds to smash the glass, and another second to depress the lever.

Sirens and bells ring out louder than a World War II London air raid.

And the blare doesn't do a bit of good.

I look out over the playground and see the throng of humanity still frantically digging like crazed forty-niners, the originals, not the NFLers.

Three minutes later, the fire trucks roar into the playground like the cavalry arriving to save the wagon train.

And the people keep digging!

"What the heck is going on?" The fire captain climbs down from the truck.

"They think there's money buried out there," I tell him.

"Is there?"

"No."

"What do you want us to do?" he asks.

"Stop them?"

"How?"

"Hose 'em down." I can't think of any other solution.

Streams of water let loose and mow the diggers down like dominoes in a windstorm. Many go bouncing into newly made mud and come up looking like the losers in a tug-of-war. Others get blinded by the spray and can't continue. Some refuse to quit, and dig their hands into the new holes, searching for that pot of elusive gold.

A few thousand gallons of water later, it's over.

The firemen herd the soggy, disappointed, cash coveters over to where I'm standing.

"There's no money here, people," I regretfully inform them.

"It's all a misunderstanding."

"But my daughter said—" one person says.

"My kid told me there's hundreds of dollars out here."

"Yeah, mine, too."

"I saw it on Facebook."

"I got a tweet."

I turn in time to see Kelly look at Care and Care look at Kelly. When they finally look at me their two sets of very wide eyes have enough fear in them to rival the opening night viewing of *Halloween 14.*

"Whoops," Care says.

"Gee, Dad, I don't know how this coulda happened," Kelly explains.

"Get in the car."

I turn back to the crowd. "Everybody go home."

"Who's going to clean this up?" Fern asks.

"Nature," I tell her.

As the people disperse and the firemen pack up, Principal Puddle drives into the playground, screeches to a stop, and hops out of his car. "What the heck is going on?"

"Fools after Fool's Gold," I tell him.

"My playground looks like a pot-holed moon crater."

"I got here as soon as I could," Fern explains. "I tried to stop them, but they were in a frenzy."

"It was like in those old movies when the prospectors get gold fever," I say. "And they go loco trying to get rich."

"This whole situation is getting worse and worse," Principal Puddle says to me.

"I know."

"Let's go inside," Eldin says. "It's too depressing out here."

I get back into my car.

"I swear to God, Dad, I only told one person," Care says before I start screaming. "And she swore she wouldn't tell anyone."

"Dad, it wasn't my fault," Kelly says. "It slipped out when we were talking about what Tugboat Togneri wore to school that day."

"And where did your comment just happen to slip out, Kelly?" I ask as I drive over to the back door where Eldin will let me inside.

"It was at lunch."

"And nobody else heard you?"

"Well, maybe someone could've overheard me in passing, but I doubt it."

My blood pressure must be near three hundred, but I don't explode. Yet.

I park the car. "Listen you two. Stay in the car. I'll deal with you later. And don't call anyone on your cell phones. Do you understand me?"

"Yes, Dad."

I get out of the car. After four or five steps, I look back to see Care and Kelly texting away on their cell phone like stenos in the typing pool. Does anybody ever listen to me?

I go inside and meet Fern and Eldin in the hallway.

"What happened?" Eldin asks. "I'm sitting at home reading the paper and I get a call the fire department is hosing down parents on my playground."

"Somebody started a rumor that there were thousands of dollars buried on the school grounds." Fern tells him.

"Who?"

I shrug my shoulders. "Beats me."

"Somehow it got on social media and spread like wildfire."

"I hate that Facebook," Eldin says.

"Me, too," I agree with him again.

"The district is going to hear about this. What am I going to say?"

"Tell them some party planner wrote a very bad clue for the scavenger hunt," I suggest.

Suspecting more bad news, Eldin goes on, saying, "And if they hear about this, they're sure to hear about the missing milk money."

"Not necessarily," I tell him.

"Why not?"

"I don't suspect a lot of these parents are going to want to admit they're infected with a case of gold fever."

"We have to get to the bottom of this. My schools don't need this kind of publicity."

I feel sorry for Eldin. "If anybody asks, just tell them it was a gopher hunt gone gonzo."

***

"I thought I told you two not to call anybody," I say before starting the car.

"We didn't call, Dad," Care says as she finishes a message and hits *send*. "We were texting."

"There's a difference?"

"Of course."

"See, Dad, you have to be more specific when you were yelling at us," Kelly explains. "You said not to 'call anyone' instead of saying 'call or *text* anyone.'"

"Fine, Kelly," I say. "When we get back to the apartment, I'll be really specific."

"That doesn't sound good," Care says to her sister.

***

I have perfect children on this Sunday afternoon. They wash the dishes, mop the kitchen floor, scrub the counters, vacuum, dust, change the sheets, and clean every inch of the bathroom, which they hate more than anything. After those chores, they do their homework. At four forty-five I pile them in the car to return them to their mother's.

"What did you learn today, girls?"

"Cleaning a bathroom is totally gross?"

"Try again."

"That you should have a cleaning lady like mom does?"

"I should, but that's hardly the lesson I expected you to learn."

"I know," Care says. "I learned that it's really hard to find someone who you can trust these days. I told Karen not to say a word to anyone."

"Yeah, Dad, you should've made that blabbermouth come over and clean the bathroom," Kelly says.

"Oh, like you didn't have a thing to do with all those people showing up, Kelly?"

"Well, I will admit, I did see a few familiar parent faces."

I raise my voice to a lecture level. "The point here, children, is when I tell you 'Not to say a word to anyone' that means 'Don't say a word to anyone!'" I pause. "Is there any part of that you don't understand?"

The two sit quietly for a few seconds before Care asks, "Now is saying and texting the same thing because you're not really saying something when you're texting?"

"Yes."

"Would we be in trouble if we would've tweeted the message anonymously?"

"Saying, texting, Facebooking, tweety-birding, or sending smoke signals; it's all the same thing. If I say 'not a word,' it means keep your mouth shut and your thumbs in your pockets."

We approach the house I used to own.

"Okay, Dad, we got it," Kelly assures me. "And to make up for our mistake, we're going to help you break the case."

"Please don't!"

"That's okay, Dad, we're more than happy to keep helping."

CHAPTER 8

I call Tiffany first thing Monday morning knowing she won't answer. I leave a message, which she probably won't listen to either.

Next, I call Antoinette "Bree" Bisonette, which is pronounced Bis-o-nay.

"Bree, how are you?"

"What do you want?"

"I'm on a case and I need some information."

"And you want to make your problem, my problem?" This lady could use a major dose of Mrs. Chumley cheer.

Bree is one of the heads of the Richmond Insurance claims department. A few months back, I helped unravel a scam going on under her nose, which has had its share of fixing along with a few of her other body parts. Bree is also the girlfriend of Jamison Richmond III, who Tiffany refers to as "Daddy." Bree and Tiffany have had some past relationship issues, which I tried my best to help smooth over. After the case was concluded, I was happy to report that Bree and Tiffany were not only on speaking terms, but Tiffany invited Bree to join her for a night on the town, and Bree nominated Tiffany for the Richmond Employee of the Month, which unfortunately Tiffany lost out to Buddy Brubaker, who designed a foolproof system for protecting lunches from food thieves in the break room's refrigerators. His idea was quite simple. He put up a sign on the front of the fridge reading: "One sandwich or salad in today's lunches has salmonella. Eat at your own risk." Nobody has lost a lunch since.

I explain to Bree, "There is a doc in Chinatown who is breaking the bank with chemo claims and I need to find out if he's doing this with other insurance companies besides Richmond."

"Why don't you have little Tiffy do it?" Bree asks in a snarky tone, telling me my smooth issue is once again bumpy.

"I've got her working on another aspect of the case."

"What? You send her in undercover as a Geisha girl?"

"No."

"Yeah, I didn't think so. Geisha girls have to know how to keep their mouths shut. Those fat-filled lips of hers would slap her face silly if she ever rolled down the window when she was speeding on the expressway. "

"Bree, that's not very nice."

"When it comes to not being very nice, little Tiffy would give the Wicked Witch of the West a run for her money."

This is getting way out of line, I better get this back on track. "Could you make some calls? Please?"

"Do I have to?"

Something is going on here, I'm not sure what, and I'm really not sure I want to know, either.

"Well, you don't have to do anything, Bree," I pause. "But, it's the Ho Lee Dong One Stop Cancer Clinic on 23rd Place in Chinatown."

"And you want me to drop everything I'm doing and just jump at your command like an elephant in the circus?" She snaps back at me with the recoil of a giant rubber band. Her breathing is harder than if she just swam the English Channel.

"Bree, is something bothering you?"

She breaks into a crying jag worthy of a Nick Sparks' novel. Bree is bawling as if her mother, father, sister, brother, best friend, and dog were all diagnosed with cases of terminal dry skin and had only two weeks before they all flaked away.

"Bree, what's wrong?"

"Jamison put our relationship on hold."

"Why?

She speaks as best as she's able through her waterworks. "He said he needed some time."

"Time for what?"

"I don't know. He didn't say." She blows her nose into the phone's receiver. I can only hope she had a hanky handy. "He said it's best for the both of us."

This revelation certainly explains her snarky tone.

"I'm sorry."

"He's put me on hold, Mr. Sherlock. Do you know what that means?"

Actually, I don't.

"It means: Don't call me, I'll call you," she chokes out.

I've never understood how relationships get put on hold. I understand how you put a library book on hold, hold a place in line, hold a telephone call, or hold an item on a lay-away payment plan, but have no clue how to put emotions on hold. If you love someone, do you stop loving them while you're on hold? Do you stop being someone's friend while you're on hold? Does being put on hold mean you turn off all your feeling like a garden hose? It really doesn't make any sense to me. I don't know if being on hold requires you to stop seeing the person, stop talking, or reduce them from lover to good buddy status? Must you unfriend them on Facebook and remove them from the frequently contacted list in your phone? If you're on hold, do you stop being intimate? I've heard of people being on hold but still be in each other's clutches. Isn't it a bit hard to believe your relationship can be on hold, as they moan in your ear?

There are so many on hold questions to be considered. Are on-holds only for boyfriend/girlfriend situations or can you put family members on hold and not invite them over for holidays, give gifts, or send cards? And how do you get off being on hold? Is it a vote, discussion, contract, mutual agreement, or coin toss? Is there such a thing as an on hold time limit? Do mutual friends get involved or do you have to seek professional help? If a relationship is constantly going on and off hold, should an on hold relationship therapist be kept on hold?

Personally, I can't remember ever being on hold. All my women seem to have no trouble dumping me. And since I don't understand the on hold rules, I've never ventured into putting anyone on hold. When it comes to relationship on holds, I have no clue. Maybe I should find out. I'll ask Tiffany, she'll know.

"Bree, I know how you feel," I lie, "but you're going to have to get through this."

"How?"

Good question. I wish I had a good answer. "Maybe you should bury yourself in your work?"

She's still weeping like a professional onion peeler. "Do you know how hard it is knowing the man you love is only one floor away in a perfectly appointed corner office with a wet bar and HDTV on the wall?"

Actually, no because I've never gotten close to the boss' office. Jamison Richmond the III doesn't take my phone calls, and if he did, I doubt if he'd even bother putting me on hold.

"I feel like my life is over," she says.

"No, Bree, your life isn't over," I try to reason with her.

"But it's on hold!"

"But it'll pick up." I realize immediately this was a bad choice of words as she lets out a huge mucus-filled cry. "It will get better. You need some time."

"I hate time. Time on hold is the worst time you can spend. You sit next to the phone and wait forever."

Well, at least she now knows how a customer feels calling the Richmond Insurance Company to request an explanation on a claim they refused to pay.

"Bree, take a deep breath, calm yourself, and drink a glass of water. You have to keep busy, exercise, or do anything that will get your mind thinking in another direction."

She's now weeping.

I give her more time.

Now she's sniffling.

"You're going to be okay, Bree. You're strong, you're good, and you'll get through this."

"I doubt it."

I bid a quick good-bye to Bree Bisonette, which is pronounced Bis-o-nay.

***

I make sure I arrive at the school after all classes are in session. Finding out who stole the missing milk money is difficult enough without fighting the drop-off line's morning, bumper-to-bumper traffic.

"Hello, Mrs. Chumley."

"Good morning, Mr. Sherlock. Are you having a smiley day?"

"Of course," I lie. "Is Principal Puddle in?"

"Principal Puddle isn't in. He's at a meeting downtown."

"Is it a spur-of-the-moment meeting or previously scheduled?"

"He goes every Monday morning."

Mrs. Dorthea Chumley looks like she was born in the chair she now sits. She's transcended being a mere employee of the school to become a fixture as permanent as the flagpole on the front lawn. It is difficult to tell her age. I would guess somewhere between pretty darn old and forced retirement, whatever age that may be. She is famous for learning every name of every child in the school within a week of the first day, and more famous for affixing small, round, yellow and black smiley faces to the collars of the children. There is no child she doesn't like and there is no child who doesn't like her.

I stand back from her desk and slightly relax in my own comfort zone. I ask, "How long has Principal Puddle been principal?" My question catches her a bit off-guard.

"Long time." She pauses. "Why do you ask?"

"Just wondered." I pause. "You must like working for him?"

"Very much. He truly cares about the children and would do anything to help them in any way he can."

"But he's not much when it comes to accounting, I hear?"

"Really? Who'd you hear that from?"

I don't like to lie, but I seem to not have problems with it this morning. "I can't remember, but I've heard it more than once."

"I wouldn't say he's bad at numbers. He just has a lot more important things to be concerned about than debits and credits."

"He leaves that up to you?"

"I put everything down, he reviews, I re-check, and pass all to Miss Mossy for payment."

"Good system?"

"Works."

"Could I see how you do all that?"

She hesitates. "I'm not sure Principal Puddle would want me to do that."

It would be pointless to push a woman, who would be a perfect model for a Norman Rockwell portrait of kindly old aunt. She has her hair in a bun, a dress one level above "house," string of pearls around her neck, and wears ugly comfortable shoes.

"When do you expect Principal Puddle to arrive?"

"He is usually here by now."

"One other question, Mrs. Chumley."

"Yes."

"Who heads up the PTA milk program?"

"Ms. Torelli."

"Do you know how I could get in touch with her?"

"She'll be here today. I suggest you see her outside on her way in before fourth period lunch or outside when she leaves after fifth period lunch."

"Thank you."

"You're welcome and have a smiley day." Mrs. Chumley places a smiley face on my collar and I bid her adieu.

I return to my car. I'm parked in a visitor's spot, which is two spots away from Principal Puddle's reserved space. I sit in my Toyota, take out my phone, and wonders never cease, Tiffany has returned my call. I call in return of her return of my call.

"It's me," I say when she picks up.

"Mr. Sherlock, where are you?"

"At school."

"Are you learning anything?"

"No."

"Sounds like the same school I went to." She speaks before I can respond. "Mr. Fumalooma's lawyer called and said he wants to settle the case and not go to trial."

"Good for him."

"Should I call him back, and tell him, 'good for you'?"

"No." I hesitate for a second, and say, "Call the guy back—"

Tiffany interrupts me, "I asked if I should call him back, you said 'no,' and now you tell me to 'call him back.' Make up your mind, Mr. Sherlock."

"He wants you to call him back and say 'yes, we'll settle.' I want you to call him back and tell him to forward whatever he's filed with the court to us."

"This is very confusing," Tiffany says.

"We need to see what he's got, so we can go over his case."

"We?"

"Okay, *me.*"

"You're putting a lot of faith in me, Mr. Sherlock. This is one of the more complicated assignments you've given me."

"Did you have a bad night last night, Tiffany?"

"No. I had a great night."

"Bad morning?"

"Yes."

A Subaru pulls into the small parking area and a woman I have seen before hurriedly exits.

"I got to run, Tiffany. Call me back when you get the file from the lawyer."

"You sure you want me to call him?"

"I'm positive."

I hang up the phone. "Excuse me," I call out to the woman. "Mrs. Torelli?"

She stops and waits as I climb out of my Toyota. "You're the man who won the money." She hesitates, noticing from where I emerged. "Are you going to use it to buy a new car?"

"Maybe." I move toward her.

"You should."

I'm about five feet from her. "Mrs. Torelli."

"It's Ms."

One more step and I am hit so hard, right in the nose, I stagger backward. My entire head feels like it is going to explode. Senses that haven't been used in years are suddenly doing overtime duty. My eyes water, ears burn, throat constricts, and I feel a rash starting to spread over my entire body.

Ms. Torelli is wearing so much cheap perfume my eyebrows curl upward and my toenails downward. The woman is a walking stink bomb. No wonder Kelly called her Smelly Torelli.

I shift to the left and keep moving until I feel the wind at my back. My senses are returning to normal as the downwind wind saves me from permanent olfactory damage.

"Are you okay?" she asks.

"That's quite a fragrance you have on."

"My favorite."

"What's it called?" I wouldn't be surprised to hear *Eau du Streetwalker*.

"*Fleur de lies extraordinaire.*"

I suck in as much clean midwest air as possible. "Mrs. Torelli."

"It's Ms."

"I need to talk to you."

"About what?"

"The milk money."

"What about the milk money?"

"Some has disappeared."

"That's impossible."

"Nope, gone."

"Where did it disappear to?"

"Nobody knows."

"Why are *you* telling me this?"

"I used to be a detective."

"What are you now?"

"An investigator."

"What's the difference?"

"One has a pension."

"You don't look like an investigator to me," she says.

"What do I look like?"

"A guy who needs a new car."

"I wear a lot of hats," I explain. "And I've been put in charge of finding the milk money by Principal Puddle."

She straightens up with her hands on her hips. "Well, I didn't take it. I can account for every nickel every day of every week."

"I'm not accusing you, Ms. Torelli."

"It sure sounds like it to me. Why are you picking on the people who bust their bottoms for this school? I have worked tirelessly over the years in every capacity from room mother to PTA president, and have never asked for or received a dime in payment for my efforts."

This is not going well.

"Maybe this is merely a simple mistake in accounting," I backpedal, "but I still have to find out what's wrong."

"If it wasn't for parents like me, Mr. Sherlock, certain over-dressed and over-talkative students, and I won't mention any names here, wouldn't have such a fine school to attend."

"Are you referring to my daughter, Kelly?"

"I said I wouldn't mention any names, but if the purple Ugg boots fit, wear 'em."

I tried to talk Kelly out of that color, but she wouldn't listen to me.

"Sure, it's easy for people like you to stand back and throw stones at people like me," Smelly Torelli continues her verbal stink, "but I've never seen you flipping pancakes at one of our breakfast fundraisers."

"Well, that's because I don't believe stuffing a load of pancake dough in a kid's stomach is a healthy breakfast choice." Go ahead try to argue with that one, lady.

"I consider your allegations against me to be an insult to my years of service at this school." I'll bet this woman is a hoot at her book club.

"Ms. Torelli, I'm not accusing you, alleging anything, or

73

throwing any stones, I'm just trying to find some missing milk money."

"You can check with Miss Mossy, Mrs. Chumley, or the bank for all I care. Every penny brought in by me is accounted for and deposited. Good day, Mr. Sherlock."

Stinky Winky/Smelly Torelli marches off in her own odiferous cloud, heading into the school to scar the nostrils of the young and unsuspecting.

I stand alone in the middle of the parking lot like a child without a home as Principal Puddle arrives. I meet him as he gets out of his car.

"I just had the pleasure of meeting Winky Torelli."

"I hope you caught her outside."

"I did."

"Downwind?"

"After the initial shock."

"Whew."

"Being in a small room with that woman would be a form of Chinese odor torture," I say. "Has anybody ever told her she stinks to high heaven?"

"After you find out who stole the milk money, you can."

"That would be pointless. Nobody ever listens to me."

"Winky is who we refer to in educational circles as a *helicopter parent*," Eldin tells me.

"Well, she's buzzing around in some heavy duty air."

We walk toward the school. I ask, "Did anyone at your meeting mention what happened on Sunday?"

"No, thank God."

"How about the milk money?"

"No," he says, "but I do have some good news on that front."

"What?"

"The money evened out last week. Nobody stole a dime."

"No offense, Principal, but I wouldn't call that good news."

"Why not?"

"It could mean that whoever was stealing is now onto us trying to find them."

From his grunt, he obviously didn't consider the possibility.

"I'd like to go over Mrs. Chumley's accounting."

"Sure."

"I asked, but she said no."

"That sounds like Mrs. Chumley."

We enter the Principal's office.

"I see you found him," Mrs. Chumley says in her fresh as a daisy tone.

"Mrs. Chumley," Eldin says, "please allow Mr. Sherlock full access to your accounting files."

"Most certainly."

"Thank you, Mrs. Chumley."

"You're welcome." She flashes a big Mrs. Chumley grin.

During the lunch periods, I sit in an empty classroom and page through Mrs. Chumley's spreadsheets. I'm impressed and I'm shocked. I find it hard to believe anyone could be this neat. The spreadsheets are past the point of being perfect. Each 8 ½ x 14 inch, columnar sheet is a portrait of perfection. Filled out with pencils sharp enough to perform laser surgery, each number fits into its tiny box without crossing a line, and each title or description is printed so clean and exact, no confusion could ever be considered. When she did have to erase, she did so with such efficiency, no trace of what may have been written before can be recognized. If Mrs. Chimley ever changes careers and becomes a cleaning lady, I'd hire her in a minute, if I could afford one.

Being one who is yet to balance his checkbook, even with my few dollars, I'm not the one to be searching for irregularities or even sure where to begin. I start with the credit sheets and line up the last four months, left to right with the latest on the left, and try to compare items to items and numbers to numbers. This is difficult because the items are not ordered the same way month to month. The items are also not consistent month to month or referred to in the same manner. For example: plumbing, plumbing supplies, and pipe routing, which I would consider pretty much the same expenses, appear and disappear one month to the next. The dollars and cents are also all over the map. The expenditures for tech supplies are boom or bust and the cost of library maintenance goes up and down like the April temperatures in Chicago.

I find the milk money on the pages and try to make some sense on how all the numbers should make sense but fail miserably. The credit is $400 one week and $200 the next. There are skipped weeks, partial weeks, and even one rebate from a prior week. I find the corresponding monthly debit sheets and try to match the milk money's debits and credits, apple juice to apple juice and orange juice to orange juice, but find it impossible. My head is spinning like lotto balls before the nightly drawing.

"You have to leave now," Mrs. Chumley tells me, entering the room.

"Did I do something wrong?"

"No, they need the room for a class."

The bell rings. I hurriedly pack up the sheets strewn across the desk as the kids file in. Mrs. Chumley helps me, making sure no sheet is wrinkled in the process. "Did this help?" she asks as we make our way into the hall amidst scurrying kids.

"Not really."

"That's a shame."

"I had a difficult time understanding your accounting procedures."

"Really?"

"There doesn't seem to be any rhyme or reason one month to the next."

"That's odd. It works for me."

The next bell rings, and in seconds, the hallways are deserted.

We return to the principal's office. "Would it be possible for me to get copies of these spreadsheets?" I ask.

She doesn't answer immediately because inside the closed office of the principal there is quite a ruckus. We can't see, but we can hear.

"It isn't fair," a male voice calls out.

"Yes, it is." Principal Puddle's voice remains calm.

"You people are kowtowing to a bunch of illegal immigrants, who don't even belong here in the first place."

"Your child can be put on the waiting list."

"She should be first on the acceptance list," the man screams.

"She had a seventy-nine on the exam."

"I don't care if she had a nineteen," the man answers. "She's a straight A student, on the student council, a math-a-lete, and president of the dance thing you got here. That should be plenty!"

"There's nothing I can do. The cut-off was a ninety on the test."

"And let me tell you something else, buddy—" I can picture this jerk pointing a finger in Eldin's face. "I'm not the only one mad. There are plenty of parents who feel the same way I do. We're sick and tired of these illegal aliens coming in and getting the benefits meant for real Americans."

"All I can do," Eldin pleads with the man, "is suggest you prepare your thoughts and present them at the next board meeting in a calm and restrained manner."

"Don't you talk down to me," he says. "I pay more taxes than anyone around here. I'm the guy you should be bending over backwards to please."

"You know," Mrs. Chumley says to me between breaks in the in-office verbal battle, "I was going to ask about the copies, but I think I'll just go ahead and make them for you."

"Thanks."

"You're welcome."

I stick around for one last rant. "You people let them foreigners into the better schools, then they get into the best colleges, and then when they're done, they take it all back to China or Guatemala and use it against us to put American workers out of a job."

I wonder who cleans this guy's house and cuts his lawn. I wouldn't be surprised if he did stand-up comedy at Klan rallies for fun.

✳✳✳

In the afternoon, I get two phone calls. The first is from Bree Bisonette.

"Mr. Sherlock—"

"Hi, Bree." I almost ask, "How are you?" but hold my tongue. If I open the door, I might have to go through it.

"Mr. Sherlock, I have news for you," she tells me.

I hope this isn't about being put on hold.

"This Doctor Dong guy is burning up accounts payable."

Whew.

"So it isn't just Richmond?"

"We do seem to be leading the pact, but he has multiple claims at all the big insurers." Bree speaks as if she is in a high level corporate meeting.

"How long has the streak been going?" I ask.

"Seven months."

"That many that quick? Is this normal?"

"Clinics will go up and down. It isn't unheard of if they change their client base or they get a rash of referrals from the same specialists and see a bump in business."

"Does it look kosher, or at least Szechuan, to you?" I ask.

"I don't know. It's hard to tell."

"Maybe he's running a two-for-one special, advertising on Asian TV, or does a daily raffle for a free Peking duck dinner?"

"You're the detective, find out."

Bree must be getting back to normal. "You sound much better than you did earlier," I compliment her.

And she breaks out in another fountain of sorrow.

Oh jeesh.

"I'm still on hold," she chokes up. "I could die waiting for him to call and take me back." She sniffles between sentences and weeps through others. "I have all this love and no place to put it. My heart's in a million shattered pieces. What am I going to do, Sherlock?"

Why did I have to open my big mouth? "Bree, you just have to hang in there."

"And if he never calls until our matching Rolexes run out of battery life, what am I going to do?"

"You're just going to have to buy a new battery and reset it."

"Easy for you to say. I bet you don't even own a watch."

I don't. I had to pawn it.

She gives me one more anguished wail of absolute sorrow and hangs up. Thank God she didn't put me on hold.

The second call is from Tiffany.

"I got the stuff from the lawyer, Mr. Sherlock."

"Okay, please describe."

"Well, it's brown with my name on the front and his name in the left hand corner."

"I didn't mean the envelope, Tiffany. I meant what's inside."

"Of course, I knew that."

"What was inside?"

"I didn't see a check, and was disappointed."

"Why would you expect to see a check, Tiffany?"

"I don't know. I must have been in a birthday mood or

something."

"What was in the envelope?"

"Fancy junk mail and a few pictures."

"Pictures of what?"

"Cigar butts."

"What?"

"Piles of cigar butts, ashes...really disgusting stuff."

"Kind of like *ashes to ashes* and *dust to dust*, huh, Tiffany?"

"Mr. Sherlock, take some of your new money and get yourself a cleaning lady."

CHAPTER 9

H erman McFadden is in love.
"Get in here, Sherlock. I want you to meet Ludmila."
Herman, my obese, computer genius, financial whiz friend has returned from his wife-finding sojourn to Mother Russia. After unsuccessful attempts at finding a mate on Match-dot-com, Overeaters Love Lines, and Two Tons of Fun, he decided his best bet for finding true love would be to go overseas where women will do just about anything to get to America and a better life. To properly prepare for the trip, he trimmed eighty pounds off his frame. If this sounds like a lot of weight to lose, it is usually, but not for Herman. His losing eighty pounds is akin to an Army jeep rolling off a C-17 transport plane.

"You're going to love her, Sherlock. She's as precious as a Faberge egg soufflé."

I enter his apartment, which is surprisingly the picture of neatness. This is a far cry from the usual array of dog-eared porn magazines strewn about, old cheese wrappers stuffed between couch cushions, empty pickle jars, and couch stains whose origin I hope to never know.

"What happened, Herman?"

"I told you, I'm in love."

"No, I mean this place."

"Ludmila, my little morsel of moonpie, is also a neat-nik."

I take a long gander at Herman because it takes some time to take all of Herman in. "And what happened to the rest of you?" Obviously, Herman not only found the weight he lost but added some.

"It was a little difficult staying on my diet while I was in Russia. I could eat khachapuri for my five meals a day."

"Herman, you have to start taking better care of yourself."

"Don't worry, I'm going to start going to the gym any day now," he assures me.

"What's stopping you?"

"Right now, the doorframe."

We move into his apartment. "Come on out, Ludy, and

meet Sherlock."

A woman emerges from the hallway. She's, at best, pushing twenty-five years and eighty-five pounds. She is about as wide as one of Herman's ankles and as high as his chest when his chest isn't sinking to his navel. Ludmila has straight, brown hair, dark eyes, pure white skin, two nose rings, and a full color tattoo of Josef Stalin on her left shoulder. I have a feeling there is quite a story behind that tattoo.

"Ha...low," she says haltingly.

I approach her and put out my hand to shake. "Welcome to America."

"Wit lee-ber-tee and jew-stasch for all," she says, smiles, and adds. "Amen."

Ludmila could use some English lessons and dental work.

"Isn't she delicious, Sherlock?" Herman says, the pride in his voice evident. "I've already started getting her ready for her citizenship test."

"I would have never guessed."

'The minute we laid eyes on one another," Herman says. "We both knew it was true love."

It takes a lot more than a minute to lay your eyes on Herman.

"She's dessert to my dinner," he adds.

I bet Ludmila saw Herman as a billboard of imperfection, surrounded by dollar signs.

"Why don't you whip us up a snack, Ludy, and go watch your TV show?" Herman uses his meat hook hands to enact a chef's actions over the stove.

Ludy gets the message and heads for the kitchen.

"She cooks, she cleans, and she obeys. What more could you ask of a woman?" Herman states. "I'm in love."

"I'm really happy for you, Herman. Now, I need a favor."

"I have one to ask of you, too, Sherlock."

"Me first."

We sit at his dining room table. His chair squeaks as if screaming out about what it's being forced to endure. "I need you to make sense of these debits and credits." I spread Mrs. Chumley's accounting records across the table.

"Why?"

"Somebody is stealing money at Care and Kelly's school."

"How much?"

"At least a couple of hundred a week."

Herman takes a closer look at the columns of numbers. "Whoever filled out these sheets must bring a whole new dimension to anal-ality."

I certainly hope he is referring to Mrs. Chumley's penchant for neatness.

"This is so neat, it's scary."

"Will you go through them and see if you can make sense of this, Herman?"

Ludmila re-enters, carrying a plate of what looks like double-stacked, fried potato pancakes topped with sour cream. Herman grabs one right off the plate and starts munching. "Wait 'til you taste these, Sherlock. They're scrumptious, just like my little Ludy."

I take one nibble and almost faint from deep-fried anaphylactic shock. "Herman, these are like gut bombs. You might as well just slap them right onto your love handles because that's where they're going to end up."

Herman finishes his first and starts in on his second. "I'm starting in on my new diet any day now. Gotta think about getting into a tux."

I can just imagine these two out and about. They'll look like an elephant and trainer.

Herman reads over the numbers slowly. A little bit of grease drips onto Mrs. Chumley's pages.

"I don't have a lot of time, Herman."

The TV goes on at the other end of the room. I hear Ludmila repeat what Burt says to Ernie, "Ru-bur Duck-ie, ou da one, who make bat-time fun."

Herman looks away from the pages, and asks in all seriousness, "You don't think I'm too old for Ludy, do you, Sherlock?"

"Age difference is the least of your problems, Herman."

"Do you think we make a good couple?"

"You two make a lot more than a couple. You're more like a one couple gang."

"Because we're soulmates?"

Any type of mating for these two, soul or otherwise, is a frightening thought.

"Ludmila wants to wait to do the deed until we're married, Sherlock."

I can't say I blame her.

"She's a real old-fashioned girl," he continues.

"I'm sure she's just like dear old Mama Russki," I tell him, especially if Mama had a Stalin tattoo on her shoulder.

"And now I have a favor to ask you," Herman says.

"Uh, oh."

"Sherlock, I want you to be my best man at our wedding."

Oh jeesh.

***

Care sees the Toyota, runs to it, and jumps in.

"Did you learn anything new at school today?" I ask, which is my usual customary question when I pick her up from school.

"Maybe."

I can't believe what I just heard and whip my head around. "What?"

"Maybe."

"What maybe? What did you learn?"

"I'll tell you at McDonalds when we stop on the way home."

"Sorry, ain't gonna happen."

The second strange earth shattering experience of the day happens about a hundred yards up the pick-up line. Kelly is standing alone on the curbside, actually waiting for me to arrive, so she can hop into the back seat as fast as her sister.

"What got into you?" I ask.

"You're not going to believe what we got, Dad," Kelly says excitedly.

"What?" I'm thinking she's going to pull out a letter from the school nurse about an outbreak of head lice.

"Don't tell him," Care tells her sister, "until he takes us to Burger King."

"Dad, this is big. I'm telling you, it's *big*." Kelly stokes the fires of my imagination.

"How about Arby's, Dad?"

"No," I say to Care, and I say, "Tell me," to Kelly.

"What we got is going to blow the case apart," Kelly says.

"I thought I told you two that you're off the case."

"We didn't listen," Kelly informs me of what I already know.

"How about Dairy Queen?"

"All right, what is it? Tell me."

"We can't tell you, we have to show you," Kelly says.

"At Thirty One Flavors," Care adds.

It's a nice spring afternoon, so we sit outside. They each have two scoops. I have one. "Are you going to show me or not?"

They each take out their cell phones. "We secretly taped the lunch line and I think I know who's making off with the money," Kelly says.

"I told you not to do anything."

"Dad. We're your eyes and ears inside the big house."

"The big house is a prison," I inform Kelly.

"Okay, the big school house then. Dad, you're so picky."

They each replay video taken during their lunch period. Because there is so much sunlight, it's near impossible to see the picture, but what I can see on the small, cell phone screens could be interesting.

"What do you think, Dad?"

"A little hard to see right now."

"We'll watch them again at home," Care says.

"But what do you think of what we did?" Kelly asks.

"I think I told you not to do any of this."

"What do you think we should do next?" Care asks.

"Nothing."

"We should get the suspects in the room, and we'll hot-box them until they confess," Kelly suggests.

"Hot-box them?"

"Yeah, that's where you play the good cop, I'll play the bad cop, and we grill 'em until they spill their beans." Interesting cafeteria metaphor. "What do you say, Dad?"

"Finish your ice cream."

Back in our apartment, Kelly finagles her cell phone pictures into my computer and we are able to watch the video on the monitor. Kelly mans the mouse as Care and I sit behind her to watch the show.

Kelly shot the first scene from where she sat, an angle directly across from where Esther Stiffarm and Stinky Winky Torelli collect the money from the kids. It was taken at the height of lunch line frenzy.

The two cashiers are a contrast in styles. Esther is nonchalant, she's done this so many times she could do it in her sleep. When a kid pays cash, she punches the keys on the register with an almost automaton quality. Stinky Winky is the opposite. She counts out each quarter, even though there are usually only two, and if she does get a bill, she holds it up to the light to check the authenticity before accepting it as legal tender. The kids pass through Esther's line with ease, but go through Winky's as quickly as possible, no doubt due to the cloud of putrid perfume invisibly hovering like mustard gas over trench warfare.

"Watch this, Dad."

Kelly points out when, after Esther Stiffarm rings up a sale, she places the bills in the cash drawer, makes change, and writes a small notation on a slip of paper on the edge of the small stand. "What do you think she's doing?"

"Writing something down."

"Now watch this."

Kelly points out Esther punching certain keys on the register as kids pass though the line and not pay for their food.

"She's recording the kids who have a lunch card," I say.

"But she's pushing different keys," Care says.

"Good eye, Care," I compliment my youngest.

The picture ends. The next scene on the computer screen is in the cinema verite' style of storytelling. Kelly is obviously walking as her phone records. Problem is, the shot is bouncing up and down faster than a dribbling basketball. In a horrible rapid succession are shots of food trays, shoes, spaghetti, shirt backs, linoleum, and flashes of the florescent lights on the cafeteria ceiling. The more Kelly roams around, the more dizzying the shot becomes. This scene's rendition makes me as nauseous as some of the food they're serving in the lunch line that day. The Swiss steak looks especially disgusting.

"Now watch this one part, Dad," Kelly warns me.

The shot zooms in on Esther adjusting her beehive under the webbing of her hair net.

"See?"

"See what, Kelly?"

"This is how she's smuggling the money out. She palms a few bills, stuffs them in the middle of her white man's afro." Kelly adds for my benefit, "All that hairspray holds the money in place."

"It's mostly one dollar bills she's working with," I tell her.

"To get two hundred out, her head would topple over."

"I don't know, Dad," Care says. "That's some really big hair she's got to work with."

The scene ends with Esther reaching down to scratch herself. The health department would be in shock.

Kelly hooks Care's phone into the computer. The two change places, and the second part of the double feature is ready for its movie debut. Care's rendition of the scene is much different than her sister's. Her shot is static, taken from the area maybe ten feet from the area of cash transactions. At least two-thirds of the picture is of Stinky Winky.

Care pauses the shot. "Look behind her, Dad."

"Okay."

"Who's that?" Care asks.

I look closely. "Teddy Tulleners."

"Terrible Teddy Tulleners, Dad." Kelly says. "Watch."

Care clicks on the play button.

Teddy hangs around like a bad smell next to a bad smell.

"Now watch closely."

I do. Teddy doesn't do much.

"See?"

"See what?" I ask.

"He's plotting his next move, Dad."

"How would you know that?"

"Because we've learned how to get into the mind of the criminal," Kelly says.

"Was there a class at school you took?"

"No, Dad, we learned it by watching a lot of TV."

"Great." Education is everything.

Both lines run out of customers. Winky straightens the stack of bills in her tray while Esther puts a key into the top of the register and turns it to the left. Behind the two of them, Terrible Teddy does come in and out of the shot as if he is sizing up his possibilities.

"I don't know what you'd do without us," Care says at the conclusion of the movie.

I do, but I won't mention it until they are much older.

We rerun parts one and two a few more times. I make some mental notes, which I will not share with my undercover agents.

"What do you want us to do next, Dad?"

"Nothing."

"Maybe we should put a tail on Terrible Teddy?" Care suggests.

"Or mark some bills, then shake Esther Stiffarm's fro, and see if any spill out," Kelly adds.

"No. You've both have done plenty already."

"I could go undercover as a cafeteria worker," Kelly tells me.

"You'd have to wear a hairnet, Kelly."

"Oh, forget that idea."

"You two being involved is not a good idea. I'm taking you both off the case. You are not to stick your noses anywhere they don't belong or into anyone else's business. Do I make myself perfectly clear?"

Neither responds.

I might as well be talking with Ludmila.

"Go do your homework."

***

"I got some bad news for you, Tiffany."

"I hate bad news. What?"

"Herman McFadden is off the market."

"Herman the vermin? The man whose fat content rivals the national debt? Whose thigh is bigger than an expressway column?" She pauses. "That Herman?"

"He's taken."

"Whoever took him must drive a forklift."

"I guess you'll just have to find someone else, Tiffany."

"Or grow my own at a fat farm."

I sit down at the Starbuck's table where she's sipping her drink. "Let me see the file."

Tiffany hands over the Manila envelope. I open the clasp on the back and pull out about a ream of paper. I start to page through as Tiffany gets up to get her second double, steam, cream, and jellybean latte' from the barista. "You want anything, Mr. Sherlock?"

"A better life if they have one."

"I'll ask."

The first thirty or so pages are legal mumbo-jumbo nobody, especially lawyers, reads. The court documents are next. Day, time, courtroom, judge, docket number, dress code, and decorum for the day. There is a copy of the policy, signed documents, proof of payments, and other pages I don't bother with. If the legal system in America would streamline this process, think of the number of trees we'd save from perishing in paper mills.

The lawsuit is on one page and stated in one short paragraph. It basically says three hundred premium classic cigars were insured for full value against theft, fire, flood, and natural disaster. Full value of said items to be reimbursed to plaintiff according to the stipulations of the insurance contract. The last pages are actual pictures of the destroyed cigars stacked in a mound of ashes and butts. It looks like the American Tobacco Company's version of Mt. Vesuvius. Charming.

Tiffany returns to the table. "Figure anything out yet, Mr. Sherlock?"

"No."

"Why not?"

"There doesn't seem to be anything to figure out. The policy says the cigars are insured against fire. He paid his premiums. And the cigars burned up." I show her the picture of the remains. "I don't know what we could argue."

"Does that mean Daddy has to pay up?"

"Yes."

"Daddy hates that."

"What do you want me to do, Tiffany?"

"Find a reason, so we don't have to pay up."

"But that's the whole point of buying insurance. The company will pay up if there's a fire or whatever."

"You don't get rich in the insurance business by paying out, Mr. Sherlock."

"You have to be fair."

"No, you don't," Tiffany says. "You've even said, 'Nobody said life was going to be fair,' Mr. Sherlock."

My words come back to haunt me.

As I stuff the pages back into the envelope, Tiffany asks, "How are we doing with the Holy Dong guy?"

We? I think to myself before answering, "Not really well."

"Why not? Is he *holier* than thou?" Tiffany laughs at her attempt at humor.

"No, dong-gone-it." I laugh at my own clever wit.

"I don't get it," Tiffany informs me.

It is best to return to the topic at hand. "The only direction, which seems to make sense, is to talk to some of the patients from the clinic."

"What are we going to talk about, Mr. Sherlock?"

"Care."

"Your kid?"

"No, the care they're receiving from Doc Dong."

"Well, we best be care-full then, Mr. Sherlock."

Tiffany should try stand-up.

CHAPTER 10

I've never missed a back-to-school night or a parent teacher conference, but when it comes to school board meetings, I'm at the other end of the attendance spectrum. The meeting is taking place in the school gym. A cafeteria table is set up in front of the expandable wood bleachers, which are filled with parents, teachers, administrators, and whoever else has nothing better to do this evening. I notice the majority of the audience is Caucasian, even though both schools enroll a number of minority students. Principal Eldin Puddle sits at the mid-point of the table facing the crowd. There is one microphone on the desk directly in front of him. To Eldin's right and left are sets of three people, two women and one man to the left and the opposite set up on the right. These are the school board members, who sit as if they were politicians waiting to debate. Off to the far side is a card table where Winky Torelli sits alone; this is no doubt by olfactory design. To Winky's left is a stand-up microphone; probably also placed there by design to insure no one speaks for too long. Bad perfume is a known deterrent to effusive oration. There are probably a couple hundred people seated on the wood bleachers, a far cry from the numbers of the Ann Margaret cheering section rooting their Metronomes on to victory.

I stand off to the far right. There is one guy to my right, who, at the sound of Eldin's gavel coming down to start the meeting, says to me, "Fasten your seat belt, this could be a bumpy school bus ride."

Eldin announces, "The meeting of the Ann Margaret and Pat Nixon school boards will come to order."

***

If you are wondering how the Pat Nixon and Ann Margaret Schools came to be named after the wife of a crooked president and a person best known for her sexy, Las Vegas lounge act, and her unforgettable portrayal of little Kimmy MacAfee in *Bye Bye Birdie*, it is actually an intriguing story. When the K through 8 school was founded years ago, it was christened Dan Walker School in honor of the recent Governor of Illinois Dan Walker (as if you couldn't guess). The name worked great until Dan Walker was convicted of some political chicanery and was sentenced to the state pen. Dan's name came off the school in less time than it takes to say, "We the jury find the defendant guilty." The school then became CPS School 147, which was not only a non-descript, boring moniker, but nearly impossible to attach a relatable mascot. The CPS School 147 *Number Crunchers* isn't a name students could rally around. After Dan Walker was locked up and no longer big news, the school board decided it was time for a new name. Keeping with the governor theme, the next name they chose for the school was George Ryan School, another leader of the just and fair State of Illinois. If you didn't think lightning could strike twice, well it certainly did because George followed in Dan Walker's footsteps right into the same prison for mishandling a driver's license scandal while he was governor. Once again, left with no name to call its own, the school board was forced to return to CPS 147, which made nobody happy. After the Ryan scandal died down, the school board took an *At first you don't succeed, try, try again* attitude and decided that the odds against this governor incarceration problem happening again were so remote, why not give it another go. They chose Rob Blagojevich School as a name that would be good for decades. Wouldn't you just know it, Rob went up the same river as his namesakes for selling Obama's senate seat to the highest bidder while he was governor. Three bad choices in a row. I wish I would've had a bet down on this happening. Interestingly enough, each of the governors had and continues to plead "not guilty" for the crimes attributed to them. They all said in some way, "We just did what every politician does in Illinois. We worked the system, played the game, did the favors, and when it was our turn to cash in, we did. What's so wrong about that?"

To coincide with the final school nomenclature problem was a severe dip in the real estate market with Sauganash taking quite a hit in the home value category. To try to alleviate the sales slump, one overly-aggressive real estate broker in a sea of overly-aggressive brokers came up with a plan to differentiate Sauganash from the other areas of the city and get more money per square foot. He figured if Sauganash had both a grammar school and a middle school, instead of a K to 8, it would be much more like the adjacent, and more expensive, north shore suburbs; thus Sauganash would seem *suburban* and could garner higher home prices.

All that was really needed was to give the appearance that the schools were separate, which would be easily accomplished by merely adding an additional marquee to the front of the pick-up area in front of the school.

If coming up with one name wasn't difficult enough, now the school board had to come up with two. Nobody ever said life was going to be easy for the school board, either.

Destined not to make the same mistake four times in a row, one board member came up with the idea of sponsoring a contest to find suitable people worthy of the honor of having their name on the beloved schools. To their surprise, hundreds of names were entered. From Michael Jordan to Jor-El, Pippi Longstocking to Pope Paul the 23rd, and Moses to Mahatma Ghandi, any name would be considered. The only requirement was that each entry had to pass a background check. When the nomination period came to an end, the school board met in private and made secret back room changes to the rules. First, they tossed out all the politicians. After being burned three times in a row, they didn't want to chance that happening again. This ruling unfortunately eliminated Lincoln, Washington, Millard Fillmore, Franklin Roosevelt, and others well deserving of being honored, but it also ash-canned Hitler, Idi Amin, and Papa Doc Duvalier, who were nominated by anonymous nominators. Next, the board eliminated any sports star such as Mike Ditka, Leon Spinks, Tinkers, Evers, and Chance. They did this because of the steroid and doping scandals happening at the time, or an unknown expose' of a dead star long past.

The board wanted someone famous, but local, who had some ties to the community. They preferred someone dead, or at least old enough not to get in any serious trouble and end up in a prison housing former governors.

How Ann Margaret got the nod, out of the hundreds of names nominated, remains a mystery to this day. Ann was born and raised in the Chicagoland area, did graduate from New Trier High School, and attended Northwestern University, both schools not too far away from dear old CPS School 147.

Granted, Ann did make a pretty fair name for herself in show biz, although most of her time in the spotlight was in Las Vegas, hardly the bedrock of purity. Rumor has it, one of the board members had quite a *thing* for Ann. He thought if he could get her name in the school lights, she would show up, he'd get to meet her, woo her, and maybe get lucky. If all that didn't happen, he'd at least be able to say he hobnobbed with her and would be able to cross her off his bucket list. This board member must also have had a lot of dirt on the other board members because he was able to push her name through as the winner. Thus, Ann Margaret Middle School was born, or newly named in this case.

If you are also wondering how Care's school became to be named the Pat Nixon Grammar School that's actually quite simple. They ran out of money during the aforementioned real estate slump and the new playground being built was left with standards with no backboards, fields with no grass, and teeter-totters that couldn't teet or tot. Thankfully, a big donor, who just happened to be a Republican, came forth and anted up the rest of the dough with the provision the school would be named after President Richard Nixon, a personal favorite of his. The school board took his money and finished the playground, but with Watergate not yet in distant memory, they stiffed the wealthy donor by refusing to add Tricky Dick to the front marquee or official school stationary. There was a big fight. The donor threatened to sue if Richard Nixon Grammar School didn't become a reality.

Thankfully, a compromise was reached.

***

Principal Puddle continues with his introduction, "The agenda will include the year end budget, capital improvement, hiring of new teachers, new tech expenditures, and—"

"That crap can wait." A daddy of one of the students commandeers the stand-up microphone like a senior senator interrupting a first-termer during a debate broadcast live on CSPAN. "We wanna know why a bunch of foreigners got into the magnet schools and not our kids."

Behind him a rousing chorus of *yeahs*, boos, and invective raspberries are hurled at Eldin like tomatoes at a bad vaudeville act.

"If you'd like to add a topic to the agenda, you may do so with the secretary of the board," Eldin informs him.

"We want answers and we want them now!"

"We had the largest number of students admitted in the school's history," Eldin answers.

"They didn't pick my kid!"

Other parents converge at the microphone, figuring there must be strength in numbers. They don't take turns, as they were taught in first grade, and instead, attempt to out shout each other with their personal vilifications. Their invectives immediately become a cacophony of calamity.

"My kid's a four-point-o."

"Mine's the student body president."

"My son's a genius in math."

Other verbal thoughts are heard from the peanut gallery, which are not shall we say, pure in the spirit of quality education or proper grammar. It would be pointless to repeat them in fear one may become a rallying cry for disgruntled parents in the future.

From the first row of bleacher seats, one guy comes forward to voice his two cents, busting through his fellow protestors like a bowling ball heading for a strike. His voice sounds much like the one I heard in Eldin's office. "My name's Lou Lauder and I want to know how her kid got in and mine didn't." He points at Winky Torelli. "I heard her kid's as dumb as a dirty sweat sock."

Winky is up and out of her chair faster than an ICBM out of a silo. "How dare you insult my child."

"If her kid got into Buttkick Prep and my kid didn't," Lou yells at the entire school board, "I'd say something isn't kosher in this deli."

"The reason your child didn't get in is because of his half-wit, heathen heredity."

"Well, somebody put a little too much chlorine in your gene pool, lady."

"Rotten apples don't fall far from the rotten tree," Winky fights back.

Eldin gavels, and screams into his microphone, "Enough."

"We want answers, Principal," another shouts from the bleachers. "Something's not right."

"There's only so many placements available," Eldin says, "and each student had to meet certain requirements."

"Like being a citizen," Lou, the same man I heard in the office, bellows out. "I know one kid who got into an academy doesn't even live in this district."

"Who?" A voice questions.

"Some illegal bean picker's kid," the man answers.

Eldin tries to speak but is drowned out by a volley of vulgar vilifications.

"Them foreigners don't belong in our schools."

"We pay the most taxes, we should get the best schools."

"America is for Americans."

"All the applicants took the same test, were under the same grade restrictions, and had to have the same letters of introduction," Eldin says to little avail.

"Before any kid goes to any school, there should be a full investigation of the applications, process, and the people making the decisions on who gets in and who doesn't," the lead man of the mob orders.

"It's about time somebody sent home a report card on you," another man offers his suggestion.

There is a resounding cheer from the audience, accompanied by shaking fists, yelps, and one "Right on," from a protestor obviously flashing back to the 1960s.

Eldin freezes as if he doesn't know what to do next. The desk microphone begins to pass from one board member to another, each trying to quell the horde of howling parents. Nobody has much luck.

As the comments continue to fly like poison arrows, I merely fold my arms and try to take it all in. Whoever said, "A mob has no brains, only heads," was truly right on.

I notice to my left a woman, who would get lost in a crowd of two. She looks as meek as an Easter lamb. I catch her eye, smile, and point at the obnoxious jerk leading the pack of angry wolves, "I bet this guy would be a good chaperone for the eighth grade dance."

She doesn't laugh. "He's never been to a dance," she says in a restrained matter of fact tone.

"How would you know?"

"He's my husband."

"Oh, sorry."

"He's very angry our daughter wasn't accepted into Butkis Prep."

"I know, I heard him in the principal's office the other day."

"He only wants the best for our child."

"I can't blame him," I say, but I could easily blame him for being such a total jerk about it.

We stand together listening to the continuing bombast.

"Did yours get shut out, too?" she asks.

"No, my daughter didn't even try. If they had a clothes shopping academy, she would've applied there."

"Elsa has one of the highest grade point averages in the school." The lady is so soft-spoken, she sounds like air coming out of a pressed pillow.

"Maybe Elsa didn't get in because she didn't do enough other stuff," I say.

"She was head cheerleader, on the student council, and a member of the debate team."

"Really?" Elsa must take after her dad, who must be a divorce lawyer, labor negotiator, or the minister at tent revival meetings.

"My husband refuses to give up when he thinks he's been cheated," she says.

"Well, he certainly knows how to put up a good fight."

"Yes, he certainly does." The woman walks away and quickly disappears behind a portable flagpole with no flag attached.

At the microphone and in the bleachers, parents continue to scream at the school board, but they all seem to be preaching to the choir or showing off their lack of anger management. At the point when all ways of shouting the same nasty comments are exhausted, Eldin says, "I am not supposed to reveal this, but an investigation on this matter is currently in progress."

All six school board members turn and stare, as do all the vociferous parents, who are suddenly quiet as church mice.

Eldin continues, "If there are abnormalities in the selection process, they will be found and measures taken to correct the situation. I expect a report by next week."

The crowd sits in a stunned silence.

"This meeting is now officially concluded." Eldin gives them one more gavel thump and that's all the minutes to be written for this meeting.

Eldin's up, out of his chair and out of the gym before the crowd catches its breath. It's all over, especially the shouting.

This goes to show you never really know about people. As I was trying to find the missing milk money, Eldin also had an investigator looking into malfeasance in the magnet school process. I must be losing my detecting touch because, not only did I miss seeing another investigator sleuthing around, none of the people I interviewed mentioned someone else on a trail of magnet school malfeasance. For all I know, every office is the place is bugged, hidden cameras are recording each minute of the school day, and a number of detectives are working round the clock to seek justice. Who woulda thought Eldin woulda been way ahead of me on this one?

The parents hurry out of the gym as if they were all trying to get home to avoid paying an extra hour's wages to the babysitter. I wait for the crowd to thin before I head for the door, and I am almost through it when I stop and hear one last announcement over the PA system. "Would Richard Sherlock please report to the principal's office immediately?"

***

"You want me to do *what*?"

"You're already here on the missing milk money," Eldin tells me. "One more mystery can't be that much more to add."

"I thought you told the parents you already had someone on the case?"

"No, what I said was I already had an investigation in progress,'" Eldin explains. "I didn't say what was being investigated."

"The milk money and the magnet issue could be two totally unrelated matters," I tell him.

"Either one of which could ruin the school's reputation. You have to help us, Mr. Sherlock."

"I'm already helping."

"So this can't be much more to add," Eldin reasons.

"But I don't even know where to start."

"The parents are one step from becoming a lynch mob," Eldin says. "If they don't get some concrete answers, they'll go to the district, this whole thing will blow up, and Ann Margaret will become yet another ink stain on the Chicago Public School blotter."

Oh jeesh.

CHAPTER 11

"Are you sure this is going to work, Mr. Sherlock?"

"No."

"Then why are we doing it?"

"Because I don't know what else to do."

"That's not a good answer, Mr. Sherlock."

"Do you have a better idea, Tiffany?"

"I think it would be a good idea if they passed a law forbidding homeless people from being homeless in my neighborhood. Maybe they could have a homeless neighborhood just for the homeless?"

"I was referring to a better idea on this case."

"I can't be expected to solve all the world's problems, Mr. Sherlock."

We remain seated in her Lexus, which is parked in a handicapped space, and wait until a patient exits the Ho Lee Dong One Stop Cancer Clinic.

"Here comes one, let's go."

We pile out of her car and intercept a senior Asian woman on her way out. "Excuse us," I say to her. "We're from the state's department of health and are wondering if you could answer a few questions for our monthly survey?"

The woman clatters out a diatribe in Mandarin or some other eastern language. When she finishes, she spits on the sidewalk and walks away.

"That was enlightening, Mr. Sherlock."

A second patient comes our way and I try again. And get the same result but without the spittle. A third, a fourth, a fifth do the same. Doesn't anyone speak English in this neighborhood?"

"Told you this was a dumb idea," Tiffany informs me. "All these people talk like a place setting falling on a terra cotta floor."

I try again. "Excuse me."

More Mandarin.

Tiffany points to the latest to exit the clinic. "That guy looks like he can speak English, Mr. Sherlock."

"That's the UPS driver, Tiffany."

"That shade of brown is hideous."

Another Asian senior departs. Hoping for the best, I approach her. "Excuse me."

"Yes?"

Finally.

"I hate to bother you, but I'd like to know what you think of Dr. Dong. I'm looking for a treatment center for a friend of mine."

"Dr. Dong good man. Said I sick, could make me better. Now I feel better."

"If I may ask, what kind of cancer do you have?"

"Cancer in blood."

"Did you have surgery?"

"Can't have surgery on blood."

"Duh," Tiffany chimes in.

"Medicine goes in blood." She shows me the patch of gauze taped in the crook of her arm.

"Is doctor expensive?"

"No, free."

Tiffany asks, "How is the magazine selection? Do they have a masseuse on staff? Can you arrange for an on-site mani-pedi during treatment?"

"Huh?" The woman looks at Tiffany as if she's speaking in a foreign tongue.

"Thank you very much."

The woman walks away.

"What did you learn out of all that, Mr. Sherlock?"

"I'm not sure."

"Why not?"

"Because sometimes you don't fully understand something until more information comes your way," I tell her. "You have to wait until you have all the pieces of the puzzle before trying to put it together."

"Maybe that's why all the stuff they tried to teach me in school hasn't made sense yet."

"Possibly."

I decide to end the Q and A part of the day. It was pretty much a waste of time.

"I have to visit Care and Kelly's school this afternoon, want to tag along?"

"Not really," Tiffany answers. "Schools have never been my arenas of expertise."

Darn. I wanted her to drive me.

"But since I've got nothing better to do today, I'll go."

"I also have to stop by and see Herman McFadden. Want to join me there, too?"

"I'd rather clean out my ear with an ice pick."

We're back in her Lexus on Kennedy heading for Sauganash when I ask, "By the way, Tiffany, have you ever put a guy on hold?"

"Naw, why bother?"

"Has a guy ever put you on hold?"

"No."

"Why not?"

"Because I'm a dumper, not dumpee, Mr. Sherlock."

I should've known.

"Tiffany, let me ask you, when one person puts another person on hold, they aren't really putting them on hold, they're actually ending the relationship, right?"

"Exactly."

"But in a nice way?"

"Not really."

"No?"

"Trying to be nice when you're giving someone the shaft is about as dumb as wanting to stay friends after you split."

"I don't understand."

"If you try to be nice and the idiot doesn't get it, the guy may think he still has hope. It's cruel to give someone hope if there is no hope to give." Tiffany educates me. "It's simple. Once someone tells you they don't want to see you, they don't want to see you. It's not a hard concept. Mr. Sherlock."

Poor Bree.

"You got some chick you want to dump, Mr. Sherlock?"

"No."

"Someone put you on hold?"

"No."

"Oh, come on, Mr. Sherlock, something's going on and you want my advice."

Before I get a chance to answer, she launches into her lecture. "Let me school ya on how it all goes down. If you want to dump somebody, don't apologize. None of that 'It's me, not you,' or 'I'm going through some tough times right now,' or 'I'm not a good enough for someone as good as you.' That's a bunch of crap. You ain't in a discussion, you want do the dump as quick as you can. You say, 'This ain't working out. We're done. I'm outta here' or 'Ex-nay on our relationship-nay' if they speak Latin." Tiffany's on a roll and there's no way I'm going to stop her. "Second, if she starts with the waterworks, step back. Your shoulder is now like the rest of you, off limits. And third, no matter how itchy you may get for a little action, don't go back. You just take care of that by yourself."

"Any of that ever happen to you, Tiffany?"

"No, and if it did, I wouldn't admit it."

***

"Hello, Mrs. Chumley."

"Nice to see the two of you." If they ever remake the Andy Griffith Show, Mrs. Chumley would be perfect for the Aunt Bea role.

"Is Principal Puddle available?"

"I'll tell him you're here."

One minute later we're in his office. "Did you figure anything out or learn anything new?" Eldin asks right out of the box.

"He learned how to dump a girlfriend," Tiffany tells him. "Thanks to me."

"Principal Puddle is referring to the missing milk money, Tiffany."

"Then he should be more specific, Mr. Sherlock."

Eldin, obviously accustomed to hearing children's thought processes, repeats, "Did you?"

"I'm working on it."

"Well, work harder, please. People are starting to ask a lot of questions that I can't answer."

"I know the feeling," Tiffany says.

"I need to see the test results from the kids who got into the magnet schools," I tell Eldin.

"That's privileged information."

"I need to see it."

Eldin unlocks a file cabinet drawer, slides it open, and pulls out a thick file. "Don't forget, it's just not test scores that grant a student admittance."

"Okay, I'll bite."

"There can be extenuating circumstances," he explains.

"Kinda like if a kid's father builds the school a new library in order to get his kid enrolled?" Tiffany questions.

"That would probably suffice," Eldin says.

"Worked for me," Tiffany admits.

I pull out the ranking page, scan it quickly, and one name pops out. "Arleta Torelli got a ninety-eight on the test?" I ask, remembering what Kelly told me about Arleta's mental capacity.

"The child tested through the roof. Nobody expected it."

"And that's how she got in?"

"You can't argue with a ninety-eight."

"Xi Chinsui got a perfect score?"

"Which didn't surprise anyone."

My eyes go down the page. "Juan Hernandez?"

"Could be the next Fermi."

The majority of the seventy-six students, which were admitted, all scored at least a ninety-five on the test. Many students achieved ninety and above but didn't make the cut. I suspect their parents were the most vocal at the school board meeting.

I keep going down the page until I find an Elsa Lauder, whose score was a seventy-nine. "What about this one?"

"Surprised all of us."

"Who else has seen this?"

"The panel making the choices and the CPS administration. Again, it's privileged information." Eldin repeats his most salient point. "It is not released to the public."

I close the file and shove it under my arm. "One other item," I say. "Explain to me once again how the accounting system works around here."

"Mrs. Chumley collects all the bills, lists them on her spreadsheet, gives them to me, and I review each cost, okay, deny, or amend. She makes the changes and passes the information to Miss Mossy, who facilitates payments."

"Who handles the checkbook?"

"Miss Mossy, but few checks are written compared to years past. It's all done on the computer now."

I'd like to have my computer pay all my bills, but I can't

find a computer that comes stocked with money.

"Don't you people have iPhones?" Tiffany asks.

"Richard," Eldin says in all sincerity, "this school goes above and beyond to give the children the best educational advantages possible. It's not easy working within the system, but we have been able to maintain one of the finest track records of any school in the city in getting our students into the top tier high schools. And this year we did better than any school in the city. If anything disrupts our apple cart, I'd feel quite a failure in my career as an educator."

"Ah, don't feel bad. My school career wasn't all that good either and look how good I turned out." Tiffany tries to make Eldin feel better as only she can do.

"I need you to take care of this situation, Mr. Sherlock," Eldin begs me.

"I'll do my best, Eldin. I will."

"Could you put a rush on it?"

We leave Eldin's office.

"Have a smiley rest of your day." Mrs. Chumley bids us adieu and puts a smiley face on Tiffany's lace camisole. It's easy to see why that face is smiling.

Out in the hallway, I say, "We have another stop to make, Tiffany."

"I told you, I'm not going to see Herman the vermin."

"Not there."

"Where?"

"Cafeteria."

"You got a taste for corn dogs, Mr. Sherlock?"

The trays are put away and the stainless steel is spotless. The staff is gone. I look for a beehive buzzing over the hanging pots and pans but don't see Esther Stiffarm. I see the janitor and ask him to unlock the storeroom.

"Come on." I lead Tiffany inside, flip on the light, and close the door behind us. "You start on this side and lift up every can. If you find any money, let me know."

"Do I get to keep it?"

"No."

"That doesn't seem fair."

"Tiffany, you're filthy rich. What do you need more money for?"

"Because it makes me feel good."

104

I find ten dollars under a can of tomato soup and five under a can of refried beans. Tiffany finds a total of either fifteen dollars or fifty-five dollars. "I keep losing count because I have to put the money back, Mr. Sherlock."

I lock the door behind us when we exit.

"That was certainly a poor excuse for a treasure hunt," Tiffany says.

We make a brief stop into the office of Miss Mossy.

"I'm sorry to bother you, but I have a couple of questions."

"Sure, come on in."

There is a stack of both new and used laptop computers piled on her desk.

"What can I do for you?"

"How do you think Esther Stiffarm has been able to keep her staff intact while the turnover in other school cafeteria staffs is sky high?"

"In other words," Tiffany says as if my question needs explaining, "why don't her people get burned out?" She then adds, as if her joke needs additional explanation, "Get it, 'burned out in the cafeteria'?"

Nobody laughs, except Tiffany.

"All I can say is the employees like working here," Miss Mossy explains. "Our average teacher has been here over sixteen years, Mrs. Chumley has been here almost forty, even our janitor has been here twenty-five. Environment and working conditions are extremely important in the field of education."

"One more item," I warn her. "I'm going to need to go over the monthly expenditures."

"Didn't you get those from Mrs. Chumley?"

"I need to see yours."

"Why?"

"Because what I've seen so far is incomplete."

"I'm not sure I can help," Miss Mossy says.

"Why?"

"Because I pay some bills electronically, some by check, others the district pays; it's complicated."

"But didn't you say you had it all on a spreadsheet?"

"I didn't say that."

"What did you say then?"

"I'm not sure, but I don't put them on a spreadsheet. Mrs.

Chumley does that." Her evasiveness is intriguing.

"Miss Mossy, what would be a good time for the two of us to sit down and go through a typical month?"

"Why don't you text me and we can set something up?"

"Mr. Sherlock is allergic to texting," Tiffany informs her.

"How about tomorrow during fifth period?" I suggest.

"I can't."

"Sixth period?"

"No."

"Seventh?"

She realizes I'm not going away. "I'll clear my schedule."

We're back in the Lexus before the afternoon pick-up line begins to form.

"Sure you don't want to stop by and say hello to Herman?" I ask as Tiffany pulls out of the school's parking lot. "You could meet the woman who beat you out in the contest for Herman's affections."

"I'd rather stick a fork in my nipple."

***

"What did you find out, Herman?"

"Nothing."

"Nothing?"

Herman knows he owes me big time. If it wasn't for me, he'd be doing fifty-to-life in Joliet. "I can't concentrate."

"Why not?"

"I'm too much in love." Herman pulls on his jowly neck fat. "I sit here and watch little Ludmila cooking and cleaning, and it's like I'm floating on a lemon cake's meringue."

One thing Herman will never do is float. He could be on a pontoon the size of a football field in the Great Salt Lake and he'd still sink like a stone.

"Herman, I need your help on this."

"Sherlock, haven't you ever been in love?"

"Herman—"

"Your heart pounding in your chest, bells ringing in your ears, that tingling feeling all over your body?"

Tingling in Herman's entirety would be tantamount to a minor earthquake.

"Herman, I have to find out what those numbers mean. The

only direction I have in this case is to follow the money."

"Both columns matched in the end," he says.

"How about the middle part?"

"Parts is parts, Sherlock."

Ludmila comes into the room with a feather duster in hand. She smiles at me before dusting the bookshelf. I notice when she moves her arm rapidly, Josef Stalin's facial expression goes from sour to downright evil.

"Look at her, Sherlock. She's my torte, fruit pie, angel food, crème puff, and puff pastry, all squeezed onto the same dessert tray.

One squeeze from Herman would cause Ludmila to burst at the seams.

"Would you please go over these numbers?"

"I can't, Sherlock. I look at those numbers, and they go into my mind like a jigsaw, and come out in a jumble of junk. I can't concentrate."

"Why not?"

"Because I'm in love."

CHAPTER 12

I do my best to make my daily phone call to my kids right before dinnertime. It's the best time to call because they're home, hungry, and Mom's busy getting dinner on the table. I'm surprised when my phone rings at 5:45 P.M. and I get beaten to my punch.

"Dad, it's Kelly."

"Yes, I recognize the voice."

"It's me, too, Dad. I'm on the other phone."

"Hello, Care."

"We're spending this weekend with you," Kelly tells me.

"You are?"

"We have to," Kelly says.

"I don't remember getting a note from your mother." Instead of calling me and having a normal conversation, their mother sends me notes concerning last minute schedule changes, needing more alimony, more child support, and more time to explore her inner self. This communicating via scribbled note was not listed in my *How to be a Good Divorced Parent* handbook.

"We have a lot we have to get done this weekend." Kelly is emphatic.

"I'm not taking you shopping."

"No, Dad," Care says. "On the case."

"What case?"

"The case of the missing milk money."

"I took you off of the case, remember?"

"I know," Kelly says, "that's why we've been working undercover."

"No. Bad idea. *Stop.*"

"Dad, look what a great job we did with the video," Kelly argues.

"I almost lost my lunch watching that one you shot, Kelly."

"I told you mine was better than yours," Care needles her sister.

"Dad, you need us on this case," Kelly says. "We're your eyes and ears inside the scene of the crime."

"Did you discuss the change with your mother?"

"She's going to a seminar on how to transfer positive energy by wearing a crystal pyramid on her head while she does housework. So, she doesn't care."

"I thought you had a cleaning lady."

"We do, but Mom wants to experiment."

We couldn't afford a cleaning lady when we were married, so how she can afford one now baffles me.

"Pick us up tomorrow after school, Dad," Kelly orders.

"And can we stop at McDonald's on the way home?" Care asks.

"No."

"Be on time," Kelly adds. "We've got a lot to get done this weekend."

"Yes, boss."

I spend the remainder of the evening going through the test results file Eldin reluctantly handed over. I am amazed at the number of eighth graders who took the test, 153 to be exact, which is more than fifty percent of the class. The fact that almost half of those, 76, were accepted to an academy or magnet school is quite commendable. Whatever Eldin is doing, he's doing it well.

It's obvious why most made the grade—exceptional scores on the test. The average test score was close to ninety-six, well over the cut-off score of ninety, which is required to be considered.

Besides Xi, two other kids got a ninety-nine on the test as well as straight A's on their report cards; both of these were Asian, or kids with very odd first and last names. Juan Hernandez won two science competitions in the past year and got invited to Washington D.C. to compete in a national competition. Two other winners had lists of do-gooder activities that would make Mother Teresa jealous. Arleta Torelli must have made the magnet grade via her test score because her grades were mediocre at best and her list of accomplishments seemed questionable. Volunteering at a spay and neuter clinic and being the Junior Board Chairman of the Bullying the Bully Society didn't seem to be the type of charitable activities, which would jettison Arleta to the top of the Deserving Students category. The biggest question mark in the report is Elsa Lauder. Her grades were almost straight *A's*, and besides the debate team and student council, she played field hockey. Maybe she didn't get in because her father is so obnoxious or her mother is so meek. Go figure.

The file takes almost forever to read. The only consistent similarity is a test score above 90%, or a spectacular capacity in one area of study. GPAs seem to play a role, but some kids, Juan Hernandez included, must've had trouble with certain subjects because a few *Cs* and *Ds* popped up on report cards.

All this reminds me of taking the SAT test when I was a senior in high school. Half of the questions asked I had no idea and the other half I guessed at.

By ten o'clock I'm going cross-eyed. I call it quits and go to bed.

***

"You have to do something, Mr. Sherlock," she screams into the phone.

"What do you want me to do?"

"Figure out a way to get out of paying for Mr. Fumigation's dumb cigars. My daddy says his insurance company shouldn't have to pay for cancer sticks going up in smoke."

"But it's Richmond's fault for writing the policy in the first place."

"I don't need excuses, Mr. Sherlock. Excuses are only as good as the paper they're written on."

I don't think she got that right.

"This is not the way I wanted to start my day, Mr. Sherlock." Tiffany's day doesn't start before eleven. "My stress level is off the charts." Compared to the stress level of a normal person, Tiffany's disruption would be more like a pebble plopping into Lake Michigan. "I haven't even had time for my skin regimen, foot massage, or kale/acai/pomegranate power shake." It'll be a miracle if she makes it through the entire day.

"The policy is clear. There is nothing I can do, Tiffany."

"We have to be in court next week, Mr. Sherlock."

"Then I guess we go to court."

"We're running out of time."

"If Richmond insured the cigars against fire and they burned up in a fire, Richmond's got to pay up. There's really no way to argue that."

"Mr. Sherlock you need to make some good adjustments to your bad attitude."

"Yes, Tiffany."

Two minutes after Tiffany hangs up, my phone rings again. It's Bree Bisonette, which is pronounced "Bis-o-nay."

"Mr. Sherlock—" She doesn't sound real good.

"Yes."

"There's something that doesn't feel right."

I wonder if she's lost all hope. "What is that, Bree?"

"The Doctor Dong guy you asked about..."

Whew!

"The chemo he's prescribing has changed dramatically over the last couple of months."

"How?"

"He's gone from the cheaper generic to the exclusively generous."

This is interesting.

"Dong is treating some heavy duty cancers in his clinic," Bree continues.

"Can you give me an example?"

"What kind?"

"A patient."

"No." She snaps at me like a puppy nipping at an obnoxious child.

"Why not?"

"I can't release personal medical information; you know that."

I do, but it sure would make my life easier if she could match me up a few names with a few diseases of a few people, who spoke English, and I could go talk to them and get this cleared up in an hour.

"I could really use this information," I tell her.

"Well, I'm not the one to ask!"

I remind myself that depression and anger often travel in the same carpool.

"Bree, are you okay?"

"No." There is a slight pause. "He told me not to call him, but I called him anyway."

"And what did he say?"

"He didn't. He put me on hold."

Talk about adding phone insult to relationship injury.

"It's not odd. Mr. Richmond does that to me, too," I tell her.

"Did he also sleep with you three times a week?"

I will consider that a rhetorical question.

"I was so stupid. I stayed on hold so long, I felt like a person who calls Richmond to discuss a rate increase," Bree admits.

"Bree, sometimes you have to just throw in the towel, move on, and get on with your life."

"But I don't want to. I love him and I want him to love me, too." She bursts into tears worthy of a spring thunderstorm then hangs up the phone before I can offer any of my pathetic condolences.

I have to admit, Tiffany's right. Giving *on hold* hope is much more painful than just getting dumped and moving on with your life.

*****

The mail comes right after I finish my tuna sandwich. I get an offer to install solar power, a free three-month subscription to Hot Rod Monthly, a Bed, Bath, and Beyond coupon for 20% off (I've got about fifty of these), and a discount on cremation services if I sign up with a deposit now. On the bottom of the stack of junk is my monthly bank statement. Usually when seeing this envelope, I treat it as if it is infected with anthrax spores; nothing I want to touch, read, or certainly spend any quality time with, but today is different. I rip the envelope open like a present under the Christmas tree. I unfold the pages and see I have a balance of thirty-four hundred sixty dollars and eighty-seven cents. This is even better than I expected. I read closely and see my credit card has rebated me sixty-three dollars for interest paid in advance. I'm even richer than I thought I was.

I'm on a roll.

CHAPTER 13

The pile of laptops has grown like weeds. We have to move them to the floor, so we can use her desk.

"Why so many laptops?" I ask.

"Students have to return them at the end of the school year."

"But we have a few more weeks to go."

"If we wait too long, we don't get them back."

Makes sense to me.

Fern pulls out three Manila folders and empties the bills, statements, and invoices onto the desk as if they were trash going into the recycle bin.

I immediately recognize the one on the top. "Why would the milk bills be different each month?" I ask, picking the page up. "Don't the kids drink pretty much the same amount every week?"

"Some weeks have vacation days, some days are hotter and the kids get juice, and some weeks we get a discount," Ms. Mossy explains.

"A two-hundred dollar difference?"

"It can happen."

I don't verbalize, but that was a bad answer.

I wade through the invoices, statements, and receipts spread across her desk. "This one, tech support." I hold it up so she can see. "If I compare what you paid to what is on Mrs. Chumley's spreadsheet, it's a big difference."

"We pay a monthly retainer with that one and the district makes up the difference." Not as bad as the last answer but still pretty lousy.

I pick up another payment receipt. "What's a stoker?"

"He's the guy we pay to maintain the boiler that heats the two schools. He has to get here early and stoke it each morning."

"Why stoke now? It's springtime."

"He also looks in on the A/C."

I pick up another page. "But you paid the air conditioning guy six hundred bucks."

"The stoker stokes, he doesn't condition."

We go at this for over forty-five minutes and I'm more confused than when we started. I scribble notes and try to list as many payments, which can be compared to Mrs. Chumley's sheet, but I only add more numbers to the accounting chaos.

"This is all very dizzying, Ms. Mossy."

"Welcome to my world."

The bell rings to signal the end of seventh period. The kids will be waiting on the pick-up line in a few minutes.

"It's the same in any of the city's branches." She leans back in her chair. "Starts out real simple, then they pass a rule, which changes a small part, then they pass another rule, which changes both parts and adds one more duty. Every time they fix something or try to make life easier, it just screws it up all the more. You do this ten years in a row and you have a system so convoluted a PhD in economics couldn't figure it out."

From the mess on her desk, it's obvious she's right on.

"Thanks for your help."

"You're welcome, Mr. Sherlock, but I knew this would only make matters worse for you."

I exit her office, not entirely buying her *not helping me to help me*.

The pick-up line out front looks like the Edens on a Friday afternoon, and since I'm coming out of the back parking lot, I have to butt my Toyota into the line of SUVs and minivans. The drivers are not happy and they tell me so with a cacophony of horn honks.

Care's waiting and jumps right into the car.

"Hi, Care. Did you learn anything in school today?"

"No. Can we stop at Burger King on the way home?"

"No."

Kelly is back with her gaggle of girls, but this time she carries a small notebook, in which she's currently scribbling. I have to honk my horn to get her attention.

She doesn't respond right away; what else is new? When she does get in the car, she says, "Dad, I've been asking people if they've seen anything suspicious around school."

"Kelly, that's not a good idea."

"Dad, 'See Something, Say Something,'" she quotes the new terrorism mantra. "I'm trying to get people to say something about what they've seen."

I'll bite. "Okay, Kelly, what have you learned so far?"

"Marcie Bailey has a big crush on Tommy Gilmore, Brenda Marshall has jumped two cup sizes, and Terrible Teddy Tulleners wasn't at school today."

Can't wait to put those clues up on *The Original Carlo*.

"Where was Teddy?" I ask.

"He probably suspects we're onto him," Kelly says, "and he's now on the lam."

I better alert the border crossings.

Kelly continues, "I think we should revisit the scene of the crime, make a list of our most likely suspects, and you should call a CSI guy and bring him in to do a thorough DNA sweep of the scene."

"Really?"

"The sooner the better," Kelly says.

"Dad, can we stop for a donut on the way home?" Care asks.

"No, but we do have some stops to make, none of which are food oriented."

"Please?"

"No."

"You two have anything else on the case that you're not supposed to be on?" I might as well ask and get it out of the way.

"Not yet, but we're working on it."

I drive down Peterson Avenue about a mile from their school and pull into a small shopping center.

"What are we doing here?" Kelly asks.

"Did you change your mind because there's a hot dog place on the corner?" Care asks.

The center has a store, second from the end, being refurbished. The store in the center of the center, which is the largest of the center's five, has a glass front and a neon sign above the door reading: Uncle Larry's Tutor Tent. Stenciled on its glass windows are a list of their offerings: SAT Prep, Magnet School Exam, Math Immersion, Summer Sessions, and in the biggest letters, Guaranteed Results.

"Ever hear of this place?" I ask.

"No," Care says.

"Oh, yeah," Kelly says. "A lot of parents force their kids to go here."

"Maybe I should do the same, Kelly."

"No, Dad, bad idea."

We get out of the car, walk up to the entrance, and find the door locked. "This is odd," I say, looking in windows.

Care points out for my benefit, "The sign says 'Closed', Dad. What part of closed don't you understand?"

The only thing worse than your kids mimicking you, is when they're correct when mimicking you. "I didn't see the sign."

"No excuse," Care tells me. "I should get a hot dog for being right and you being wrong."

"Why would the place be closed on a school day?" I ask, trying to peer into the place from the vacant, being refurbished, storefront next door.

"Nobody wants to get tutored on a Friday afternoon, not even the Asian kids," Kelly informs me.

I make a mental note of the dot-com address and their hours of operation. We'll come back tomorrow.

Back in the car, "Where to next, Dad?"

"We're going to make a visit to one of your classmates, Kelly."

"Is he hot?"

"I'm going to pretend I didn't hear that."

I get off Peterson and head north.

Sauganash is one of the better areas in the city of Chicago. It is in the northwest corner, and for years, has been the home of police chiefs, judges, city officials, and rich politicians, mainly because if you are employed by the city of Chicago you are required to live in the city of Chicago. This is where I used to live.

The majority of the houses in Sauganash are of the upper middle class strata, but in recent years, many houses have been torn down and in their place mini-mansions have arose. If my ex ever sells, my ex-house will undoubtedly have a similar fate. I'm the one who buys the worst house on a great block instead of the reverse. There are numerous parks, trees, nice shopping centers, and great schools in Sauganash. The most unique feature of the area is the number of cemeteries dotted about the area. It might bother some, but the well-maintained graveyards are very quiet and add a history to the area. I wish I still lived in Sauganash.

I pull up in front of one of the aforementioned mini-mansions, which sits on two lots instead of one.

"Who lives here, Dad?" Kelly asks.

"Juan Hernandez."

"The Hispanic science geek?"

I consult my notes from the file Eldin gave me. "Yep."

"Well, his parents must have spent all their money on the house because they sure don't spend it on his clothes," Kelly says. "The guy dresses one step away from something you'd wear to illegally cross the border."

I sit and stare at the residence.

"Dad, can we first get something to eat?" Care asks. "I think I'm getting faint."

"I'll take you both to dinner after this. You stay here and decide where you want to go. I'll be right back."

I leave the girls in culinary excitement and make my way to the elaborate front door. Before ringing the doorbell, I check to see if there is a name on the mail slot. There isn't. I ring twice. No one comes to the door. I make my way back to the car.

"Nobody home?" Care asks.

"Nope."

"Did you look in the back?" Kelly asks. "Juan Science Dude might be in the garage getting ready to send a rocket to Pluto."

"Not a good idea to be snooping around a residence with security cameras everywhere, Kelly."

"I knew that. I was just testing you, Dad."

"I guess you can just say, 'Juan gone, Juan to go.'" Care sums up the situation.

"So, you decide where you want to eat?"

"We got it down to Applebee's, Olive Garden, or Chili's," Care says.

We live in one of the greatest restaurant cities in the world and my kids pick three theme restaurants where you can get the exact same meal in each of the fifty states and numerous foreign countries.

"I know where we'll go."

I pick an Italian place, the Vernon Park Tap. The place has been there since Capone was a kid. You walk in the front door and are transported back in time. There may be fifteen tables in the place. You order off a blackboard, pasta is made with loving hands, there isn't a dish that isn't delicious, and you always get plenty to take home. The kids love it, especially the gelato dessert. We just about roll out of the place we're so full.

"Dad?"

"What, Care?"

"Can we stop and get donuts on the way home?"

"Are you kidding me? You ate enough in there for an Army brigade." How Care stays as skinny as a rail is beyond my comprehension.

"I'm thinking about breakfast tomorrow. You got to plan ahead."

***

Saturday morning, with kids or without, is reserved for errands, but today the only stop we make is at the Jewell. I let them buy one junk food snack each. A perfect parent I'm not.

"Dad, we got to get on the case," Kelly informs me. "The thieves could be inside the school right now, cleaning out the place."

"Patience is a virtue, Kelly."

"I hate patience, Dad."

"I've noticed."

In the afternoon, we're back at the Hernandez mini-mansion. This time the girls accompany me up the walk to the front door. "Maybe Juan's dad is a drug dealer and they make him dress crummy so he won't cast suspicion," Kelly surmises.

"Kelly, that's not a very nice thing to say."

"Dad, I'm trying to think outside of the box."

"Go back in the box, Kelly, and do your thinking there."

I ring the doorbell. We wait. The door opens.

"Yes?" The very attractive woman is maybe thirty, red hair, thin, and overly stylish for a Saturday afternoon. She wears a diamond the size of a cat's eye on her ring finger.

"Mrs. Hernandez?"

"Who?"

Kelly interrupts, "I love your outfit. Is it Dior?"

"Ralph Lauren."

"I was going to guess that next," Kelly says.

I interrupt the fashion Q and A. "Are you Mrs. Hernandez?"

"No."

"Does Juan Hernandez live here?"

"I certainly hope not."

"We're sorry to bother you," I apologize. "I must've been given some wrong information."

Kelly asks the woman, "How long do you go between haircuts?"

"Three to four weeks."

"You don't have any split ends at all," Kelly says, staring at the woman's do.

A man approaches from the rear. "Everything okay here, dear?" He's about sixty with a muffin top around his waist.

"These people are looking for someone named Hernandez," she tells her husband.

"In this neighborhood?" he asks.

"I was given some bad information," I repeat.

"Wait," the man says to his wife. "Isn't our cleaning lady named Hernandez?"

"I wouldn't know," his wife says. "She won't take a check, only cash."

Enough said. I back away from the door. "Sorry to bother you."

"One more thing," Kelly says. "Where did you buy your shoes?"

I have to pull my daughter away from the door before she asks about the woman's skivvies.

Back in the car, Care comments, "That guy looked like the lady's dad, not her husband. Are we going to investigate them too?"

"Not today."

Next stop is back to Larry's Tutor Tent, which is open for business. The three of us walk in the door.

"Hi, Mr. Mizzi," Care says to the man who sits at the front desk.

"Hi, Care. Hi, Kelly. Are you here to get smarter?"

"No," Kelly says.

"We didn't know you worked here," Care says.

"This is what I do after school when I'm not grading papers." He stands and puts out his hand to shake mine. "Hi, I'm Larry Mizzi."

"Richard Sherlock. I didn't know you all knew each other," I admit.

"Mr. Mizzi is the computer science teacher at school."

"Welcome to the Tutor Tent. Are you here for our summer immersion program? It's never too early to get a jump on next year."

"Maybe," I say.

"I don't think so, Dad," Kelly says.

"Math's my best subject," Care says. "I don't need this."

"As Mr. Mizzi said, it's never too late to get a jump on next year, girls."

Before my two argue, I say, "Why don't you two go down to the corner and get yourselves something healthy to drink?" I give the girls ten bucks and get them out of the tent before they spill the few beans I've been able to gather in this case.

"Obviously, it might take some convincing on my part," I tell Larry, "but please tell me what you have to offer."

Mizzi gives me a brief tour of the two-room facility. In each room there are two cafeteria tables with five or six laptop computers on each. It's a little hard to talk since we're in the midst of a nail gun staccato from the re-doing of the unit next door.

"We offer six different small group programs and individual instruction," he says as he hands me a tri-fold brochure.

"What are the most popular?"

"The SAT and magnet school prep classes."

"And how much are those?"

He points to the last page of the brochure. "Four to six-thousand dollars."

Knowledge doesn't come cheap in this place.

"And how exactly does the guarantee work? If we sign up for the prep class and she doesn't get accepted into a college prep school, do I get my money back?"

"Only the top tier individual courses are guaranteed and the guarantee is only for the results the student gets on the test, not whether they get accepted into a magnet school."

"What's the guarantee level?"

"Ninety percent on the test or better."

"Wow," I say. "That's pretty good, but what happens if the kid isn't that bright to begin with? Isn't that pretty risky for you?"

"Before we accept a student into our premier level classes, we thoroughly test them. We only accept students into the program who have the capability to succeed." He pauses. "Would this course be for Kelly?"

"No, Kelly couldn't care less about going to a magnet school. She's more interested in going to a best dressed academy."

"Then you're thinking about Care?"

"Next year," I tell him.

"We're already eighty percent booked for next year."

"Business booming, huh?"

"It's never too early to get a jump on the competition."

It's time to go. "Thanks very much, Mr. Mizzi." I take a brochure with me.

"You're welcome."

I find my two kids at the end of the strip center sitting at an outdoor table slurping down sugary concoctions that will rot their teeth and cost me thousands of dollars in dental bills.

I sit. "Why didn't you tell me you knew Mr. Mizzi?"

"We didn't know he'd be here," Care says.

"You like him?"

"Not really," Care says.

"He's a little on the geeky side," Kelly says, an interesting comment from a kid who spends most of her time staring into the screen of her cell phone.

"He is a computer science teacher," I say. "He should be a geek."

"A lot of kids think he's a perv."

"Kelly, that's another word I don't like to hear out of your mouth."

"I'm just telling you what people say about him," Kelly says.

"And why would they say that?"

"Because he's creepy."

"How?"

"I don't know, just creepy."

"Do you know anyone who he tutors?"

"Lots go," Kelly says. "All the Asian kids and losers get tutored."

"Some real dumb-dumbs in my grade go," Care says.

"Do you know if Arleta Torelli was tutored in the tent?"

"Well, she's not Asian, but she is certainly a loser. And if she did," Kelly adds, "I bet her mother was right next to her the whole time."

"How well do you know Arleta, Kelly?"

"Hardly at all. She'd be the last person I'd ever hang out with."

"Then you have no reason to say mean things about her."

"I didn't say anything mean."

"You just called her a loser."

"Well, I didn't mean it in a negative way."

"If you don't have anything nice to say about someone, don't say anything at all, Kelly."

"Okay, I won't. I'll put it on Facebook instead."

Technology for our children, isn't it wonderful?

I pile the kids into the Toyota.

"We should go back to the scene of the crime, Dad," Care suggests.

"It's Saturday; the place will be locked up tighter than a drum."

"You sure there's no big money buried out in Esther's garden, Dad?" Kelly asks.

"Almost positive."

"Maybe we should take another look? I need some new shoes."

"Forget it."

Back at home I prepare a new recipe I got off one of those TV food channels. The kids take one look at my gourmet chopped turkey brocaflower fricassee', turn their noses up, and run to the fridge to get out the leftover pasta from last night and zap it in the microwave. I personally think my gourmet meal has some very unique flavors. The only problem is the flavors seem to be at odds with one another and end up like two bull goats with locked horns fighting for dominance inside your mouth. It might be a while before I repeat this meal.

After dinner, Kelly finds my tin box with the blank recipe cards and pushpins. She takes it into the living room where she and Care start filling in the cards and tacking them up onto *The Original Carlo*, a particularly bad work of art I bought years ago for eight dollars, which depicts a dilapidated barn behind four mailboxes, set against a bright yellow sky, painted by a guy named Carlo or a painter using the name Carlo because he was horridly ashamed of this creation.

By the time I finish cleaning up the kitchen and join the two super sleuths in the front room, they have ten cards pinned up. Terrible Teddy Tulleners' card rests dead center.

"Teddy's your number one suspect?" I ask.

"He had motive, access, and is known to carry lethal weapons," Kelly answers.

"Like what?"

"Somebody said they saw him carrying an AK-47 once."

"Do you know what an AK-47 looks like, Kelly?"

"No, but I'm sure the person who saw him carrying it did."

My first rule of life, *Assume Nothing*, has somehow been lost on my children.

I can see from the handwriting that Care put up the Esther Stiffarm card. "You think Esther did it?"

"She looked pretty suspicious on my video, Dad, and she could pack a lot of quarters in that hair of hers."

I look at the rest of the names and comments on the cards. "You think Principal Puddle is stealing from his own school or Ms. Mossy has something to do with this?"

"Ms. Mossy's got shifty eyes, Dad," Care says.

"And since she can't find a husband, she probably needs the money for her retirement," Kelly adds.

"And Arleta's mom?"

"Stinky could be depositing a lot fewer quarters than we think she is, Dad," Kelly says.

"Don't call her Stinky."

"I heard you call her Stinky the other day, Dad. Why can't I?"

"Because it's not nice, Kelly."

"So, I'm not allowed to call her 'Stinky' even if you call her that and she really is?"

"I will admit Mrs. Torelli is a bit on the odiferous side."

"What's odiferous mean?" Care asks.

"It means she stinks," Kelly says.

I sit on the couch as they continue to tack cards up on the *Carlo*. "So, if you suspect Winky Torelli, how much do you think she's getting away with every week?" My question catches them by surprise.

"I don't know," Care says.

"Do you suspect she has an accomplice?"

"You mean she may be in cahoots with somebody?" Care asks.

"It could be an organized crime family," Kelly says.

"Terrible Teddy could be Arleta's distant cousin and they have that onamonapia thing going."

"Omerta?"

"Whatever."

"And do you suspect the missing milk money is the only crime being committed at the school?" I continue as the devil's advocate.

"I don't understand, Dad," Care says.

"Maybe the milk money is just the tip of the iceberg."

"And this is all a huge educational conspiracy?" Kelly continues to surmise.

"Dad, you're making this way too complicated," Care says.

"Life is seldom what it may seem, Care."

"But I'm pretty sure I saw Miss Stiffarm stash some money into her hair."

"Ten dollars' worth of quarters up there and she'd tip over, Care."

"Dad," Kelly says. "I think you're onto something here. A conspiracy."

"By the way, Kelly, why haven't you ever brought home a school-issued laptop?"

"Only kids in advanced computer science classes get them."

"And that left you off the list?"

"I'm advanced but not in computer science."

"Where are you so advanced, cell phone science?"

"The science of fashion, Dad."

The girls continue to write on cards, pin them up, and move them around like chess pieces. I keep peppering them with questions, trying my best to put as much confusion into their thought processes as possible. It's not hard to do. By the time they're ready for bed, their brains are spinning like a dreidel during Chanukah.

CHAPTER 14

On Sunday morning, I rise much earlier than my girls. I make the coffee and sit in the front room. I have to laugh at the total disarray of cards adorning *The Original Carlo*. The bad painting looks like it has been covered by flaking white paint chips.

I retrieve the test file Eldin supplied and find the phone numbers for Juan Hernandez and Winky Torelli. If these two are landline phones, this will be easy. If they are cell phones, it gets a little harder. I dial the reverse directory number I used to use as a CPD detective and put in Juan's number first. His address comes up in seconds, and not in the Sauganash neighborhood we previously visited. The Torelli number doesn't come up, only a recording, which says the number is unpublished. I'm one for two.

It's well past nine o'clock when my sleeping beauties get out of bed and find their way in front of the TV set, and begin to exist in a semi-somnambulist state of being.

"I thought it would be a great idea if the three of us went to church this morning," I announce.

"Really, why?" Kelly grumbles.

"Because you people need spiritual guidance in your lives."

"Mom gives us that," Care informs me.

"How?"

"If the pyramid thing works for her, she's going to get us our own."

"Wearing a pyramid on your head, Kelly, will ruin your hair."

"Oh my God, I didn't think of that."

I make scrambled eggs and toast for breakfast. They complain. "Any of that pasta left from the other night?" Care asks.

"No, but I have some turkey brocaflower fricassee left over."

"We want to eat, not barf."

"Eat the eggs. We're leaving in a half-hour, girls."

"But *Friends* won't be over by then," Care, the more

diligent TV viewer of the two, says.

Care and Kelly each have seen every rerun of *Friends* at least thirty times. They're better friends of *Friends* than the friends on *Friends*. "If you want to be a detective, you got to learn to get up pretty early in the morning."

"Even on Sunday?"

"Half an hour. We're leaving."

The address is well west of Logan Square, between Fullerton and Division. It's not the ghetto, but it's not too many steps above it. Most of the businesses don't sport signs in English.

"What are we doing here?"

"If we knew you were taking us out for Mexican food for lunch, why did you force us to eat those awful eggs?" Care asks.

Although my Toyota fits in well in the neighborhood, I am a little leery about being here with the kids. A lot of stray bullets find unintended targets in these neighborhoods. But it's Sunday morning when, according to statistics, the least amount of violent crime takes place. All the hoods are in bed after an exhausting night of shooting at each other.

Juan's address is 1829 1/2, which means it's a house or apartment in the rear. I pull up across the street and park in front of 1830. The houses in this neighborhood can't be called decrepit, but this is nowhere near the 'next up and coming' hot investment opportunity. The homes are small, on twenty-five foot lots, all in need of some repair. Whoever had the franchise for selling burglar bars made a fortune on these blocks.

"Come on, Dad, tell us what we're doing here."

"Watch. Maybe you'll learn something about life."

"Oh, great," Kelly says. "I've always wanted to learn how to gangbang in Spanish."

We wait. When noon hits, the neighborhood starts to come alive. People return from church or breakfast and walk up and down the block, chatting up neighbors. Some residents come out and sit on small front porches, watching their kids play in front yards.

"See anyone you know?" I ask.

"Are we supposed to?"

"Hopefully."

Five minutes later, a kid about Kelly's age walks up the gangway between houses.

"Hey, that's Juan Science Dude."

I start the car and pull away before Juan recognizes any of us.

"That's not very polite," Care says. "Shouldn't we at least stop, and say, 'Hola'?"

***

In the afternoon, I drag them away from *The Original Carlo*, which now has enough cards pinned up to make it look like flaking skin after a horrific sunburn. "Homework time. Get in there and get it done."

At five o'clock, I load them into the Toyota and take them to their mother's.

"What do you want us to do on the case tomorrow?" Kelly asks.

"Nothing."

"Nothing? You got to be kidding, Dad!"

"If I need anything, I'll call you."

"Why don't you give us some of those bugging devices we can secretly plant on people and track where they go?" Kelly suggests.

"Or show us how to tap into their cell phones and record their conversations?"

"We could measure people's footprints."

"Or dust for fingerprints?"

"If I need you, I'll call you."

"Dad, that's like being put on hold," Kelly says. "I hate that."

She has no clue just how much she could hate being put on hold and I hope she never has to find out.

I pull into what used to be my driveway. I get out of the car, give the girls each a kiss, and tell them I love them. As I watch them run through the open front doorway, I feel a very strange sensation go through my entire body. The feeling must be from the crystal pyramid my ex is wearing on her head.

CHAPTER 15

L loyd's of London has been selling insurance since the late 1880s. They have made quite a name for themselves by insuring what other insurance companies would never consider insuring. They insured Jimmys Durante's nose, Bob Dylan's vocal cords, Tina Turner's legs, even a Playboy Playmate's breasts. I'm not sure if Lloyd's does this merely for publicity, but I am positive that each of these policies are written in their favor. A nose would have to be flattened, a finger cut off, leg amputated, or a breast sagging down to the navel before Lloyd's would pay out a farthing.

Richmond Insurance has never made a practice of this type of insuring. It amazes the heck out of me why they would ever insure classic, imported, expensive cigars against fire, flood, and natural disaster but they did. And now they have to live with the consequences.

"I've reread the policy twice, Tiffany. There is nothing I can do."

"My daddy doesn't want to shell out a buck-and-a-half for a bunch of crummy cigars."

"Then they shouldn't have written the policy in the first place."

"But it's not fair."

"What's not fair about it? Fumadoro has receipt of purchase, proof of ownership, and has documented the cigar ashes both by photograph and scientific analysis," I try my best to convince her. "He's followed the terms of the policy exactly how Richmond wrote it."

Tiffany gives me a big humph.

"If you don't believe me, read the policy."

"I can't read that thing, it's boring." Tiffany has a hard time getting through a People Magazine without nodding off. "We have to go to court on Friday. What are we going to do?"

"Pay him off."

"Oh, Mr. Sherlock, Daddy hates that." Tiffany fumes and sulks the rest of the trip to Sauganash.

"Park in the street. I can't let him see me."

Tiffany parks in a handicapped spot. I hate when she does this. "Now tell me again what do you want me to do?" she asks.

"Go in, ask for the owner, tell him you want to go to college, and you have to take the SAT test. Got that?"

"I guess so."

"Tell him you want the best SAT prep course they have."

"I only go first class, Mr. Sherlock, you know that."

"And then he should ask you to take a test."

"I hate tests, especially the medical kind."

"Take the test. If he says you passed, sign up for the course."

Tiffany gives me one of her many *What?* looks. "Why am I doing this, again? I don't want to go to college. People go to college to learn how to get rich, so what would be the point of me going?"

"Pretend, Tiffany, just pretend."

"Yeah, I can do that."

"And ask for the guarantee."

"Yeah, yeah, yeah."

I watch Tiffany make her way into the strip center. I have to point and direct her past the refurbishing unit next to the Tutor Tent. Once she's inside, I get back into my car, get out my cell phone, and call Herman.

"Herman, have you gone over those numbers, yet?"

"I'm ready, Sherlock."

"Good. When can we go over them?"

"Over what?"

"Mrs. Chumley's spreadsheet."

"Oh, I'm not ready to do that."

"Then what are you ready for, Herman?"

"I'm ready to pop the question."

"What?"

"I'm in love. I want to make a commitment."

"Herman, you might be rushing things a bit. You two don't even speak the same language."

"The language of love, Sherlock, has no syllables. We speak to each other through our hearts."

"Herman, wait. Don't rush into this."

"I'm going to get a ring, get down on my knees, and propose."

"Trust me, Herman, don't do that."

"You're right. I won't." He agrees with me immediately. Whew.

"If I get down on my knees, I may never get up. I'll ask her sitting down."

"Herman, wait."

"I can't wait."

"There's no hurry."

"I've waited my whole life for such a love to cross my path."

"Herman, your path is like a four lane expressway. Wait, there's no rush. There could be a lot more fish in the sea for you to meet."

"I can't swim."

"Herman, be reasonable."

"As soon as I can get out the front door, we're going bridal dress shopping. I'm thinking we can both wear white."

Herman in a white tux will look like a cumulus cloud.

"If I fast for two or three days, I can squeeze out the back door."

I got a two-day reprieve.

"Herman, promise me you won't pop the question until we talk in person."

He breathes deeply into the phone.

"Will you do that for me, please?"

"The only 'do' I want to hear, Sherlock, is the 'I do' from Ludmila."

Oh, jeesh.

As I hang up the phone, I look up and see Tiffany getting back into the Lexus. She's been gone less than ten minutes. "What are you doing back so soon?"

"What, you're not happy to see me?"

"Did you go in there and do everything I told you to do?"

"Yes."

I quickly figure Larry Mizzi had a one minute conversation with her and decided she wouldn't be 'right' for his program. "So, you didn't take the test?"

"Of course, I took the test. Isn't that what you told me to do?"

"Yes."

"See, I can follow directions. I just don't like to follow directions."

Now, I'm thinking she took the test but never got past the

name line and Larry was nice enough to not embarrass her any
further.

"And?" I ask Tiffany to continue.

"He said I had all the skills and pre-somethings needed to
ace that dumb STA test."

"Did you sign up?"

"Six grand."

"Did you get the guarantee?"

"What guarantee?"

"The one I asked you to get."

Tiffany gives me one of her odd looks. "You know you can't
expect me to remember everything, Mr. Sherlock."

What was I thinking?

Tiffany starts up her car. "Wanna get something to eat? All
that thinking made me hungry."

"Sure."

Tiffany pulls out of the handicapped spot.

"What did you think of Mr. Mizzi?"

"Creepy."

"How?"

"His eyes never left my chest. I can't say I blame him since I
have perfect breasts, but if I would've had a mirror, I coulda put
it in my cleavage, and he coulda stared right back at himself the
whole time."

Not only is Larry a creep, he may also be a crook.

When Tiffany gets on the expressway to go back downtown,
I remember to tell her, "Don't forget to cancel the charge on
your credit card, Tiffany."

"Why would I do that?"

"You don't want to pay for something you won't use."

"No, I think I'm going to take the course. If I do as well as
Mr. Mizzi said I'll do, I might go to college after all."

"Tiffany—" I have no clue how to break this to her.

"I heard that Harvard is a pretty good school, maybe I'll go
there."

***

Tiffany treats me to lunch at one of her favorite gourmet,
organic, all sprouts, un-genetically modified restaurants called
The Unbearable Lightness of Bean.

ULB wouldn't be my first choice, but she's paying. She orders the rhubarb/cucumber/cauliflower/kale medley. Yum. I go for the Veggie Potpourri, which tastes pretty much like the potpourri you'd find in the restroom. Not Yum. And the portions on the plate are so tiny I'm famished by the time lunch is over. But I must admit the presentation was nice. I've never seen a slice of rhubarb in the shape of a Gumby doll before.

"Where to now, Mr. Sherlock?"

"Back to the Ho Lee Dong Cancer Clinic."

"Why? I hate that place. It's so depressing."

"Sometimes you have to do things you don't like, Tiffany."

"Only when you can't hire someone to do them for you, Mr. Sherlock. And that's a problem I've never had."

I forget with whom I speak to at times.

It's mid-afternoon and the clinic is as busy as Union Station. People come and go like commuters on a Monday. Something is horribly wrong and I don't have a clue what it is. I sit in the Lexus and watch, wait, contemplate, and try my best to ignore Tiffany's constant, "Can we go, now?" Granted, I've only been here twice before, but I don't recognize one face. The clientele is 100% Asian with an 80% majority of women, and at least an 80% percentage of seniors. There is no parking; everyone walks. The only vehicle which pulls up in front is the UPS truck, whose driver must be having the same kind of day I'm having because he wheels in a full cart and ten minutes later he wheels out the same stuff. I know the feeling.

Some patients are quickies, in and out in less than a half-hour. Most of these do seem to have a little more bounce in their step on the way out than they did on the way in. Some patients enter and disappear. I wish there were windows, so I could see inside. I also wish I had an excuse to go in, but I don't. There is not one question I can come up with, which would give me a reason to visit.

"Mr. Sherlock, may I remind you how bored I am?"

"No, I have a very good memory, and since you've already reminded me about thirty-five times how bored you are, I think I got it."

Two seconds later, "Mr. Sherlock—"

"Yes, Tiffany?"

"Can we go now?"

The thirty-sixth time's the charm.

Tiffany drops me off at Lake and Wacker, so I can take the Brown Line north. There's plenty of empty seats since it's one of the first stops. Sitting in the last row, I stare out the window lost in absent thought the entire trip home. I'm not having a good time.

One hour later, I can't believe I am about to do what I am about to do, but I can't think of anything else to do. Right before dinner, I call my daughters. It's not the calling I can't believe, it's the *what I am going to say* that truly disturbs me.

Kelly answers the phone. "Hi, Dad."

"Kelly, get Care on the other line."

Twenty seconds later, "Hi, Dad."

"Hi, Care." I hesitate a few seconds, and I'm about to begin, but I can't bring myself to say it just yet. Instead, I ask, "Are you both wearing your pyramids right now?"

"No," Care says.

"Why not?"

Kelly explains, "Care got hers stuck and couldn't get it off."

"The only energy I got was pain."

It's no wonder so many of the Pharaohs died young.

"Kids," I say, "I need your help."

"You want me to help you pick out new clothes?" Kelly asks.

"Make out this week's shopping list?" Care asks.

"No. I need you to do something for me at school tomorrow."

"You mean we're back on the case?" They both explode into the phone.

"First, you have to promise not to say anything about this to anyone."

"No problem," Care assures me.

"Are you going to be there, Dad?" Kelly asks.

"No."

"So you won't embarrass me, thank God."

"Second, you will do exactly what I ask, nothing more and nothing less. Understand?"

"Will we need a disguise?" Care asks.

"No."

"Will we be packing heat?" Kelly asks.

Oh, jeesh.

I pause to let them calm down a bit, which doesn't help a

lick. "Care, here's what I want you to do."

"Tell me."

"After lunch is over, hang around the cafeteria where you won't be noticed. Watch Esther Stiffarm. I know she'll go into the storeroom."

"Okay."

"After she comes out, stay where you are and see if the other cafeteria workers go in after her. If they do, count how many."

"Ten-four, Dad."

"Kelly—"

"Yes, Fearless Leader."

"Tomorrow, I want you to talk with every kid who got into a magnet school and find out who and how many took Mr. Mizzi's course at the Tutor Tent."

"Cool."

"Write down the names of who took the course and who didn't. Then hint around, see what you can find out about the course. Find out if it helped or if it didn't. Ask if it was taught on a computer or by Mr. Mizzi himself."

"I'm on it."

"Be sure you talk to Arleta Torelli, she's the most important person, and get as much information as you can without telling her why you're asking."

"Dad, you can count on me."

"You both have to be very careful. Don't tell any of your friends what you're doing."

"Our lips are sealed."

After hearing the last assurance, I'm now positive this is a very bad idea, but I'm too far into it to back out now.

"I'll pick you up tomorrow after school. I love ya."

"Dad, we're going to break this case so wide open, you'll be able to drive that awful car of yours right through it."

CHAPTER 16

I'm up at the crack of dawn, get a cup of coffee into me, do my back exercises in front of *The Original Carlo*, take a shower, and am out the door before six forty-five.

I take Ashland all the way to Fullerton, turn right, and, in a few more minutes, pull up in front of the home of Juan Science Dude. I need to speak with his mother. I wait an hour. In that time, neither Juan nor, his mother, exit the residence. I drive off with the realization I have wasted the first two hours of my day.

Figuring the expressway will be a parking lot, I get back on Ashland and stop-and-go all the way south to Chinatown. I pull up across the street and slightly down the block from Ho Lee Dong's clinic. I sit in my Toyota and watch.

There has to be something I'm missing. What is wrong with this picture? What doesn't make sense? How can this guy be this busy? What's he doing that other clinics aren't? I waste another hour watching and waiting. After two hours, I have no better idea of what's going on than when I arrived.

I call Tiffany at eleven o'clock.

"Hello."

"Are you awake?"

"Yes, Mr. Sherlock, I've been awake for minutes."

"I need you."

"That sounds creepy, Mr. Sherlock."

"I need you to stand guard, to make sure nobody sees what I'm doing."

"That sounds really creepy."

"Tiffany, it's not creepy."

I can almost hear the cogs turning in her mind through our lousy cell phone connection. She blurts out, "Do you want me to stand guard while you break into Mr. Fumatorium's house and find out what he really did to those dumb cigars?"

"No."

"Why not? We have to do something before Friday, so Daddy won't have to pay him any money."

"Tiffany, I've told you a hundred times, there's nothing we

can do. It was Richmond's fault for selling him such a ridiculous policy."

"I never thought of you as a quitter, Mr. Sherlock, but I do now."

"Sorry to disappoint you." I pause. "Will you help me or not?"

"Where?"

"At the Ho Lee Dong Cancer Clinic."

"I hate that place. Are you going to be doing something creepy there?"

"You might think it's creepy, but I'd put it more in the *disgusting* category."

"Are you doing it with someone or alone?"

"Alone."

"Is it animal, vegetable, or material?"

"None of the above."

"Are you going to keep your clothes on, Mr. Sherlock?"

Oh, jeesh.

"Maybe this is a bad idea, Tiffany. Forget we ever had this conversation. Whatever it is I have to do, I'll figure out a way to do it by myself."

"Oh, no, no, tell me. Now, I really want to know."

"No, forget it. Sorry I asked. It's probably too much for you to take. I should've never mentioned it in the first place."

"No, tell me. I can handle it. What are you going to do, Mr. Sherlock?"

"I'm going Dumpster diving."

"Yuck."

✳✳✳

No matter what a person does to make living, whether he's a butcher, a baker, or a candlestick-maker, I'll bet there is at least one aspect or duty of their job they absolutely hate. A fireman friend of mine loves everything about being a fireman except polishing the truck. A plumber I know loves pipes but hates crawling under houses. I read once of a Lincoln Park zookeeper who hated penguins. Snakes, armadillos, and iguanas didn't bother him in the slightest, but penguins gave him the willies. Go figure.

Personally, this isn't the case for me because I hate

everything about my job. With me, it's not what I hate but what I hate the most. Topping that list is going through someone's garbage. Do you have any idea of how disgusting it is retrieving used dental floss, coming across a dismembered thumb, or scooping up a sample of a fresh burrito regurgitation? I can't tell you how many times I've waded through a mound of disgusting filth in search of the proverbial *bloody glove* and came across something so disgusting I did the regurgitating.

Tiffany pulls up a half-hour later, dressed in a designer Hazmat suit. "I'm ready to stand guard, Mr. Sherlock," she says, parking her car illegally.

I get out of my car and climb into hers. "I love your outfit, Tiffany."

"You're probably wondering where I shop."

I point to the back of the clinic's lot. "Drive around to where they dump the trash."

I have her position the car so she'll be able to see if anyone comes out the back door of the clinic and heads for the two trash containers at the back of the lot. "Will I be safe from germs and bacteria here, Mr. Sherlock?"

"Since you're in that suit, in a locked car, and one hundred feet away from the Dumpster, I think you'll be out of harm's way."

"Who's this 'harm's' guy, anyway?"

"I'll tell you later."

I, at least, had the forethought to bring a couple pairs of latex gloves and a pair of booties to cover my shoes. I put these on, and before exiting the Lexus, give my lookout directions. "Now, if you see anyone come out of the clinic and head for the trash, honk the horn."

"Do you want beeps, honks, or an ah-ooh-gaa?"

"Beeps."

"How many?"

"Two."

"Do you want beep-beep, or do you want Beeep.... Beeep?"

"If you see anyone, just honk the horn."

"You just said you wanted beeps. Make up your mind, Mr. Sherlock."

I get out of the car and head for the Dumpsters. The one on the right is dirty gray, about five feet deep, eight across, and six high. It is shorter in the front than in the back, and one of its two swing-open covers is open. I peer inside; it's maybe half full. This is the regular trash. I boost myself on the edge and am careful not to strain my back lifting myself upward. Once on top, I sit on the closed cover with my feet dangling down, and search with my eyes. I can't see much of anything except used lunch bags, scraps of paper, old newspapers, empty food containers, wadded up paper towels, and other assorted gunk. If nothing else, I could have Dr. Dong arrested for not recycling properly.

I don't have much choice, so I tighten the gloves, cinch up the booties, and jump down. My feet hit the pile and sink into the slop like they're hitting quicksand. I start to sashay around, pushing the mound of filth every-which-way, looking for some type of clue, and have no luck. It stinks. I get the immediate realization that patients of the clinic are not Clean Plate Club members because there's enough old rice in this trash to feed a family of four in Beijing for a week. I pick out discarded papers, searching for financial information or mail, and find only junkmail. The Ho Lee Dong Clinic got the same offer to install solar as I did. I search for invoices, mailing labels, and anything I can link to the clinic's business. Nothing.

I keep searching. After another five minutes of trash prospecting, my cellphone rings out either Katy Perry, Fergie, or some other singer I wouldn't know if she hit me in the ear with a flugelhorn. I have to get my kids from adding ringtones to my phone without my permission. "Hello."

"Sherlock, Eldin Puddle. You have to get up here right away." He's one degree away from frantic.

"I'm kinda buried right now, Principal."

"All hell is breaking loose."

From outside the trash bin, I hear: Beep-beep. Beeeep. Beap, beep-beep, beep.

"Can you hold on one second?" I beg in a muffled voice.

"You have to help me. I need you right now."

I look up and see the top of a full plastic trash container reach the top of the Dumpster, tilt my way, and empty its contents on top of me like a tub of Gatorade on the winning Super Bowl coach.

The empty plastic can retreats from where it came. A few seconds later I hear a long *hooooonk*.

I get back on the phone. "Eldin, I'll be there as soon as I

can."

"Please hurry."

Maybe Tiffany's right. I am a quitter because I give up. I can't take this trash any longer. I brush off what I can, hoist myself up, and climb out of this disgusting bin of bad bacteria.

Standing and inhaling a breath of somewhat fresh air, I look down on myself and see enough stains and splotches on my clothes to qualify as an entrant to a modern art show.

Before I begin my cowardly walk of shame back to Tiffany's car, I stop at the second, much smaller trash container. This one is painted red with big white letters informing all of its purpose: Medical Waste Only. The top of this container is padlocked, but the plastic is somewhat see-thru. I pause to take a gander at what's inside. There must be a dozen foot high, four inches deep, plastic containers, chock full of used syringes. I've seen these receptacles in ERs. They fit into a wall-mounted disposer where the syringe is inserted on top and drops into the plastic case below. Once inserted, it cannot be retrieved; the exact same principle as a USPS mailbox. The only other items I'm able to make out are empty, used, four by six inch, plastic bags with long tubes attached. There's hundreds of them. Each has an open circle on the top to allow it to hang on an IV pole. I can't read the finer print through the opaque plastic, but the words I can read are *Saline Solution*. There are other items in the red receptacle, but none nearly as numerous as the two I've mentioned.

I walk back to Tiffany's car. She rolls her window down and greets me with, "Pretty good beeping, huh, Mr. Sherlock?"

"So good, I thought it was the Archangel blowing his trumpet at midnight."

"Is that some guy in a rock group?"

"So to speak."

"And how did you like my *All Clear Honk*?" Tiffany asks.

"It was magical."

"That's me, *magical*," she agrees.

I walk around to the passenger's side, try the door, but it's locked. The window rolls down.

"You don't think you're getting into this car smelling like garbage, do you, Mr. Sherlock?"

"Guess not."

"I hope you don't need me for a couple of hours," Tiffany

says. "I'm feeling kinda icky being around all this trash and could use some aroma therapy at my spa. Ta-ta, Mr. Sherlock." The window rolls up and off she goes.

Hating my job every step of the way, I walk back to my car.

CHAPTER 17

I lock my car whenever I park anywhere in this city, but this time, I let it sit in front of my building with all the windows rolled down to air it out. I go in and take a shower. And boy, do I need one. I toss my Dumpster-diving outfit on the back porch.

It is well past the end of fifth period or one o'clock by the time I see Ann Margaret and Pat Nixon.

"Hello, Mrs. Chumley."

"Well, good afternoon, Mr. Sherlock." Each time Mrs. Chumley opens her mouth, she puts the chip in *chipper*.

"Is Principal Puddle in?"

"He can't wait to see you."

Before I leave the front of her desk, I ask, "By the way, would you happen to have a new spreadsheet for the week just passed?"

"I don't yet, but I will."

"May I get a copy?"

"If Principal Puddle agrees, it would be my pleasure."

"Thank you, Mrs. Chumley."

"You're welcome, Mr. Sherlock. Have a smiley day."

I give a slight knock before entering Eldin's office.

At the sight of me, Eldin jumps out of his chair. "Sherlock, it's about time." He closes the door behind me and pushes me inside. "Where have you been?"

"Getting trashed, if you really must know."

Puddle hurries back into his chair. "All hell is breaking loose. The school board wants explanations, I've got parents banging on my doors, a lawsuit's been filed, the missing money hasn't shown up, somebody has reported us to the authorities, and teachers are starting to jump ship."

"Slow down, Eldin. Take a deep breath."

Eldin is past frantic. "I can't slow down. Pretty soon this is all going to start having an effect on the kids, and that's something I can't let happen."

"Fine, let's start at the end. Who's jumping ship?"

"Our computer science teacher quit this morning and I

hear there's more right behind him."

"Mr. Mizzi quit?"

"This morning."

"Why?"

"He didn't say."

"What authorities got reported to?"

"Immigration."

"What would that have to do with you?"

"I don't know."

"What lawsuit and who filed it?"

"I don't know that, either."

"I'll bet it's Loudmouth Lou Lauder."

"Okay." He pauses. "Did you find the thief, yet?"

"I'm still working on that."

"You have to hurry." Eldin's cheeks are bright red and his receding hairline seems to be increasing before my very eyes.

"Eldin, try to calm down."

"I can't. This is a nightmare. All we want is to give our students every advantage possible in their educational development and all this craziness is going to ruin that. I'm dealing with children's lives here, Mr. Sherlock, and I can't let them down."

"You won't, Eldin. You're the one voice of reason in this place, but if you go off the deep end, the whole ship will go down with you. Be strong."

"What can I do?"

"First, get Loudmouth Lou in here. Let me talk to him."

Eldin nods.

"I know what he wants. All I got to do is figure out how to shut him up."

"Then what?"

"I need a copy of Mrs. Chumley's current spreadsheet and copies of any prior ones in the past three months."

"You suspect Mrs. Chumley?" Eldin asks.

"I suspect everybody."

"You're wrong, Mr. Sherlock. There is no one who cares more for the children than Mrs. Chumley."

"Okay, I'll put her at the bottom of my list."

"Who else do you suspect?"

I pause, look him straight in the eye, and say, "Be honest with me, Eldin, do you trust Fern Mossy?"

"Implicitly."

I'm beginning to suspect Eldin also trusts Terrible Teddy Tulleners.

I lean back in the chair and begin to think out loud. "The problem, Eldin, is that there are only three streams of cash flowing through this school from which to pilfer. There's the money from the cafeteria sales, which is totally controlled by Esther Stiffarm, the milk money controlled by Winky Torelli, but passed through Fern Mossy, and the money from the PTA, which comes in big clumps."

"Could someone be pilfering our cash account at our local bank?" he asks.

"Which is dribs and drabs and so convoluted, the US Treasury Secretary couldn't figure it out."

Eldin doesn't disagree.

"So I'm left with Stinky Winky," I say, and immediately regret referring to her as "Stinky."

"I find it hard to believe she's a thief."

Actually, I have Fern and Stinky as leading candidates but don't discuss my current standings.

"What are you going to do?" Eldin asks.

"Talk to Ms. Torelli," I answer. "I'm going to need her address."

Eldin spins his Rolodex, pulls out the card, and hands it to me. "If I were you, I'd talk to her outside."

"If you could have Mrs. Chumley make me those copies, I'd appreciate it."

"Done."

I have about forty-five minutes before school lets out today. I take a walk to the cafeteria and find it locked up tighter than a bank on Labor Day. Next, I stroll outside and meander to the patch of garden to see, even after the "Big Dig" of a couple of Sundays ago, the radishes are popping up, the tomatoes are budding, and the squash flowering. Isn't nature wonderful? With my windfall of money, I'm going to buy a couple of tomato plants and put them on my back porch. Few things in life are as good as home-grown tomatoes.

Back inside the school, I head for Ms. Mossy's office. I knock on the door before entering. Hearing nothing, I twist the doorknob, and push the door open slightly. "Hello?"

Entering the office, I once again see the laptops

haphazardly stacked off to the left. A lot of the kids didn't bother to remove the decals, selfies, and personal flair on the tops of the computers. On the file cabinet, I see the accounting for the daily milk money. I take it, open the file, and quickly scan the numbers inside. Today's pretty much match up with Monday's and the totals from last week are identical to the previous week. I return the file to its rightful place. Although I probably shouldn't, I check to see if the drawers of the desk are locked. They are. Adding to what I already shouldn't be doing, I go back to the office door and lock it from the inside. Returning to the desk, I pull a small penknife out of my pocket, get down on my hands and knees, jimmy the lock, get back up, and pull the bottom drawer out as far as it will go. The milk money lockbox is unlocked. I open it. The money inside is small bills and change. I count; its total matches the total on the sheet I just read. The bell rings. I hear hallway doors burst open and the sounds of happy children knowing they're done for the day. I close the lockbox, shut the drawer, and relock the desk with my penknife. Two minutes later, I pick up the spreadsheets from Mrs. Chumley. Five minutes later I'm in the pick-up line.

Care jumps in the car.

"Hi, Care. Did you learn anything new in school today?"

"No. Dad, can we stop at Wendy's on the way home. After all my detective work, I'm really hungry."

"No."

"Dad, if I don't get some food in me, I might not have the strength to tell you what I found out."

"I guess we'll have to risk it then."

Kelly is not in the middle of her usual gaggle of girls. I have to slow up to find her, and when I do, horns honk. I get a quick déjà vu back to my time in the Dumpster.

I finally see her talking to an Asian girl. "Kelly, come on."

She doesn't respond.

"Kelly, come on!"

She finally makes her way to the car and gets in. "What's your hurry? I was doing what you asked me to, Dad."

"I don't remember asking you to hold up the pick-up line."

"And I didn't ask you to embarrass me," she says. "Some things have to suffer in the pursuit of the truth, Dad."

"Like being embarrassed?" I question.

"No because you have to draw the line somewhere," she

144

says.

I pull the Toyota away from the curb and we're on our way.

"Dad, can we stop and get a churro on the way home?"

"No."

"The reason I'm still hungry is because I spent so much extra time in the cafeteria, my appetite went into overdrive," Care tells me.

"Did you spy on Esther Stiffarm?"

"Yes."

"Good."

"You were right. After she finished taking the money from the hot lunch kids, she went right into the food closet."

"How long was she in there?"

"A couple of minutes."

"Then what happened?"

"Just like you said, Dad, two of the other workers went in."

"Together?"

"Separate."

"When?"

"They waited until Esther told them to go."

"And how long did they stay in the storeroom?"

"Minute, max."

"How about the other ladies who work in the cafeteria?"

"They didn't go in."

"Anything else, Care?"

"Esther caught Terrible Teddy hanging around, grabbed him by the arm, pulled him back into the kitchen, and I think she was whuppin' him with one of those big metal spoons."

"Really?"

"Terrible Teddy was wailing."

"Good job, Care."

"For my reward, I'd like to stop at Superdawg on the way home."

"Who said anything about a reward?" I ask.

"There's always a reward," Care says. "Look at any *wanted* poster."

I turn onto Peterson Avenue. "Your turn, Kelly."

"I talked to a whole mess of kids who got into magnet schools."

"What they say?"

"Almost all took the Tutor Tent course, the ones who didn't

are already so smart, they could've like pitched the tent." Kelly pauses. "Get the joke, Dad, pitched the Tutor Tent?"

"I got it. What did they say about the test?"

"They all said the test was easy."

"All of them?"

"All except Arleta Torelli."

"What did she say?"

"The chick is strange. She got real weird when I chatted her up about it. First, she told me she didn't finish the course, then she told me her mother made her go back, then she said the test was really hard, then she told me she aced it."

"How was she weird?"

"Dad, the girl is always weird, but this time she was like nervous-weird."

"And what's nervous-weird, Kelly?"

"Like she just figured out wearing a prom dress to a swim meet isn't cool."

I pull the car up across the street from the strip center where Larry Mizzi spends his after school hours. The place has changed. The refurbished unit next door is finished, and now the front door of the Tutor Tent sits between the two units, which have become *The New, Bigger, Better, Tutor Tent where Learning is Fun and Success is Guaranteed!* Business must be better than good. Larry has more than doubled his space. No wonder he quit his day job.

"What are we doing here?" Care asks.

"We've already been here. We've already done this, Dad," Kelly so kindly reminds me.

A car pulls up in front of the improved and expanded tent and parks. A woman is behind the wheel. My kids scream, "Hi, Miss Mossy!"

"Quiet!"

Thank God the windows are rolled up. Miss Mossy doesn't turn our way.

"What's the matter, Dad?" Care asks.

"I don't want her to see us."

"You always tell us to be polite," Care reminds me.

"Well, we're making an exception today."

"You should tell us when we're undercover, Dad," Kelly admonishes me.

"Watch what she does."

The assistant principal gets out of her car, pops the trunk, and lifts out a stack of thin, flat boxes; it's hard to tell how many, four, maybe six.

"What's she got?" Kelly asks.

"Looks like pizzas," Care says.

"Laptops. It's right there on the top of the box," I inform them of the obvious.

"Oh, yeah."

We watch Fern carry the computers into the new digs. I think back to a picture of my last trip to her office and compare it to what I see now. Putting the scenes side by side in my brain, I search for similarities and differences.

"What's going on, Dad?" Kelly asks.

"I don't know."

We wait. A few minutes later, Ms. Mossy comes out of the Tutor Tent. She is stuffing an envelope into her purse. I start the car.

"Are we going to tail her?" Care asks.

"Yep."

"Cool," Kelly says.

"We should've worn disguises," Care adds.

I stay about three or four car lengths behind as Fern proceeds down Peterson. When she makes the light and I have to stop, the kids go nuts.

"Run it, Dad."

"Don't lose her."

"I don't want to get a ticket."

"You should have a siren on the car, Dad."

I wait for the light to change and pick up the pace down the street.

"There she is," Care yells, pointing up ahead.

Ms. Mossy pulls into a bank's parking lot a few blocks down.

"Maybe she's going in to knock it off," Care surmises.

"I told you we shoulda packed heat," Kelly says.

I pull up a hundred yards from where she's parked and wait. A few minutes later, she comes out of the bank, gets in her car, and drives off.

"Aren't we going to follow her, Dad?"

"No, I got to get you home. You both have homework to do."

"We can't stop for something as dumb as homework. We're in the middle of a case and the perp is getting away," Kelly argues.

"Maybe Ms. Mossy is on her way to a secret rendezvous or meeting up with a couple of guys from the mob?" Care thinks out loud.

"Maybe she's going to use the money for a sex change operation? She becomes a man, and we'll never recognize her."

I have to get parental controls on my TV set. "We're going home."

"But, Dad, if we let her get away, she could skip town and disappear."

"I guess we'll have to take that chance."

CHAPTER 18

"What do you want for dinner?" I ask after we settle in at the apartment.
"Take-out."
"Pizza."
"I was thinking something more along the lines of goose liver pate or stuffed rutabagas."
"Gross."
The phone rings. Care answers. "It's Tiffany, Dad. She wants to come over."
"Tell her to bring a pizza," I suggest.
Care quickly covers the phone receiver with her hand. "No, Dad, we hate all those veggies. We want meat on our pizza."
"Give me the phone; you two go do your homework."
I listen to Tiffany complain, then tell her, "You can come over if you want, but it's not going to change anything, Tiffany."
"But, Mr. Sherlock—"
"That's my story and I'm sticking to it."
"Well, I hate that," she says before hanging up.
Next call I make is to Giordano's. Ninety minutes later, the girls finish their homework, the pizza arrives, and Tiffany shows up.
"Hello there, little dudettes."
I pass out plates, silverware, plop the box in the middle of the table, open the cardboard top, and we dig in.
"What are these little round, greasy things on the top?" Tiffany asks at her first sight of the night's entrée.
"Pepperoni," Care informs her.
"And these little, brown bumpies?" Tiffany asks, surveying the pizza as if it were a science project.
"Sausage."
"Oh, God," Tiffany says. "Pig guts."
"Bon appetite."
As the girls devour the pie, Tiffany scrapes everything off the top of the pizza except the pepper, mushroom, and tomato sauce. On her plate is a pile of ingredients a carnivore would die for.

"Did you know, Mr. Sherlock, that the average overweight American has over one pound of meat byproducts trapped in his colon?"

"No, I wasn't aware of that fact, but thank you very much for letting us know while we're eating," I tell her.

"You're welcome."

Tiffany's fact doesn't do much to upend my daughters' appetites they attack the pizza like seagulls attack an unwatched sandwich at the beach.

Between bites, Tiffany glances up at *The Original Carlo*. "Good to see you've covered up that hideous painting, Mr. Sherlock."

"We're trying to solve the case of the missing milk money," Care tells her.

"I should help," Tiffany says. "The last time I worked on the painting, I ended up a genius."

"If you're already a genius, Tiffany, why would you want to go to college?" I ask.

"Meet genius men." I hope my girls heard that one.

After dinner the three women mix, match, add, subtract, trade, and cancel cards on the Carlo.

"The principal did it," Tiffany says. "He's a principal with no principles."

"How did you come up with him?" I ask.

"It's obvious. He's the stud in the middle of the wheel."

I don't think she got that right.

"Everything that goes around, comes right back around," Tiffany finishes her thought. "It's got to be him."

"I don't think so," I respectfully disagree.

"It's Ms. Mossy," Care concludes. "She can reach into her desk at any time and pull out as much milk money as she wants."

"And that's why she was at the bank?"

"Exactly, Dad. She was laundering the money."

"Ah, dirty money," Tiffany concludes. "Do you know there are more germs on a twenty-dollar bill than a toilet seat?" The facts just keep on coming.

"If you have a few filthy twenties you don't want," Kelly tells her. "I'll take them off your hands for you."

"No, I'm good. When you're born rich, you're immune to money germs."

Fitzgerald was correct. The rich are different.

"Well, Care," I get the conversation back to my youngest, "do you think Ms. Mossy and Mr. Mizzi are in this together?"

"Together in the biblical sense, Mr. Sherlock?"

I wish Tiffany wouldn't ask these questions in front of my kids.

"Yeah, Dad," Kelly says, her libido taking over her brain, "they could be doing hands-on projects in the name of better sex education."

Oh, jeesh.

"I bet it gets pretty lonely in those hallways, Mr. Sherlock. Maybe they take their own recess and grade each other's papers?"

Kelly says, "It's got to be one of the Torelli's. The only one weirder than Arleta is her mother. She out-tigers the Asian tiger moms, and she's on Arleta like tacky comments on a dumb Facebook post."

"You really think she aced that magnet school test, Kelly?"

"I don't know how she could have, she's as dumb as a bra strap."

"Don't be mean, Kelly."

"Arleta couldn't figure her way out of a bathroom stall even if the door was open." Kelly is on a roll.

"What's wrong with being mean?" Tiffany asks. "Especially if the person deserves it."

Another question never to have been aired in this forum.

"What do you think, Dad?" Care asks.

"I don't know," I admit. "But it has to all tie together somehow. These are all pieces of a puzzle that some way have to fit."

The recipe cards continue to move up, down, across, and back. Theories are voiced, shot down, reworked, and resubmitted, but none solve the puzzle.

"I have a question," Tiffany announces after an hour passes and bedtime nears. Oh, no. Here comes another. "What are you going to do about Mr. Fukashima and his exploding cigars? We're running out of time for coming up with an excuse not to pay him."

"Face it, Tiffany, you're just going to have to bite the bullet on this one."

"No way. I could break a tooth."

"Pay the money. Treat it as a lesson to never write a policy as ridiculous as the one Richmond wrote for this guy."

"I can't believe you're such a quitter, Mr. Sherlock. The only winner I ever knew who was a quitter was a guy who was in rehab."

"Thanks for putting me into such lofty company, Tiffany."

"Winners never quit and quitters never win by quitting."

So to speak.

The kids go to bed. Tiffany goes home. I sit staring at *The Original Carlo*. My eyes get tired after an hour. I put sheets on the couch and go to bed. I secretly hope the electrical impulses in my brain go to work while I sleep, and in the morning I awaken with the case wrapped up as pretty as a Christmas present with red and green bows.

But that doesn't happen. Instead, I bolt awake in the middle of the night, drenched in sweat. In my dream I was behind the wheel of a runaway UPS truck, headed for a fleet of wheelchairs filled with people smoking big, fat cigars, rolling themselves toward the Ho Lee Dong One Stop Cancer Clinic.

No doubt about it, I'm losing it.

CHAPTER 19

"Rise and shine."
Neither stirs.
"Get up."
Kelly rolls over, mumbling, "It's not time yet. It's too early."
"We're leaving early. Let's go."
I have to jostle Care to get her up. "What's for breakfast?" is her awakening question.
While the girls reluctantly get ready and dressed, I fix lunches and scramble eggs. They are about half-awake when they get into the kitchen.
"What are we doing up so early?" Kelly questions. "I need my beauty sleep."
"You need a lot more than that," Care tells her sister.
"Shut up."
"Don't tell your sister to shut up."
"She's pissing me off, Dad."
"Don't say 'pissing.' That's one of our no-no words."
"What should I say, Dad, she's 'urinating' me off?" Kelly questions.
"Eat your breakfast."
We arrive at the school fifteen minutes early. The drop-off lane is deserted. "This is stupid. What are we doing here so early?" Kelly asks.
"The early bird gets the worm," I tell her.
"Who wants worms?"
I pull to the opposite side of the drop-off lane at the spot Ann and Pat meet, drive up the curb, and park half on the road and half on the parkway. When Tessie the Terminator, the school's Gestapo parking officer comes up, bangs my car with her stop sign, and tells me to "Move it, mister," I'll tell her, "My car won't start." One look at my car should give me a reprieve.
A few minutes later a big orange school bus arrives and parks directly across from us. The passengers stand to file out the front door of the bus. The first kid out walks with a slight limp. "There's Terrible Teddy," Care announces. "I bet he took one heck of a whuppin'."

"Does Arleta take the bus, Kelly?"

"Yeah, I think so."

"Point her out to me."

After about ten kids unload, Kelly says, "That's her, the nerdy one with Clark Kent glasses falling off her nose."

One look and I immediately feel sorry for the girl. The way she's dressed, how she carries herself, and the look in her eye all scream, "I'm weird and hardly proud of it."

"How about Juan Hernandez? Does he take the bus?"

"How would I know, Dad?" Kelly answers my question with a question and adds another, "Do I look like the school's Director of Transportation?"

Kids these days.

The cars begin to enter the lane. Students jump out of mini-vans and SUVs and head into their respective schools.

"Dad, can I get out now?" Care asks.

"Sure. Have a good day and learn something new."

"Yeah, right, Dad."

Across from me I see a familiar woman dropping off her daughter. "Is that Elsa Lauder, Kelly?"

"Yeah."

I wait until Elsa's mom pulls away in her massive SUV. "Kelly, go over and ask Elsa if she took the Tutor Tent magnet school class."

"What? You want me to just pop over there, and out of nowhere say, 'Hey, Elsa, you didn't happen to take the Tutor Tent class, did you?'" Kelly pauses for effect. "God, Dad, I'm going to sound totally lame."

"Don't argue with me, go do it."

"It'll be embarrassing."

"Go."

Kelly bounces out of the car, runs through traffic, and approaches Elsa. I see her ask the question, then point to me as if I'm the weirdo in this the picture. In a few seconds, she comes to the edge of the opposite curb, and yells out to me, "Yeah, she took it, hated it, and it really pissed her off."

Wait until I get Kelly home.

***

As I mentioned previously, Sauganash is about as suburban

as you can get while still being in the City of Chicago. Having lived here, I know the layout pretty well, but for some reason, I can't find the address Eldin gave me. I burn up a half a tank of gas before I pull up in a dead end alley behind a hardware store, slightly off Bryn Mawr Avenue. Above the storage area of the store is an illegal apartment. I park, make my way up the rickety stairs, and knock on a useless screen door. No answer. I pull the screen door; it's locked. I push my hand through one of the many tears in the screen and pound on the wood door. Again, no answer.

Being the quitter I am, it's back down the rickety staircase. Just as I reach terra firma, a Subaru, about the same vintage as my Toyota, arrives and parks.

"What do you want?"

"I'd like to speak with you."

Winky Torelli exits her car. "Well, I don't want to speak with you."

"I only have a couple of questions."

Winky is dressed in a white, waitress uniform with the name Norma in blue script across her heart. She is either working undercover, likes to use an alias, or that was the only waitress outfit that fit her.

Winky doesn't smell like she did before. Now she harbors a distinct odor of kitchen grease. Still stinky, but I'll take this smell over her over-perfumed odor any day. The scent makes me hungry.

"Questions your daughter forgot to ask my daughter?" she asks.

"My daughter?"

"Don't try to play dumb with me," she says.

I must be too dumb to play dumb.

"Your little miss fashionista has never said 'boo' to Arleta and all of a sudden yesterday she starts chatting her up?"

Shouldn't I be asking the questions, here?

Winky continues, "Why? What's so interesting all of a sudden? Is Kelly inviting Arleta to a sleepover?"

"Maybe."

"You're harassing us for no reason," she tells me.

"Nobody is harassing anyone. I just like to ask questions."

"Whatever you want from me, you can't have it. I don't care what you want to know, what questions you want to ask, or what you *need* to know."

I wonder if she uses this same brand of inquisition when a customer orders an omelet?

"You men always think they can run roughshod over us single moms."

"I'm not trying to run over anybody. There's some money missing from the school and I'm trying to find it."

"Oh, you're accusing me? You suspect *me*?"

Although she is first on my list, I answer, "No."

"I work my tail off for that school and this is the thanks I get?"

"I just want to ask a few questions."

"I'm only trying to do what's best for my daughter, so why don't you just leave me alone?" Winky rushes past me like an unblocked tailback. She's up the stairs and out of sight in seconds.

Sure am glad I stopped by. It's so much fun popping in on someone, spur of the moment.

CHAPTER 20

For decades, Children's Hospital was a beloved Lincoln Park institution. Located at the intersection of Lincoln, Fullerton, and Halstead, the tall, white building was a welcome tenant in one of the most affluent neighborhoods in the city. Yes, the sirens were a little much and the heliport on the roof could be obnoxious, but having such a positive place, doing such great work for generations of children, the upscale neighborhood appreciated Children's being a part of their community.

A couple of years ago, Children's became the Lurie Children's Hospital with a multi-million dollar donation from the Lurie Family. It was decided to move the new Children's downtown to East Chicago Avenue, folding it into the Northwestern Medical Complex, which had already taken over most of the prominent Streeterville neighborhood. The new Lurie Children's is a bigger, modern, up-to-date facility noted for being one of the finest pediatric research hospitals in the world. It has modern art on the walls, sculptures designed for children, clever pathways, and polished chrome. It rises twenty-three stories high and literally gleams when the afternoon sun shines down. But I miss the old Children's. The place had a kindness and warmth you felt the moment you stepped inside.

Today, I'm standing at the reception area on the Hemoc/Oncology floor.

"Is Toni around?"

My friend Toni has been an RN for over thirty years, most of which has been spent at Children's. She works in what is called the Day Hospital, where cancer-stricken kids, and some adults, come in for their chemo to be administered. Toni's job is to make sure the right medicine goes into the right veins. Her hands are steadier than a diamond cutter's. I've seen her find a vein in a four-month-old, puncture it with a needle, and insert an IV when the child was wailing like a screaming meanie. I got to know Toni when I was doing some good-deed-doing years ago. It has always amazed me how she can treat so many patients, who she knows upfront have little chance of ever seeing adulthood, and keep smiling on a daily basis.

"Toni."

"Sherlock, what brings you downtown?"

"The *L*. I can't afford to park around here." I follow her into the small lunchroom. "Help me out, would you?"

"I hope not in the treatment sense."

"No. I want to know what you do with your trash."

"My husband puts it out every Thursday morning."

"I meant at the hospital."

"Some we toss, some is recycled, and a lot is sold to drug companies. What kind are you referring to?"

"The chemo stuff. What do you do with the plastic bags after they're empty?"

"Medical bin."

"Does all chemo come with a saline chaser?" I ask.

"Some, not all."

"If the chemo is mixed in with the saline, does it have to say saline on the pouch?"

"I don't know why it would. Saline is a cleaning agent. It's used to increase blood volume, rehydrate, and add glucose to the blood."

"Use a lot of it?"

"Quite a bit. You want a little shot? I can hook you up in a minute."

"Does it make you pee?"

"Yeah. Are you having trouble down there? I know a great rear admiral if you need one."

"I got a lot of problems, but that isn't one of them." I pause. "So would an empty saline bag go in the same medical recycle bin as a bag that dispensed chemo?"

"That's the way it's done here."

"Is it done everywhere the same way?"

"I'd guess," she says.

I pause again to contemplate the info. She's given me a lot to consider. I only wish I knew why or how.

We talk for a few more minutes. I know she has to go back to work. I promise I'll buy lunch one day, but she knows it'll never happen, and I'm merely being nice.

"Great to see you, Toni."

"You, too, Sherlock."

158

***

Being a good rule follower, I turned off my phone when entering Children's. I turn it back on when I leave and see Tiffany called. I walk across the street to the park behind the fire station, find a bench, and return her call.

"Tiffany, you called?"

"Yes, Mr. Sherlock. I wanted to get an update on the progress you're making on Mr. Fumanchoo and his cigars."

"Tiffany, how many times do I have to tell you?"

"Tell me what?"

"The cigar case is closed."

"A closed cigar case? Wouldn't that mean there's still cigars inside the case?"

"No."

"Mr. Sherlock—"

"That race has run, the trip completed, the day passed. Time to move on."

"Quitter."

"I'm not a quitter, Tiffany. I'm a realist."

"Well, if you're a realist, you should keep fishing and reel something in, Mr. Sherlock."

"I couldn't catch a cold going fishing on this case."

Tiffany harrumphs.

"I need a ride back to Doctor Dong's Dumpster, want to give me one?"

"No."

"Please?"

"I can't believe you, Mr. Sherlock. You'd rather play around in somebody's trash than investigate a very important case."

"I know. I'm losing it. Maybe I should be committed."

"Before you can make a commitment, Mr. Sherlock, you have to start dating."

"I need a ride. Please?"

"Oh, all right."

It takes Tiffany a half-hour to go from her penthouse to where I'm waiting, a distance of a couple blocks. In the interim, Principal Puddle calls. "Lou Lauder is coming in at three."

"Eldin, don't start the screaming until I get there."

***

We arrive at the clinic just in time to watch the garbage truck empty Dong's container. Timing is everything in life.

"This is as boring as the last time we did this, Mr. Sherlock," Tiffany informs me as we sit in her car parked in a handicap space across the alleyway street of the Ho Lee Dong One Stop Cancer Clinic.

"Did I ever say detective work is a thrill every minute type of activity, Tiffany?"

"No."

"Then why do you expect it to be?"

"Because it's that way on TV."

"TV isn't real life, Tiffany."

"Documentaries are."

The cancer patients walk in and walk out with the same regularity as a Starbucks. I only wish I owned a business this good. Maybe I could invest my raffle winnings and start a business that would make me rich. I hear illegal ivory, stomach stapling, and microwavable cannibal cuisine have big profit margins.

"Remind me, what are we doing here, again?" Tiffany asks.

"Looking for something fishy going on."

"We'd do much better at a sushi place, Mr. Sherlock."

Twenty minutes elapse in which I see nothing out of the ordinary occur.

"This is boring," Tiffany reminds me as if I need reminding.

"Look." I point.

Dr. Ho Lee Dong and the nurse we met on our first visit come out the front door. The questionable good doctor points out Tiffany's car to his nurse then retreats back inside his clinic. The nurse walks our way, up to the car, and taps on my window, which I roll down.

"Hello." If I had a Mrs. Chumley smiley face, I'd put it on her collar.

"Aren't you people tired of hanging around here?" she asks. "You've staked us out, chatted up our patients, and gone through our trash; what do you want?"

I'm feeling like Terrible Teddy probably felt when Esther Stiffarm caught him in the storeroom.

I don't have an answer, but Tiffany has a question. "How did you learn English so quickly?"

"I grew up six blocks from here," the nurse answers.

"What does that have to do with speaking English?" Tiffany argues.

"If there is something you want to ask or see inside, why don't you just come in?" she asks me.

"Would you mind?"

"It would be a lot better than you hanging out around here like some perverted creep."

Wouldn't most creeps already be perverted?

Tiffany and I get out of the car and follow her inside. We go right through the crummy outer office into the treatment room where every chair is filled and other patients reading or watch the big screen TV on the wall as they wait.

"Does it look like we're doing anything wrong in here?" she asks as we walk through the rows of oversized chairs.

"No."

She stops at one patient. "Lynn, tell the man what you think of Doctor Dong?"

The woman perks up but is careful not to move her hooked up arm. "Dr. Dong is wonderful. Makes me feel better every week."

What else can I do but smile?

We stop at a second patient. "Miss Chen, tell this man how you feel."

"Better, so much better."

I've had enough after two customer reviews, but our tour guide nurse adds three more satisfied customers for our listening pleasure. They all sing the praises of wonderful Dr. Dong.

"Enough?"

"Sorry to bother you," I tell the nurse. Every time I walk out of this place, I seem to have my tail between my legs.

"It's funny," Tiffany says once we're outside. "All the people you chat up can't speak English, but the nurse picks out people who could work as telemarketers. It must be Birther Baby Day at the clinic."

When we get back to Tiffany's car, a parking ticket is pinned to the windshield wiper. "Oh, darn. You should've reminded me to put my gimp sticker on the rearview mirror, Mr. Sherlock."

"So it's my fault you got a ticket?"

"Yes. You can't expect me to do everything."

As I try to think through what just went down, Tiffany speeds out of Chinatown towards the lake. I take out my cellphone, look up a number, and hit the spot that makes the call. The connection is made. "Hello. Is Bree Bisonette available?" I am careful to pronounce her name "Bis-o-nay."

Tiffany jumps hearing the name, and says, "My dad just dumped her lipo-suctioned butt."

"Don't be mean, Tiffany," I say as I'm put on hold.

"Bree 'Bare-her-butt' Bis-o-nette is now barren of a body buddy."

I do my best to ignore her comment.

In a few seconds, I hear on my phone, "Bree Bisonette speaking."

"It's Richard Sherlock."

I watch Tiffany pretend she's upchucking by the means of two fingers going down her throat. "Bree, is there any way of finding out how many of Dr. Dong's patients have either passed away or are no longer getting chemo?"

"No."

"Is there any way to find out the length of time the patients at Dong's clinic receive their chemo?"

"No."

"Are you sure?"

She doesn't respond.

I say, "Could you at least give it a try?" I listen again, and say, "You don't have to, but I sure would appreciate it."

She sighs. I thank her and hang up. I don't want to take the chance of her going into another negative, emotional upheaval with Tiffany sitting right next to me, listening to every sob.

"I don't want to hear one mean word out of you, Tiffany."

"I wouldn't think of it," she says with a snarky smile on her face.

"You know, Tiffany, it does you absolutely no good to be mean to someone."

"Bree's mean to me. She said my chopsticks were too short to get to the food."

"And you said her thighs could be a cellulite factory."

"She was trying to put a ledge between me and my dad."

"No, she wasn't." I continue after a pause, "The point here is that being mean to someone doesn't do anyone any good, so stop it."

"Become a quitter just like you, Mr. Sherlock?"

"In this case, yes."

"How about in the Fumatorium case, should I quit that, too?" she asks.

"Yes."

I look up and see Tiffany is getting on the expressway north. "Where are we going?"

"I have an appointment."

"Where?"

"At the Tutor Tent. My new class started a half-hour ago."

CHAPTER 21

I have Tiffany drop me off at my apartment, so I can get my car. I arrive at the schools a little before 2:30 p.m.

I may be losing it, but my detective sense is in full sensory mode as I walk through the hallway toward Eldin's office. There is tension in the air thicker than the pollution over a steel plant during a building boom.

One step into the principal's outer office, I see a man in a suit hunched over Mrs. Chumley's desk. "You're now past one-hundred-twenty days. We need to get paid," he says to Mrs. Chumley one angry octave above matter-of-fact.

Mrs. Chumley answers as chipper as ever, "You've always been paid in the past, why would you think you wouldn't be paid this time?" She then looks over at me, and says, "Hello, Mr. Sherlock, how are you today?"

"Fine, Mrs. Chumley. How are you?"

"I'm just smiley."

"Mrs. Chumley," the man says, interrupting our greetings, "don't make me take this to the district."

"Oh, this isn't a district expense. They won't ever consider paying a bill that isn't a district expense."

"If we have to keep going through this every time, Tech Connections may have to stop doing business with Ann Margaret, Mrs. Chumley."

"If you stop doing business with us, other schools will hear about it and stop doing business with you," she tells him.

"We don't have payment problems with them. Why do we have to have them with you?"

"You'd probably have to ask them, I guess."

"Could you just write us a check?" he pleads his case. "Even if it isn't for the full amount, we'll have something on our books before the school year lets out?"

"I don't write the checks."

"Could you have whoever does write one for us?"

"I'll see what I can do," she tells him.

"Now?"

"Oh, no, not now. I have to play the piano for the spring

play practice in the boys' gym. They're doing *Spamalot*."

"Today?"

"Oh, sure."

As the man takes an exasperated sigh, I ask, "Is Principal Puddle in?"

"Oh, yes, Mr. Sherlock, he can't wait to see you."

I say, "Thanks," as I head for the door.

"You're welcome. Have a smiley day."

I poke my head inside his office, "Principal Puddle?"

Eldin is seated behind his desk but facing the back window. He slumps in his chair, his head resting on his closed right fist. His eyes look out on the school playgrounds.

"Is this a bad time?" I ask.

Eldin swings around to recognize me. "All the times lately have been bad times, Richard."

I enter and sit in one of the two chairs facing his desk.

He hands me one sheet of paper from the top of his desk. "Look."

I read quickly. It is a listing of rankings, numbers, and grade categories. Ann Margaret is at the top or near the top of every column.

"We have the second highest combined reading and math scores for all schools in Chicago."

"That's great."

"In the technology sector, Ann ranks in the top three for technical achievement and in the top two for science."

Since he hardly looks thrilled at the news, I ask, "Shouldn't you be happy with this?"

"Yeah, thrilled," he slurs.

"You don't look it."

Eldin leans forward. "I'm worried. We've been able to do so much more for our students, but with what is going on now, it could all come to a screeching halt."

"Why?"

"Parents are never satisfied. They're mad their kids aren't getting into magnet schools. They're going to the district to complain. They're saying the money they've spent isn't helping their kids. They want more."

"But you had more kids get into magnet schools than ever before."

"Parents don't care about the results of all the kids; they

only care about their kids. A lot of these parents held their children back, so they could mature another year before they started kindergarten. Some fathers hold their sons back so they can be the biggest kids in their class and excel in sports. Parents force us to put their kids into certain classes, and if they don't get their way, they scream louder than their spoiled kids."

"That doesn't seem fair."

"Fair has nothing to do with it. Parents have figured out how to work the system. They'll do just about anything to put their kids ahead of the other kids. It's a never ending, escalating battle."

Eldin hesitates and reaches out to retrieve the page he handed me. "And now this."

"I don't understand."

"The district is considering coming in and investigating what we do for our students."

"I still don't understand."

"The other schools are mad. We get these kinds of scores, it brings the average up, and their schools look worse. They hate us. They say it's not fair."

I have to play devil's advocate, asking, "Can you blame them?"

"No, but it's not fair to blame us, either. My job is to prepare our students for their next educational steps, especially into high school. I can't let the district hold us back because we're better than the rest."

"What can the district do?" I ask.

"If you can't bring the bottom up, Richard, you bring the top down." There is a pause in our conversation. "All they need is a good reason," Eldin says, "and this immigration case might be the tipping point."

As if on perfect theatrical cue, Eldin's intercom buzzes and Mrs. Chumley's voice rings out, "A Mr. Lauder is here to see you."

"Send him in."

Lou Lauder walks into the office in a suit worth three times the worth of my Toyota. "Who are you?"

"This is Mr. Sherlock. He's a consultant for the school."

I am?

Lou says, "Aren't you the guy who won all that money at the last benefit?"

"Lucky me."

"I bought three hundred dollars worth of tickets for that drawing," he says. "How many you buy?"

I repeat, "Lucky me."

"Please sit down," Eldin says as he and I sit.

"I don't want to sit," Lou says, standing defiantly with his arms crossed.

I stand up. The last position I want to be in is one lorded over by an over-dressed jerk.

Eldin asks, "Mr. Lauder, could we discuss your dealings with the district office?"

"My lawsuit?" he questions sarcastically.

Certainly not your thousand-dollar suit, I think to myself.

"Yes," Principal Puddle answers.

"It's already been filed."

"It has?"

"And I've alerted Immigration."

Immediately exasperated, Eldin asks, "Why?"

"Because it's the right thing to do."

"No, it's not," Eldin argues.

"Don't sit there, buddy, and act innocent with me," Lou says to Eldin. "I know what you're doing."

"You do?" Eldin says.

"You're shipping in kids to bring up your averages, so you can receive some performance bonus."

"Principals don't receive bonuses."

"Why not?"

"Because we're educators, not salesmen."

"You're stocking the team with high draft numbers, so you're sure to blow away the competition." Lou's metaphor is pretty lousy; he's probably a Bears fan.

"No, we're not."

"Oh, you're going to tell me that little science spic lives in Sauganash?"

Eldin pauses, a sure sign of guilt.

"The kid lives in the city, takes three buses to get here every day, and his mother swam him across the Rio Grande before he was four," Lou continues.

"How do you know that?" I ask.

"I put one of my guys on it. The kid is illegal as a crop-picker named Brocero."

Eldin slumps in his chair. He's been had. As his consultant, I take up his sword, and ask, "What good does all this do for you?"

"This burrito bandito gets into a magnet school and my daughter doesn't?" Lou asks rhetorically. "You call that fair? Rewarding these criminals at the expense of kids whose parents pay all the taxes to keep these schools in business? Something's got to be done and I'm the man to do it."

"Juan is a budding genius. He needs a superior education," Eldin says.

"Well, he's going to have to get it in Juarez because that's where he's going to be headed soon."

"You wouldn't?" Eldin asks

"Why wouldn't I? It's about time we sent these criminals back where they came from."

Calling this guy a jerk is unfair. Jerk is much too nice a term for this jackass.

"And don't assume I don't know about all the slant eyes you got coming here too. I bet they're sneaking into the schools just like the little taco bender. And you're looking the other way, Puddle."

Eldin stares at his shoes.

I ask, "What do you want, Lou?"

"I want my kid in Butkis Academy."

"But she didn't score high enough," Eldin says. "She was below the ninety-nine percent cut-off on the test. If she's accepted, every other child who got a seventy-nine will demand to be accepted, too."

Lou leans on Eldin's desk, lording over him like an over-sized third grader peering down on a first grade wimp. "So, kick out the illegals, the territory cheats, and the ones who don't belong in this country, and there will be plenty of room."

"You know that's not going to happen," I state the obvious.

"Then we'll start with one and go from there."

"You do that," Eldin says, "and you'll destroy everything this school has accomplished in thirty years."

"Why would I care? My kid's not going to be in it anymore."

Lou's the type of next-door neighbor you'd like to have if all the lots in your neighborhood were fifty acres in size.

'The ball is in your court, boys. I want my kid in Butkis Academy. What are you going to do about it?"

Eldin doesn't speak and I have no clue how to respond, so I say, "We'll be in touch."

"It better be soon." Lou adjusts his gold cufflinks and exits the office.

Eldin slumps down in his chair.

"I bet Lou's a fun guy at the father/daughter dance." I try to lighten the load.

Eldin removes his glasses and rubs the palms of his hands against his eyes. When his hands come down, I see tears.

"He's nothing but a big bully, Eldin."

"Way too big for after school detention." Eldin pauses. "There's no way I can get Elsa Lauder into Butkis Prep now. The last thing the district would do is grant me a favor."

"Don't panic, Eldin."

"You have to believe me, Richard, I only do what's best for the students."

"Don't worry, I'll think of something."

"What?"

I wish he wouldn't push me on this point because I have no idea.

I leave Eldin to stew in his own juices.

In the outer office, the salesman is gone. Mrs. Chumley informs me, " I tried twice to give Mr. Lauder a smiley face sticker and he wouldn't take it."

"The nerve of the guy."

Mrs. Chumley sticks a sticker on my collar before I exit.

I walk down the hall and knock on Ms. Mossy's door.

"Come in."

"Do you have a minute?" I ask as I enter, finding her behind her desk.

"Sure."

The computers are now stacked neatly in piles of eight on the right side of the room. "Weren't there some new computers in the pile before?" I ask.

"Matter of fact, there were," she says as if to compliment my detective skill. "We had to send those back."

Really?

"Why wouldn't you just save them if you needed them for next year?"

"If we need new units for next year, we'll order them next year," she tells me.

"Wasting a lot of postage, aren't you?" I continue.

"Not really."

I sit and take a few seconds before I drop the topic, which I can tell she doesn't want to continue with. "Can I ask you a question that would be just between us, Fern?"

"Well, I'm not sure I'll answer, but you can ask," she says, her suspicion increasing.

"Is it me or is it all men that Winky Torelli has a problem with?" I see Fern flash a smile of relief before I explain. "I've been trying to talk to her and she treats me like a Tsetse fly."

"Ms. Torelli does seem to have a slight chip on her shoulder when it comes to the male portion of our species," Fern says.

"A two-by-four might be more like it."

"I'm not sure why, but I would suspect her history with men has not been a totally positive experience." Fern says. "But she has been a tireless worker since her daughter entered our schools. She's done it all from playground helper to room mother, field trip chaperone, and PTA president."

"Does she ever let Arleta out of her sight?"

"No."

"Helicopter parent?"

"No, drone mom. Drones can fly much lower than helicopters."

"Husband?" I ask.

"Banker."

I immediately remember Fern Mossy coming out of a bank. "What bank?"

"Sperm."

On Father's Day, I can see Winky and Arleta celebrating with a test tube atop a cake.

"What can you tell me about Elsa Lauder and her mom?"

"Let's just say, after meeting Lou Lauder, I'm surprised Jane Lauder isn't more like Winky Torelli."

I stand up to leave. "One more thing, Fern, did Mrs. Chumley requisition a check to go to Tech Connections?"

"No." She looks at me like I'm a Stiffarm Special of the Day in the cafeteria, "Why do you ask?"

"The salesman was in her office and I just wondered if his begging worked."

"Hasn't so far."

CHAPTER 22

"Where's the little lady?"
"Shopping."
"For what?"
"Wedding dress."
"Herman, don't do it. There's plenty of time to get married."
"Sherlock, you're a real stick in the mud when it comes to true love."
"Herman, you barely know her. You don't speak the same language. You haven't met her family. I bet you don't even know her middle name."
"She won't need a middle name anymore because soon she'll be Ludmila Bratapova McFadden."
I wonder if she'll hyphenate it and get an extra line in the phone book.
"Herman, please listen to reason," I beg him.
"Love is stronger than those piddley-little nuances, Sherlock. What Ludmila and I have is a bond so unbreakable a team of horses couldn't drive us apart."
A team of horses would exhaust themselves driving Herman out of the stable.
"You can't understand, Sherlock, because you don't know love as we know love."
"Herman, wait a few months. There's no reason to rush to the altar."
"In a couple of months, I'm hoping Ludmila is on the nest."
If there ever were a case for artificial insemination, this would be it.
"Herman, you're going ninety-five in a school zone. Slow down, apply the brakes, and stop for gas."
"One thing I don't need is anymore gas, Sherlock."
I give up. "Herman, have you had a chance to go over those school expenditures I gave you?"
"No."
"Why not?"
"You can't concentrate on dollars and cents when your

heart is pounding in a rhythm of love."

Oh, jeesh.

"All right, forget the spreadsheets, Herman."

"I already have."

"I need you to do something else."

"Work on our vows?"

"No. I need you to hack into the Chicago School District's computer program."

"I don't hack anymore, Sherlock. I gave it up for Lent."

"You're not Catholic and Lent's already over, Herman."

"It is?"

"Yes." I pause. "I have to know if a guy on the outside could tap into their system for the answers to the test the eighth graders take to get into the magnet school program."

"That sounds like a lot of work."

"And I need it right away."

Herman shifts his bulk around. He reminds me of Jabba the Hut in the Star Wars movies. "You have to understand, Sherlock, my heart is fluttering, my body a-twittering, and my mind is in such an ethereal state of expectant bliss I can't concentrate on anything except my lovely Ludmila."

Time to play hardball.

"Herman, you still want me as your best man?"

"I would be so honored."

"Well, if you don't help me, you'll have to find another boy to be at your altar."

"At this late date?"

"Yes."

Herman pretends to be in shock. "Sherlock, you're bargaining your best man status to get me to hack into a school's computer?"

"Exactly."

"That's not fair."

"Nothing is fair in love and war, Herman."

"Sherlock, you've shocked me to the core of my existence."

Getting to Herman's core would be equal to falling into a cosmic black hole.

"Hack, Herman, hack."

"Do I have to?"

"Yes."

I fill him in on the particulars of what I need and want. He grumbles through my explanation asking me to pause twice to allow his heart to go pitter-pat as he sees Ludmila in his thoughts.

When I finish, I tell him, "Get going right now, Herman. I need it *a-sap*."

"You're being a sap forcing me to do this, Sherlock."

"Oh, the things we do for love."

***

I can't go home. It is close to dinnertime, but after being with Herman, I've lost my appetite. I drive towards the lake. My mind feels like the mesh metal container spinning around with all the raffle tickets inside, mixing to the point where it's only mixing the over-mixed, mix. I get to Montrose Harbor on autopilot and park the car. I would walk along the lakefront, but being springtime, the path is filled with runners, bikers, skateboarders and rollerbladers. Far too crowded for me. If you're a walker in this thoroughfare of wheeled speed, you are taking your life in your own hands, or feet in this instance. I walk north to where the boats are back in the water after our miserable winter and a number of fishermen are casting their nets. This is the way you catch smelt, if smelt is your fish of choice.

I contemplate as I wander on the paths.

Something is very un-oriental with the Ho Lee Dong Clinic. The facility is a dump, he has too many claims from too many patients, drugs are flowing into the place like water into a Lake Michigan lock, and the only thing I can find suspicious is he doesn't recycle his paper products correctly.

I start to get a headache, so I move on to my next case.

Ann Margaret is about to be brought up on the carpet for being one of the best schools in the city. The fact there are hundreds of dollars missing from the school's milk money has become a secondary problem since jerk-brained attorney, Loudmouth Lou Lauder is whistle-blowing an illegal domestic for using the address of her employer to enroll her science genius son in the school where he belongs. Loudmouth Lou couldn't care less about anyone besides himself and his daughter, Elsa. All he wants is his kid to be accepted into Dick

Buttkick prep academy, even though she didn't pass mustard on the admission's test. Add to that whole mess teachers suddenly quitting, laptops missing, an ornery PTA president, a guaranteed test-taking tutoring program, and Terrible Teddy Tulleners' bruised butt, and I have my second headache of the day.

The only thing I am positively sure about is Richmond Insurance will never insure any tobacco product against flood, fire, and natural disaster as long as smoking continues to cause cancer.

I walk round and round the harbor for over an hour and I don't see one smelt in a net yet. As I reach the intersection of the walking and the biking path, a rollerblader almost runs me over. I have to jump to the side to save my own life and land on my butt. The skaters, bikers, and bladers go by without a thought to stopping. From the level of a ten-speed's wheels, a thought comes in my mind: If so many of the Ho Lee Dong patients are terminally ill, why don't the people look a lot sicker?

I get in my car and head towards home when another question hits me. At Western Avenue I turn right and head north. I'm back in Sauganash in less than twenty minutes. I park the car in the alley across from a hardware store. I am about to exit and drop in for a chat with Stinky Winky Torelli when another person beats me to the punch.

Larry Mizzi arrives, driving a new Cadillac. Unlike Larry, if I ever buy a Cadillac, I won't buy one that's bright red. I stay in my car as Larry gets out of his. He locks the doors with his fob and hurries up the stairs as if he is a man on a mission. At the top, he pushes his hand through the broken screen and raps hard enough to wake Rip Van Winky. The door opens, he steps inside.

For being a creep, Larry seems to be doing all right with the ladies. If my girls were right about Ms. Mossy, and I add Winky to the stable, Larry is quite the Casanova. In a million years I would never suspect Larry and Winky to be an item, but it certainly seems the case here as I see a light go on in what I would guess is a bedroom in the apartment. I wish I could hear what's going on inside their love nest, not because I'm a creep, but I'd like to be sure their love is a love as true as Herman and little Ludmila's.

I wait about fifteen minutes before Larry emerges out the door a bit on the flushed and disheveled side. In that time, I wouldn't think they had a lot of time to chat, except for a *slam-bam thank you, ma'am* discourse, and a few sweet nothings in her ear.

I consider taking my turn to visit, but it was difficult enough trying to talk with Winky after she arrived home from a long day at the diner. Chatting her up as she lies propped up on a pillow, puffing a post-coital cigarette would not only be near impossible but definitely on the creepy side. No, this would not be a good time to pop in on her unannounced, although, I have a lot more questions now than I did before.

I sit for a few minutes, more confused than I was wandering around the smelt fishermen, and anyone who wanders around smelters must be really confused. I start the car and head for home. My mind is spinning with possibilities.

They say many things in life come in threes. Tonight, I agree because I get my third headache of the evening.

CHAPTER 23

The closest city bus stop to Ann Margaret/Pat Nixon is on Crawford Avenue about three blocks away. I sit in my Toyota and only have to wait three buses before Juan Science Dude and his cleaning lady mom step down off the CTA vehicle.

"Excuse me." I intercept the two after crossing one of Sauganash's main drags. "Could I speak with you a second, please?"

Juan stops. His mother pulls him along.

"My name is Richard Sherlock. I'm Kelly and Care's dad."

"I've seen you," Juan says.

"Ándale," Mom orders.

"I need to ask you a few questions," I explain.

"Ándale, ándale."

"We can't stop. I'll be late for school," Juan says.

I walk along with them. "Has Immigration contacted you yet?"

They stop.

"Sí," Mom says.

"What did they say?"

Juan speaks, "We got a notice."

"What did it say?"

Juan's mom answers in Español.

Juan translates, "It said we have to prove citizenship or show them the green card."

"Does she have one?" I ask Juan.

Mom answers. All I understand is the word *no*.

"Are they going to make us go back?" Juan asks.

We walk towards the school.

I lie, saying, "I don't know."

Mom speaks. I can't understand a word, but her emotional tone is universal.

"What did she say?" I ask Juan.

"We can't go back. There is no life for us there. We go back there is no school, no job, and no money. We can't go back."

The tears in the woman's eyes need no translation.

I pull out my wallet and take out my business card. I hand it to Juan. "Don't talk to anyone before you talk to me. If the phone rings, don't answer. If you have another place to stay for a few days, go. If not, don't answer the door. If they do find you and you get arrested, don't admit guilt, don't answer any questions, don't tell anyone anything before you call me. Understand?"

"What did we do wrong?" Juan asks.

"You were born on the wrong side of the fence."

Mom asks a question.

Juan says, "She wants to know why you want to help?"

"I'm out to out-jerk a jerk."

A block from the school mom stops, hugs her son, addresses him. I can only hope her comment is the Español version of "Learn something new every day." She gives him a kiss, turns left, and heads for the mini-mansion up the block.

Juan and I arrive at the schools in the midst of drop-off frenzy.

"Hasta la vista," I tell the boy. "And remember what I told you."

"Thank you, Mr. Sherlock."

"I'll do what I can."

I look around for Kelly and Care, neither are around, but I do see one familiar face. She is sitting in her massive SUV creeping along with the rest of the drop-offees. I walk alongside her car.

"Funny meeting you here," I say after she rolls down her window.

"Aren't you supposed to have a car?" she asks.

"It's not my court appointed day with my kids, so I don't need one."

I glance into the SUV's back seat, which looks bigger than my apartment. "Hello, Elsa."

"Hello."

"I'd like to ask you a favor." I'm back to Mrs. Lauder. "Could you call your husband off?"

"Off what?"

"Off getting the Hernandez family shipped back to Mexico."

Mrs. Lauder avoids my stare as she maneuvers her massive urban assault vehicle closer to the curb where she will drop Elsa off.

"They're good people. They don't deserve to get deported," I tell her.

"I'm not the person to make that decision, Mr. Sherlock."

"Is your husband?" I ask.

The SUV almost runs over my big toe as she turns toward the curb and stops. "Elsa, you have a good day at school today. I'll be here to pick you up this afternoon. I love you." Jane tells her child.

I do the honors of opening the big door for Elsa to exit. She smiles her thanks. "Wait, Elsa?" I ask before she runs off.

The cute kid looks to her mom for an okay. "What?"

"I'm sorry you didn't get accepted into Butkis Prep."

"Oh, that's okay. They don't have a dance program and I like to dance," she says

"I heard they really pile on the homework, too."

"Yeah, I hate that," she says.

A few horns honk behind us.

"Elsa, you should get going," her mom tells her.

Before the girl leaves the side of the SUV, I get in one more comment to make her feel a little better, "Maybe you can apply next year."

"Nah, I don't think so."

I wait until Elsa hurries off into a crowd of kids before I ask her mom, "Did you get a rebate from the Tutor Tent?"

Jane Lauder doesn't answer. The SUV pulls away from the curb, but I stay at the window picking up my pace. "Did you?" I ask again.

"I let my husband handle those things," Mrs. Lauder says before rolling up her window, picking up speed, and exiting the drop-off line.

The minute I step back up on the curb, I hear, "Dad, what are you doing here?" It's Kelly in a panic. "You didn't come here to embarrass me, did you?"

"No."

"Well, you are."

"How?"

"Do you see other parents getting out of their cars?" She pauses. "Ah, no."

"Sorry."

"Where is your car?" she asks, looking around.

"It's at the bus stop."

"What's it doing there?"

"Not much, I hope."

Kelly looks to see if any of her friends are looking at her. "Dad, are you trying to find someone to help get your car started?"

"No."

"Then what are you doing here?"

"I've got questions that need to be answered."

"On the case?"

"Yes."

"Well, couldn't you ask them undercover?"

"Why undercover?"

"Because it's creepy having your dad hanging around the drop-off line at school when he's not in a car." She does have a point.

"Well, Kelly, what do you suggest I do?"

"Wear a disguise."

"So, if I'm here dressed like Darth Vader, people won't notice me as much?"

"Not Darth Vader, Dad."

"How about Al Gore?"

"That would be much better." She stops to think, then asks, "Who's Al Gore?"

How quickly we forget.

The bell rings. "We'll talk about this this weekend, Dad."

"I don't have you this weekend."

"Ah, no, duh," she says before reaching her pack of giggling girls.

Kelly is almost out of earshot when I yell out, "And don't forget, learn something new every day."

Kelly's face turns bright red in absolute total embarrassment before hustling off into the school building.

Gee, too bad.

***

I wait for all the kids to disappear inside to their respective seats of learning. Tessie the Traffic Terminator sees me standing and comes over to chat. "Where's your car?" she asks.

"Parked a couple of blocks away."

"That's a good place for it."

"So nice of you to say."

"Now keep moving," she orders, and nudges me with her stop sign.

"Drop-off is over for the day, Tessie."

"Sorry, force of habit."

The final first period bell rings and I go inside, straight to Eldin's office.

"Good morning, Mr. Sherlock, are you planning on a smiley day today?" Mrs. Chumley greets me as if it's Christmas morning.

"Well, I certainly hope so."

"Oh, splendid."

"Mrs. Chumley, do you have this week's accounting spreadsheet?"

"I certainly have."

"May I have a copy?"

"With pleasure." She makes a copy at the Xerox machine, but before handing it over, she places a smiley face sticker on its upper right corner.

"Is Principal Puddle in?"

"No. He had to go to a meeting at the district office."

"That's not good, is it?"

"You never know, Mr. Sherlock. You have to be positive." I like to stay positive, too, but I couldn't exist with this woman for more than an hour before I went positively wacko.

I glance at the spreadsheet and quickly notice the payees and expenditures in no way resemble the previous spreadsheets I've studied. "Mrs. Chumley, do you and Principal Puddle go over these each week?"

"Of course."

"Are changes ever made?"

"Of course."

"And who makes them?"

"Principal Puddle."

"Have a smiley day, Mrs. Chumley."

"You, too, Mr. Sherlock."

On my slow walk back to my car, my brain is in overdrive. The problem is that I'm driving in circles. I'm so confused, I'm surprised I find my way back to my car.

The only thing that could possibly bring me out of my *going nowhere* reality bite are the words, "Oh, Mr. Sherlock."

Reality hits me with a right cross.

"Tiffany, what are you doing here?" She's leaning on the fender of her Lexus, which is parked behind my Toyota.

"We have to talk."

"How do you find me?"

"We don't have to talk about that." She pauses before she says, "We have to do something today to stop having to pay for Mr. Fume-a-lot's burned up cigars tomorrow."

"What do you suggest?" I ask.

"I don't know. That's your job, Mr. Sherlock." She's in quite the snippy mood; must've woken up on the wrong side of her custom made, ergonomically perfect, super king-sized bed this morning.

"What's got you so possessed with this case, Tiffany?"

"I hate cigars. They're bad for people, they stink, and they look disgusting going in and out of a guy's mouth."

"None of that has any bearing on the case."

"It should."

"Why? What difference does your opinion make?" I pause. "Face facts, Tiffany, Richmond made a bad decision insuring such a dumb asset, and now they have to pay the price for their own stupidity."

She raises her voice. "A hundred and fifty grand is a big price to pay for an eeny-meeny mistake, Mr. Sherlock."

"It's small potatoes compared to what's being claimed at the Ho Lee Dong clinic. Bree Bisonette said he's well over a million dollars in claims."

She raises her voice even higher. "Cigars cause cancer. We get rid of the cigars, there'll be no one sick enough to go to see Dr. Dong."

"My point, Tiffany, is we have much bigger fish to fry than Mr. Fumadoro."

"Mr. Sherlock, you know I don't eat fried foods, so that's not an issue. We have to do something." Tiffany screams, "We just can't up and quit!" She stops, as if she can't believe she is actually yelling at me.

I take a deep breath. "Fine, Tiffany, if you want me back on the case that badly, you do something first."

"What?" she snaps back.

"The only thing we don't know is where the fire took place. Find that out and I'll see what I can do."

"Are you going to help me do that?"

"No."

"Why not?"

"Because I have to go see my friend, Herman."

"The world's most disgusting human being?"

"Yes."

"Why?"

"I have to talk him out of getting married."

"Take a picture of him naked and show it to his fiancée; that should kill any engagement."

"Then I have to go see Bree Bisonette."

"Bree 'Butt's too big for her body' Bis-o-nette?"

"Yes. Wanna tag along?"

"I'll pass."

"Call me when you find out where the fire took place."

"It's not fair that you're not helping me."

"Nobody ever said life had to be fair, Tiffany."

"Thank God."

CHAPTER 24

"**D**o you have your kids this weekend, Sherlock?" Herman asks as he munches on a Baby Ruth candy bar.

"No."

"Darn."

"Why?"

"Because I need a couple of flower girls."

"For what?"

"The wedding is Saturday at eleven."

"What?"

"I'm getting married at eleven on Saturday."

"Where?"

"Here."

"Herman, I thought we'd decided you'd wait."

"If I wait any longer, my love for Ludmila is going to erupt like Vesuvius. I'll have lava-love flowing all over the apartment."

Perish that thought and image.

"You can't get married," I inform him. "You haven't had your blood tests."

"You don't need them if you're being married in the Church of the Everlasting Sanctuary of Love and Natural Goodness."

"The *what*?"

"I found them on the Internet. You get a minister, flute player, license, a flower arrangement, and a champagne-glass pyramid of flowing organic fruit smoothies. All for six hundred bucks, tip included." He finishes the candy bar and starts in on another. "They'll also cater, but it was all sprouts, fruit, and roots. You know I prefer something a little more substantial. I'm considering a six-foot Little Caesar's Carnivore Lover's Pizza with extra cheese baked into the crust."

"Herman, don't do it."

"Everybody likes Little Caesar's, Sherlock."

"No. Don't get married."

"When two people are in love, that's what they do," he says. "Be here about fifteen minutes before eleven and bring your cell phone. We're going to want a lot of pictures."

"Herman, listen to reason."

"It's going to be semi-formal. You can wear anything but camouflage."

"It's all too soon. Ludmila's family won't have time to get here."

"Her brother's already here. They're out looking at silver patterns right now."

"Herman—"

"Ludmila is as excited as I am, Sherlock. Do you think she could stay at your place the night before the ceremony?"

"Why?"

"She's very traditional," he explains. "And could you loan her a sock or hanky?"

"Why?"

"She already has something old, new, and blue."

"Herman, this is a bad idea."

"No problem, I'll get her a hotel room." Herman is finished with the Baby Ruth bars and starts in on a stack of Butterfingers.

I try to reason with him. "Herman, have you asked her father for her hand in marriage, yet?"

"I texted him."

"And—"

"He hasn't gotten back to me," Herman says. "I'm not sure they text in the old country."

"Have you discussed a pre-nup?"

"Of course not. I won't allow money to get in the way of our love."

"Trust me, if money doesn't get in the way now, it's only a matter of time before it becomes the elephant in the room." And with Herman already here, there's hardly room for a plus-sized pachyderm.

"The only thing that will ever come between us is my stomach, Sherlock."

"Herman, is there anything I can say to make you postpone the wedding?"

"Sleet, snow, nor dead of night couldn't keep me from my appointed wedding rounds."

"Are you getting married or delivering a mail order bride?"

"Both."

I put my head in my hands and painfully wish the happy couple all the best.

"Want a Butterfinger, Sherlock? You're looking a bit peeked there."

"I'm overcome with emotion."

"I know how you feel," Herman says.

I rise up slowly. "Herman, did you hack into the CPS computer system?"

"Are you wearing a wire?"

"Why would I be wearing a wire? I'm the one who asked you to do it."

"You can never be too careful in this new, unwired world."

"Did you?"

"I was up all night, Sherlock."

"Hacking into their system, I hope."

"No, dreaming about Ludmila."

"How can you be up and dream at the same time, Herman?"

"When you're in love, it's amazing what you can do."

I have to pause. I'm wide awake and having a bad dream. "Herman, were you able to get the answers to the test?"

"No."

"Why not?"

'To be honest with you, Sherlock, my heart wasn't really into it."

"Because it was too busy fluttering about Ludmila?"

"Exactly." Herman puts his hand across the right side of his massive chest. "It's fluttering right now."

There is a gurgle and a bodily release, but this one didn't come from Herman's heart. I get up to open the window before anything that could stick hits me.

I remain in the window's fresh air. "Herman, what am I going to do? If I can't prove the tutor in the Tutor Tent is a crook, there's no case."

"I'm sorry I couldn't find the answers to the test," he says, munching away.

"Me, too."

Herman finishes the Butterfinger, crumples up the wrapper, and tosses it on the couch. "I'm thinking about Maui for our honeymoon. A little beach time might be fun," he says.

Herman in a Speedo. Oh my God.

***

I have a couple of hours before I meet Bree Bisonette, pronounced "Bis-o-nay" at the Richmond offices. I go home. Once inside, I gaze upon *The Original Carlo*. It's a mess, more confusing than the case itself. I sit at my kitchen table and place Mrs. Chumley's spreadsheets side by side. I stare at the columns of numbers, payees, and reasons for payment. Then I ask myself: What is wrong with this accounting?

Since I have yet to balance a checkbook in my lifetime, I'm probably not the best person for this exercise. There is no rhyme or reason to anything on the pages. One week's expenditures never match another week's. The payees listed change more often than Tiffany changes shoes. A vendor gets paid a huge chunk one time and a pittance the next. I don't get it.

I peer down on all this, but I don't know how long before I get up and go to my kitchen's junk drawer. I have to search around, moving old padlocks with no keys, almost empty Scotch Tape dispensers, pens that no longer write, and a set of three small beanbags, with which I plan to teach myself how to juggle, and finally find the small electronic calculator given to me by Mickey D. Monroe, whose good hands sell Allstate Insurance. *If it's insurance you need, call Mickey D's.*

I go back to the table, turn the calculator on, hold it up under the kitchen's florescent light for a quick charge, and sit. I add up every column, write the totals down, and repeat the process to make sure I'm correct.

Every column totals the exact same number, $4,326.00. This is weird. I have added more confusion to my already confused state of being.

I need explanations and I can come up with only one place to start. I pack up, leave the apartment, get back in my car, and drive city streets toward downtown. The first public school seen is on my right, I stop, park, go inside, and head for the assistant principal's office.

"I apologize for dropping in without calling, but could I possibly have a few moments of your time?" The middle-aged lady, dressed Walmart chic, eyes me suspiciously before I explain, "I'm being transferred to Chicago, and my wife and I found a house we like in the neighborhood, but I thought I better check out the schools before we make an offer."

"Certainly," she says, "Welcome to Stan Mikita School. What would you like to know?"

"My daughter is in seventh grade and loves computers. Does your school have an advanced program?"

"No."

"Does any school in the area?"

"Not that I know of."

"Does your school offer laptops for the students to use?"

"Oh, no," she says. "We're under strict budget constraints. That would be nice, but no school has student laptops that I know of."

"Do you have special classes for kids who are going to test for the specialized high schools in the system?"

"No."

"Why not?"

"We couldn't afford the expense."

"Does this school get the same amount of money as a school in Lincoln Park or Lakeview?"

"Budget is based on the number of students. The district tries its best to be fair," she says. "We're all pretty much the same size."

"Would you happen to know what a private school would cost?"

"A lot."

"Thank you very much for your time."

***

I drive towards the lake, find a spot on Belmont, and park my car. I might have big bucks in the bank, but at twenty-four bucks for the first fifteen minutes, my big bucks won't last long. I take the *L* downtown.

Bree doesn't look good. Her face is drawn, her posture in a slump, and two of her most prominent fake body parts seem to sag. She asked if we could meet downstairs in the Aon Building's coffee shop instead of in the Richmond offices.

"Bree, are you okay?"

"No."

"He never called?"

"No."

"I got dumped," she admits

"I know the feeling."

"I really love Jamison. I know a lot of people thought I was after his money, prestige, and lifestyle, but I really do care for him."

"Some people have a difficult time loving other people. It's like they don't know how. Jamison is like that." I'm guessing here, since I've never had an actual conversation with the man, but I do suspect this may be true from what Tiffany has told me.

"I was trying to teach him how to love."

"Some people can't be taught."

A tear falls from her right eye.

"I'm sorry, Bree, but you can't give up. There is a lid out there for every pot. You'll find your perfect man, you just have to keep looking."

"I did find him and he didn't want me." She sniffles and takes a moment to readjust her emotional bearings. I wait patiently. "I think you're right about the Ho Lee Dong guy. Something's not kosher." Bree doesn't look Jewish.

"Such as?"

"He's using way too many doses of heavy chemo."

"Can you give me an example?"

"He has sixteen cases where he's using Gleevec. Its cost is seventy-thousand dollars a year. A typical clinic might have two or three."

"What's Gleevec?" I ask.

"It's basically what you'd use for advanced leukemia patients when there is little or no hope."

"Could Dong be specializing in leukemia patients?"

"He's administering other high priced chemo for other patients, too."

"Over the top, huh?"

Bree says, "I would say it's a bit much."

"Thanks for helping out, Bree."

"You're welcome, and sorry I've been a bit difficult to deal with the past couple of days."

"No problem. Compared to some people I have to deal with, you're a piece of cake."

We take last sips and rise from our table.

"One other thing, Sherlock. I got an email from our in-house attorney about a court date tomorrow concerning a claim about cigars. What's that all about?"

"You really don't want to know."

"He wants me to go to court instead of him."

"Coward."

"Do I have to?"

"An executive from Richmond has to be there. Sorry, if you got the call."

"Is little Tiffy attending?"

"Afraid so."

"Damn, I hate that brat."

I sit back down for a few minutes by myself. I do feel sorry for Bree, but unrequited affairs of the heart are seldom cured by anything besides time. As I am sitting, a man in a wheelchair slowly makes his way up to the counter, orders, maneuvers over to the pick-up spot, gets his coffee, and wheels over to the table next to where I'm seated. I want to ask him if he has cancer, but it wouldn't be fitting. I call Toni at Children's. After being bounced around, my call is answered.

"Toni, it's Sherlock. Are you busy?"

"We seldom lack for business around here," she tells me.

I speak softly as not to bother the person at the next table. "Do you know what Gleevek is?"

"Of course."

"It's pretty heavy duty stuff, isn't it?"

"A lot of times it's the last medication on the list."

"If a patient is taking Gleevek, could he walk?"

"Some can, a lot can't."

"Thanks, Toni."

"That's why you called?"

"Yep."

"Sherlock, the longer I know you, the stranger you get."

"At least I'm not boring."

CHAPTER 25

L ester Oland is a faux Asian. He claims he is a direct descendant of Walter Oland, an actor who portrayed Charlie Chan in a string of old movies before such films were considered racist and demeaning to Asians in general. Lester, as a CPD detective, does his best to continue the role his distant relative once played.

"Visit from Sherlock this close to weekend is bad omen."

"What? You're not happy to see me, Lester?"

"No."

"I'm on a case and need a hand," I tell him.

"When in need of hand, look no farther than end of arm, Sherlock."

We're sitting in the detective area of the District 1 station on South Halstead where Oland is the go-to guy when someone gets kidnapped in Chicago. And since kidnappings are few and far between in the city, I'm sure Lester has plenty of sand left in his hourglass.

"I got to get inside a cancer clinic to see if they're scamming Richmond Insurance."

"To get inside of anywhere, first try door," Lester tells me.

"I have, but it's closed to my kind," I tell him. "I need a certain someone of a certain ilk, who thinks they have cancer to go in for a check-up."

"Why me?"

"Everybody is Asian in the place including the janitor, who goes by the name E-Z Ernie. If I send someone in I know, they'd stick out like a cigarette machine in the place."

"What's the name of the clinic?" he asks.

"Ho Lee Dong One Stop Cancer Clinic."

"Where is it?"

"Chinatown, in an alley just off 23rd near the main pagoda."

I can tell from his expression, no gongs are being rung. "It's behind the Yu RiRi Fatt restaurant."

"Ah, yes. Excellent Peking Duck."

"Will you do it?"

"When?"

"Today."

Lester sits up. "Today, why today?"

"Never put off to tomorrow," I tell him with my own Oriental twang, "what you should have done yesterday."

"Yet, egg drop soup needs to simmer before becoming tasty."

"But better to eat while hot before dumpling gets soggy," I counter his counter.

"You win."

We sit for another twenty minutes. I give him all that I know, most of what I don't know, and what I need and want to know. He begins slowly, but by the time I'm finished, he's asking question after question.

"Seem to be a bit more interested now, don't you, Lester?" I chide his better nature.

"Detective with no curiosity is like glass eye at peephole."

***

I need somewhere to go to think and eat, although not necessarily in that order. There is a jazz joint on Hubbard below Michigan Avenue named Andy's where a piano player jams freestyle on Thursdays. I've always liked the place. It's old, creaky, a bit on the worn out side, and about as unpretentious as you can get—exactly what a jazz joint should be. I take the *L*, get off on Grand, walk over, sit at the bar, order an iced tea, and my phone rings.

"Hello, Tiffany."

"We have to talk."

"Why?"

"Because I didn't find out anything, Mr. Sherlock."

"Then what would we have to talk about?"

"Plenty. I'll be there in a few minutes," she informs me, and hangs up.

I order the chef's salad and listen to a jazz piano rendition of "Somewhere Over the Rainbow." Knowing Tiffany is on her way, I can only wish my troubles would melt like lemon drops.

Before my second bite, Tiffany storms into Andy's, takes one look at my entrée, and says, "Did you know there are more calories in a chef's salad than a burger with fries, Mr. Sherlock?"

"No, I didn't know that."

"You got eggs, ham, cheese, and enough blue cheese dressing to drown parts of Paris."

"From now on I'll cross the item off my menu list."

"You better or you'll end up looking like your friend Herman."

"He's getting married on Saturday."

"To the fat lady from the circus?"

"No, to someone more your size."

"I'm a zero."

There's a line I won't touch.

Tiffany is wearing a sleek, bouncy, little, sundress accentuating her body, which hardly needs additional accentuating.

"I drew a total and complete blank, Mr. Sherlock. I asked and asked and asked, and nobody saw any fire."

"Who'd you ask?" I ask.

I rang every doorbell on Mr. Fume-a-torium's street. God, every third house had that "Guantanamera" song. If I hear it one more time, I'm going to scream."

"And nobody reported a fire?"

"No. So thinking the neighbors were all tone deaf and couldn't see the fire because of the smoke, I went to every fire station in Bollingbrook and asked them."

"You walked into fire stations dressed like that?"

"Yes."

"I'll bet you set off a few alarms."

"They didn't know anything, either. They had no record of any call to Mr. Fume-a-lot's house."

"Okay."

"So, what are we going to do, Mr. Sherlock?"

"Nothing."

"What do you mean, 'nothing'?"

"Tiffany, the deal was you had to find out where the fire took place, so we had something to investigate. You didn't, so there is nothing we can do."

"But the fire had to take place somewhere," she argues.

"It did. He had pictures," I remind Tiffany. "That's what he used to prove his claim for the insurance money."

"They could've been photoshopped. It happens all the time on the net. Just ask anyone who's been on Match-dot-com."

"I don't think so, Tiffany."

"But that's not fair."

"The policy clearly stated all he had to do is prove destruction of the items insured and he did that."

Tiffany stews silently as I pick at my salad. Having heard Tiffany's dietary review of my lunch, I push the cheese, hard-boiled eggs, and the ham to the side and focus on the lettuce and veggies.

"We can't give up, Mr. Sherlock. We just can't."

My phone rings. I'm incredibly popular today. It's Fern Mossy on the line. "Hello, Fern."

She launches into a string of information like a nervous news anchor on a late breaking story, ending with, "I've never seen him like this before."

"Are there any sharp objects in his desk?" I ask.

"I don't know. I've never looked in his desk."

I certainly hope Eldin didn't keep any switchblade he might have confiscated from Terrible Teddy. "I'll be there as soon as I can."

I hang up the phone, pull out my wallet, and put a twenty on the bar. "Tiffany, I need a ride to Sauganash. It's an emergency."

"Oh, all right."

I leave a fiver in the jar on the piano. The player gives me a smile, I whisper my request, and he accompanies our hurrying out of Andy's with a jazzy rendition of "Guantanamera."

"Aaah! I hate that song."

CHAPTER 26

"He's locked himself in his office." Fern Mossy meets us as Tiffany pulls up and parks her Lexus in what will soon be the pick-up line. Tessie is going to have a fit.

"He won't listen to us. I'm afraid he's going to do something drastic," Fern continues.

I quicken my pace into the building. Tiffany and Fern right behind.

"You have to be quiet because the children can't find out," Fern concludes her warning and directions.

One step into the principal's office and I'm hit with, "Hello, Mr. Sherlock, are you having a smiley day?"

"Not right now, Mrs. Chumley, no."

"Soon, I hope."

I go to the door and turn the knob, but it's locked. "Principal Puddle, are you all right in there?"

No answer.

"Eldin, can you hear me?"

No answer.

"Let me try, Mr. Sherlock." Tiffany moves forward to the closed door and coos, "Oh, Eldin, it's little Tiffany, I want to come in and you can help me go over my figures."

I hear the bolt on the lock open. I twist the knob, push the door open, and burst inside. Eldin is collapsing back into his chair like a prize fighter who should have gone down before the bell rang.

"Fern, get some water, quick."

"This can't happen to me, Sherlock. This can't happen."

"Eldin, just relax. Calm down. Take a deep breath."

"It might be my last," he says.

I hear the outer door open, Mrs. Chumley cheerily greets the pint-sized visitor. "Why sure you can have a smiley face."

I tell Tiffany, "Close the door."

Fern soon finds her way back into Eldin's office with a large glass of water. She takes out a short stack of bathroom hand towels, wets them, and starts dabbing Eldin's forehead.

"I was only trying to do what's best for the children."

"I know that Eldin, just calm down."

"Should we call 911?" Tiffany asks.

"No," Fern answers. "We don't need any more excitement around here."

"What happened?" I ask.

"The district suspects we cheated to get so many pupils into the magnet program," Eldin says.

I should ask, "Did you?" But I decide to wait with that question.

"It'll be a scandal. The good name of Ann Margaret will be tarnished forever."

If Ann's portrayal of Elvis's girlfriend in *Viva Las Vegas* didn't ruin her, I doubt if too many good students will ruin the school's reputation.

"I was only trying to do what's best for the students with the extra classes, the advanced curriculum, and the magnet school tutorial."

"There's no point in apologizing for those now, Eldin."

"Immigration contacted us," Eldin adds.

"They want to come in and talk to Juan?"

"They're looking for him. They want to send him back to Mexico."

Poor Juan and Mom.

"Did the district also find out about the missing milk money?" I ask.

"Yes," he says. "They want to do a full audit of our expenditures."

"I wouldn't worry about that," I tell him.

"Why not?" Fern asks.

If Herman couldn't figure it out, I doubt if the district could, either.

"Trust me," I tell Fern, "nobody could figure out your accounting system."

Fern gives me a very odd look.

Eldin's color comes back into his cheeks. He's breathing a little easier.

Fern says, "If that loudmouthed Lou Lauder wouldn't have opened his big mouth, all this wouldn't be happening."

"The district said he wants all of our students to prove citizenship, starting with the ones who got into the magnet schools," Eldin says.

"Jerk," I respond. What else is there to say?

"What are we going to do?" Fern asks.

I don't have an immediate answer.

Tiffany, who has stood off to the side to watch our little play, speaks up. "Are you going to give up and quit on this case, too, Mr. Sherlock?" Before I can answer, Tiffany fills in for the group, "That's what Mr. Sherlock does. When he can't figure something out, he packs up his clues and goes home."

"You can't quit now," Eldin says.

"He sure can," Tiffany assures. "He's a quitter from the word Q."

Eldin looks up at me with water-logged eyes. "Please don't. The district's calling a meeting for Monday and they're going to want answers."

"I'm not quitting."

"You sure, Mr. Sherlock?" Tiffany asks. "It seems to me you've become adopted to throwing in the bath towel."

I don't think she got that right. "No, I haven't."

"Like the Fuma-cigar-looma case, Mr. Sherlock?"

"I'm not quitting on Pat or Ann. I'm still digging. I've still got more questions than I have answers. There's more loose ends dangling here than in Medusa's hairdo."

"School's almost out and I'll be out with it," Eldin says.

"I need more time," I tell the group as I go to the door and open it. "Mrs. Chumley, could you come in here a minute, please?"

"Well, of course."

She enters as springy as the first day of Indian summer.

"Mrs. Chumley, I'd like you to take Principal Puddle home. He's not feeling well and he needs his rest."

"Why, certainly." She comes around to the chair side of the desk and helps him to his feet. "Come on, Principal Puddle, let's get your things, and put a smiley on that face of yours."

"Go, Eldin. Get some rest. I'm going to need you at your best to get to the bottom of this thing."

Eldin reluctantly leaves with Mrs. Chumley.

The three of us remain in his office as the bell goes off to signal the end of school for the day. I look out the window and see the cars coming down the road and lining up in the pick-up line. Amongst the cars is a tow truck.

"Tiffany, you better get outside, your car is about to be

towed."

"Oh my God. I must've forgotten to put my gimp sticker up." Tiffany runs out of the office leaving Fern and I alone.

"Tell me about you and Mr. Mizzi," I say it quickly, and as expected, the name hits her like a bolt of Midwest lightening.

"What about me and Mr. Mizzi?"

"You two an item?"

"A what?"

"You two in a relationship?"

"I don't think that is any of your business," she states emphatically, getting past the shock of my original comment.

"I'm merely asking."

"We've seen each other socially," she admits. "Is there a crime in that?"

"No."

If I really wanted to shock her, I could tell her how Winky Torelli and Larry Mizzi were exchanging sweat gland odors. I bet that would make her day.

"The other day you visited him at the Tutor Tent."

"I don't see how that could have any bearing on what's going on here," she says, dodging my question.

"I'm not sure it does," I say.

"Why were you spying on Larry?"

"Who said I was spying on anyone?"

Fern looks away and back at me. "For your information, Mr. Sherlock, Larry and I haven't actually dated in months."

"Okay."

I wonder what's the difference between 'dating' and 'actually dating.'

"Anything else you want to know?" she snaps at me.

"Not right now, but I'll let you know if I do."

My cell phone rings. I look at the screen and see the name. Before I pick up, I see Fern is relieved at the interruption.

"Hello, Lester."

"Getting ready to pass through the eye of cancer needle."

CHAPTER 27

"That woman with the stop sign is an animal."
"She's Tessie the Traffic Terminator at the school," I inform her.

"I barely escaped with my life," Tiffany says as we aim for the expressway. "I thought she might go ballistic with that traffic sign of hers."

"I heard she once chewed the fender off a Chevy when the driver refused to move."

"I wouldn't be a bit surprised."

Traffic is getting heavy. "Tiffany, I'm not asking you to break any speed limits, but I want to get to the clinic when Lester Oland comes out."

"I don't know how you can be so involved with Dr. Dong and totally ignore Mr. Fuma-smoka-stogie, Mr. Sherlock."

"Tiffany, sometimes you have to choose which road is more important to travel."

"You want to take Lakeshore Drive instead of the expressway?"

"No, I mean you have to sometimes pick and choose your battles. You always want to pick a fight you have a chance at winning."

"I don't have clue what you're talking about, Mr. Sherlock."

"We have little chance of winning the Fumadoro cigar case. It was Richmond's mistake to sell him such a policy. You'll see tomorrow that we could argue 'til we're blue in the face, and the judge will decide in their favor."

"I don't want to get smurfed, Mr. Sherlock. Blue is certainly not my color, but I have this thing about giving up too easily."

"And when did you get this 'thing,' Tiffany?"

"When my mom died, I was so depressed I could barely apply blush. I stayed in my condo, didn't want to be seen, let my split ends grow, let the enamel on my toes split and crack," she says, weaving in and out of lanes like a Petty at Talladega. "I was in a state of personal make-up avoidance."

Tiffany's mom died suddenly during a botched liposuction operation when the surgeon mistakenly sucked out a kidney.

"I don't get the connection, Tiffany."

"I could've given up on myself, folded up my designer closet, and slunked off into looking middle-class, but I didn't. I did what my mom would've wanted me to do."

"And that was—"

"Go to the spa, get a facial, mani-pedi, and redo my boobs to become the person she wanted me to be."

"I'm still not sure I see the connection."

"Because I didn't give up. I hung in there throughout all the pain and sorrow and realized if I didn't do anything and merely walloped in my own misery, I'd be destined to buy my underwear at Target the rest of my life instead of becoming the person I was meant to be."

In a perverse way, this is touching.

"Tiffany, I promise you, if there is anything I can do on the Fumadoro case, I will."

"You don't have your fingers crossed, do you Mr. Sherlock?"

"No."

Tiffany takes the off-ramp's shoulder the last five hundred yards, and we arrive at the Ho Lee Dong Clinic close to 4 p.m.

I look frantically for Lester's state-issued detective car, which usually stands out like a cop car with a sore thumb. "There it is over there. Go that way."

Tiffany maneuvers her Lexus around the UPS truck at the entrance to Dong's clinic and parks behind the Ford with the state-issued plates. Lester is sitting in the front seat.

"Good, he hasn't gone in yet."

I hop out of Tiffany's car and hurry into Lester's, plopping down in the front passenger's seat. Tiffany follows and sits in the back.

"So nice of you to join me," Lester greets us.

"Why haven't you gone in yet?" I ask.

"Not going in. I have Number One friend do the deed instead."

"Good cover, Lester."

"Remember me, Detective Oland?" Tiffany asks.

"Difficult to forget flower who is always in bloom."

"I'm not sure what that means," Tiffany admits, "but I'll take it as a compliment."

"How long has your friend been inside?" I ask.

"Twenty minutes," Lester says as two patients come out of the clinic and have to dodge the UPS man and his loaded cart going in. "This guy has quite a business here."

"There's big money in cancer."

"Why do you suspect him?"

"Come on." I start to get out of the car.

"Wait," Tiffany says, "where are you going?"

"Back by the Dumpsters."

"Why didn't you tell me? I would've brought my Hazmat suit," Tiffany says.

I lead the two back to the Dumpsters behind the building. I first point out the contents of the medical recycle unit. "The only items in here are empty saline bags and used syringes."

"What's so weird about that?" Lester asks.

"Shouldn't there be a lot of other stuff?" I ask rhetorically.

"Not necessarily."

"Chemo bags, empty vials, glass containers, or whatever?"

"Matters what kind of chemo he's doing, wouldn't it?" Lester asks in the same manner. "Is that the only reason you brought me out here?"

"No." We move to the regular Dumpster and peer inside. It's pretty much the same trash as before with the exception of a broken swivel chair resting on top of the papers and lunch refuse. "Look here."

Lester follows my lead, peering inside the metal container.

"Why don't we bust him for not recycling properly and go home for the weekend, Sherlock?"

"Ask yourself the question, Lester. What's wrong with this trash?"

"It stinks?"

"It's trashy?" Tiffany says.

"No," I pause for effect. "There's no cardboard."

"Ah-ha!" Lester exclaims facetiously.

"UPS brings in boxes and boxes of chemo, but there's no empty boxes in the trash," I tell him.

"Maybe he's recycling properly, and has them broken down and stacked inside?"

"Or maybe he's recycling something other than cardboard," I mention.

We walk back around the building and approach the UPS guy.

"What is this? Did I win the lottery?" the surprised delivery man asks.

"Have you ever delivered cigars to a guy, who lives on Musical Street in Bollingbrook?" Tiffany asks.

"Not on my route, lady," he answers as he scans each package with a hand-held wand before putting it up onto the floor of his truck.

"Quite a big haul you got there," I say.

"In this business, size matters," he says.

"Do you ever get frustrated with your job?" I ask. "You drop off in the morning and pick up in the afternoon. It's kind of like a never ending cycle, isn't it?"

"I got a wife, three kids, a mortgage, and two car payments. What do you think?"

I'm reading the labels on the packages as we talk. "You ever worry about handling all this medical stuff?"

"I haven't yet, but I might start since you've mentioned it."

I notice many of the boxes have mailing labels in Chinese as well as English.

"Are you people from one of those undercover tracking services, seeing if I'm goofing off on my job or something?" the UPS guy asks.

"No."

"I have a question," Tiffany announces. "Do you always wear that awful shade of brown?"

"Afraid so, lady."

"Why?"

"Matches the truck."

"Well then you should have the truck painted a more flattering color."

"I'll put it in the suggestion box when I get back tonight."

"Okay, nice chatting with you," I say as we begin to walk away. If I had one of Mrs. Chumley's smiley faces, I'd put it on his collar.

"It's been a slice," the guy says.

The three of us get back into Lester's car.

"Like an emperor on a Ming vase," Lester says. "You might be onto something here, Sherlock."

Suddenly, a middle-aged Asian woman opens the door and climbs into the back seat of the car next to Tiffany. "Hello."

Lester does the introduction, "This is Anna May Long, my

number one friend at the station."

She looks familiar. "Aren't you Anna May Wong, who used to work in the Wentworth station?" I ask.

"Yes, when I was married to Ang Wong," she answers.

"I'm Sherlock. I was a detective there three years ago."

"Oh, yeah. You're the guy who punched his boss on TV," she recalls.

My past follows me wherever I go.

"Got divorced?" Tiffany asks.

"Yep."

"Why?" Tiffany has no borders when it comes to personal questions.

"I didn't like being Anna May Long Wong," she admits.

"If you married the doc in there," Tiffany says, "you'd be Anna May Long Wong Dong."

"What happened inside the clinic?" Lester asks.

"Old Dr. Dong put me through the ringer. Took blood, urine, x-rays, and poked around my chest like he was molding hard clay."

"I hate that," Tiffany says. "Nothing's worse than a guy who does a boob like he's thumping a casaba melon."

"And what did he tell you?" I ask.

"I have cancer."

"Oh my God," Tiffany says. "I'm so sorry."

I look over at Lester. "Think you can get a warrant before the UPS guy gets back to his distribution center?"

"When warrant, warrant action, Lester go into action."

***

I have Tiffany drop me off at the *Red* Line.

"Our court date is at ten, Tiffany."

A 10 a.m. court call means our case will come up around eleven. So, telling Tiffany to be there at ten, will translate to 10:45 in Tiffany time, and she'll arrive fifteen minutes early for our case, which will be an hour late.

"I'll meet you there, Mr. Sherlock," she promises. "I'll wear something blue just in case we get into an argument with the judge."

"Excellent fashion forethought, Tiffany."

It is almost six by the time I'm in my apartment. I call my

kids right away.

"Are we doing something fun this weekend, Dad?" Care asks. She's on the bedroom extension while Kelly' is on the hallway phone.

"I don't know, are you?" I semi-answer her question with a question.

"Can we go shopping, Dad?" Kelly asks.

"I don't have you this weekend," I inform them.

"Yes, you do."

"I had you last weekend," I remind them.

"But that was a special request weekend, Dad," Care says.

"So, we could help you work on the case," Kelly adds.

I don't seem to recall too much help.

"Special request weekends are over and above regular weekends, Dad," Kelly says.

"I've never heard of a *special request weekend*. When did that start?"

"Last weekend."

I pause. "Your mother has something to do this weekend and she doesn't want to pop for a babysitter?"

"How'd you guess?" Care asks.

"I don't guess. I'm a detective, remember?"

"She's going to an all-day seminar on how to change the color of her aura."

"Well, I certainly would hate to have her miss that."

Care changes the topic. "By the way, Dad, how is the case going? Are you going to have us in the room when you figure it all out?"

"I'm not sure I'm going to figure it all out."

"Will you let us help some more, Dad?" Kelly suggests.

"At the school?" I ask.

"Yes."

"With me?"

"Yes."

"What happens if I show up at school and embarrass you again, Kelly?"

"Disguise, Dad, disguise."

"Fine, Kelly, I'll wear a sign on the back of my Darth Vader outfit that says, 'I'm not Kelly's dad.'"

"Oh, Dad, that's not funny."

"So what are we going to do this weekend?" Care goes back

to the original question.

"Yeah, Dad, what should I pack?" Kelly wants to make sure she's fashion appropriate no matter what we do.

I can't think of a worse place to take them, but I don't seem to have a choice. "Bring the best you got, girls."

"Why?"

"Because we're invited to a wedding."

"Oh, Dad, that is so romantic."

I'm not sure they'll be saying those words when they see who's getting married.

***

Knowing I have big bucks in my bank account, I should go out and treat myself to a big dinner, but I'm feeling very antsy and confused. I'm not too worried about the Ho Lee Dong case. If Lester gets the warrant, the packages are confiscated from UPS, and they find what I'm sure they'll find that Dong is going to get dinged. The case against Fumadoro is pretty much a lost cause. We'll show up at court, the judge will make it clear that if we take this case any further, he'll slap us with enough additional charges to double the amount already due. A judge's main function is to keep cases out of the court that don't belong in the court. Chalk Fumadoro and his cigars up as an expensive lesson learned.

What has got me discombobulated is what's going down at the school. Eldin has pretty much lost it, Fern is lying, and I can't see Winky and Mr. Mizzi on the cover of a bodice ripper novel titled *He Schooled Me in the Lessons of Love*. Milk money is missing, but dollars show up under tomato cans in the cafeteria's storeroom, and how can a school district punish a school for doing too good a job getting its kids into their magnet school programs? I feel horrible about Juan and his mom being shipped back across the border and, if it was up to me, the word *jerk* should be tattooed across the forehead of Loudmouth Lou Lauder to warn people of what to expect when they have to deal with him. What's a detective to do?

Go to bed. I'm exhausted.

CHAPTER 28

I make one stop before going downtown to the Daley Center.

"Herman, please don't get married."

"You're just jealous, Sherlock."

"No, I'm not. I'm happy for you. I just don't want you to rush into things."

From out of the apartment's second bedroom emerges Ludmila in a flimsy little robe. She gives me a wave as if we're old buddies back from when Russia was the USSR.

"Isn't she a little pumpernickel?" Herman comments.

Following Ludmila out of the room is a swarthy looking gent.

"That's Petrov, Ludmila's brother," Herman explains. "He's going to be her maid of honor."

"Certainly will make for a unique wedding party portrait." I notice Petrov has a matching Josef Stalin tattoo on his upper arm. No sibling rivalry between these two.

"Does he speak any English?" I ask.

"No, but Ludmila's really making progress. She's got the bus system figured out, how to use coupons at the Jewel, and can operate an ATM machine with the best of them."

I wait for the two to go into the kitchen. "Herman, I'm your friend and I'm only telling you this because of our friendship."

He interrupts, "You're more than a friend, Sherlock, you're my best man."

"The best man says this isn't a good idea, Herman. You're rushing into things. There's no hurry to get to the altar. You should take some time to get to know each other better, see if the two of you are compatible, learn to communicate, and at least learn to speak each other's language."

"We already speak the same language, Sherlock, the language of love. We speak with our eyes, our hearts, and our emotions. Watch." Herman calls out, "Ludmila, my little tasty tamale."

The petite little woman bounces into the room with a look of love in her gaze. She comes right over to Herman, sits on his massive thigh, wraps one arm around him, and with her other hand, playfully tugs at the folds of fat around his neck. She giggles.

"Need I say more?" Herman asks.

I give up. "What time does the wedding start again?"

"Eleven."

"Set two extra plates. I'm bringing my girls."

"Oh, great, they can help Ludmila up the aisle. The preparations are now complete." Herman bounces Ludmila a few times to express his joy. "It's going to be lovely."

I stand up. Time to go. I give a smile to the happy couple. But before I leave, I have to ask, "You didn't think of any other ways that guy from the Tutor Tent could have hacked into the system to get the answers to the magnet school test?"

"Nope."

"Damn."

"I'm sorry I couldn't help."

I head for the door with my head hanging low.

"I really tried, Sherlock, and not just because you threatened to pull out of your best man duties."

"I know, Herman."

"Sorry, I couldn't find the answers."

"Me, too."

"But I did find the questions, would they help?"

***

I sit outside in my car. For the first time in my career, the questions are just as important as the answers. All the pieces of the puzzle are floating around in my head as if they are recipe cards finding their rightful spots on *The Original Carlo*. I am amazed how one comment from Herman can immediately improve the entire work of conspicuous art.

I'm not sure how long I sit, but I do come up with at least one conclusion.

An opportunity has presented itself and it is time to act. I, in no way, have the entire case figured out, but I do have the goods to out-jerk the jerk, and I can't wait to get at the guy. I call Eldin.

"Good morning, Mr. Sherlock," Mrs. Chumley cheerily greets me. "Are you ready for a smiley day today?"

"Of course. Is Principal Puddle in the office yet?"

"Yes."

"Is he better?"

"Much better."

"I need to speak with him."

"He's behind closed doors with Miss Mossy."

"I really need to speak with him."

"Not a good time, Mr. Sherlock," Mrs. Chumley says. "I don't think there's a lot of smiling going on inside the office right now."

"It's important."

"What do you need? Maybe I can help."

"I need to set up a meeting this afternoon."

"I can do that. Who do you want in the meeting?"

I give her my list.

"The only one I'm not sure of is Mr. Lauder," Mrs. Chumley says.

"All you have to do is tell him it's about Elsa being admitted into Buttkick Prep and he'll show up."

"And when he does, I'm going to put a smiley face on his collar."

"Go for it, Mrs. Chumley, go for it."

I call Lester. He doesn't pick up.

I have an additional thought. I call Herman back. He refuses my request at first, but when I offer to supply rose petals for tossing, he says, "Sure, no problem."

I have to hustle to get to the Daley Center and have to park in the city lot across the street. It'll cost me a fortune. I arrive in the courtroom a few minutes after ten. Bree Bisonette, pronounced "Bis-o-nay" waits for me in the back row. She looks, to be nice, on the totally worn out side of exhausted.

"Sorry, I'm late. Did they call our case?"

"Not yet."

I look to the left and five rows ahead of us, and see Mr. Fumadoro and his lawyer. They wear matching blue suits.

"What's this all about?" Bree asks.

"Some over-aggressive Richmond salesperson wrote a buck-and-a-half policy insuring aged, collectable, Cuban cigars against theft, fire, flood, and just about every other act of God. And guess what happened?"

"He got a big commission?"

"Besides that."

"They burned up in a fire?"

Bree's a good guesser.

"And a hundred and fifty grand went up in smoke?"

"Right again," I say.

Bree hangs her head as if it is her money being paid out.

"I couldn't believe Richmond would write such a policy," I say. "Lloyds of London, yeah, but Richmond?"

The bailiff comes over and shushes us. Fumadoro and his lawyer see the admonishment and add their own caustic smiles to the scolding. I get up, move across the side of the room to the front and check the docket in front of the clerk. On the sheet there are two more cases before us. I go back and signal Bree to join me outside the courtroom.

Once outside the door, I ask, "How are you doing, Bree?"

"Not good. I can't sleep."

"Why not?"

"Pillow's too wet."

"I'm sorry."

"So am I."

I take her hand in mine. "Trust me, you'll get over it. Nobody's been dumped more than me," I admit. "It just takes time."

"My clock is moving slower than little Tiffy's thought processes," she says.

I should scold her for being mean, but I'll save that for another time.

"Time is the only cure for a broken heart. You just have to get through it."

"I don't want to get through it. I want Jamison back."

I feel sorry for Bree. "Some relationships are just not meant to be and there is nothing you can do about it," I tell her.

Bree pulls out a wad of already cried on Kleenex and dabs at her wet eyes. She takes a few moments and regains what composure is regainable. "Why are we even here, Mr. Sherlock?"

"Richmond refuses to go down without a fight, even when there's nothing except their own incompetence to fight about."

"I wish Jamison would feel that way about his relationships."

At five minutes to eleven, ten minutes after her usual forty-five minute delay, Tiffany arrives.

"Oh, it's you," she greets Bree.

"And so nice to see you, little Tiffy."

"You look stunning," Tiffany snaps at her. "Are you going for the *just bit by a vampire* look?"

"And I love your make-up. When did you decide to go punk?"

"Get another facelift, Bree, and you won't have to turn around to see behind you."

"Tiffy, the girl who brings happiness *whenever* she goes."

I jump in. "Knock if off. I don't want to be here and I certainly don't want to listen to the two of you snipe at each other."

"She started it."

"Did not."

"Did too."

I interrupt, "What happened, anyway? After the last case, I thought I had you two on better terms?"

"She was talking behind my back."

"Was not."

"Were too."

"You said I was as dumb as I look," Tiffany quotes Bree.

"No, I said, 'No one is as dumb as you look,'" Bree corrects her.

I can't take any more, so I walk back into the courtroom.

"Fumadoro versus Richmond Insurance," the bailiff announces.

I follow the opponents to the bench, and stand before Judge Blunt as he pages through the case summary. Bree and Tiffany continue to snip in muffled tones behind me.

"What is this all about?" the Judge asks, skimming the material.

Fumadoro's attorney speaks, "A total waste of the court's time, Judge. You can see the policy clearly states the items destroyed were insured against fire, flood, and natural disaster, but Richmond is refusing payment."

"Yes, it says so right here," Judge Blunt says, flipping back one page.

"And," the attorney continues, "we have provided ample proof of the items' value and they're having been destroyed."

The Judge lifts up the page to reveal the photos of what's

left of the cigars. When he brings the paper down from his face, he takes his first glance at me standing before the bench. "What are you doing here, Sherlock? I haven't seen you since my time in criminal court."

"Richmond didn't want to spring for an attorney, so they sent me."

The Judge looks down at me like I'm the criminal. "This is what you've been doing since they kicked you off the force?"

"Afraid so."

Judge Blunt shakes his head to further shame me. "You're acting as quasi-counsel for Richmond in their hopeless cases division?"

"So to speak."

"Quite noble of you, Sherlock. Why didn't you perform the same gesture for the court and not show up?"

"The thought did cross my mind, but so did the fact that I have to make a living, Judge."

The Judge points a finger at my head. "You should've never punched that boss of yours, Sherlock, *especially* on TV."

"Yes, Judge, I'm well aware of that now."

The judge lifts the documents up. "Sherlock, do you have a rebuttal to these claims?"

"No, not really."

"Since cigars are known to be bad for you," Tiffany pipes up from the peanut gallery. "We don't think it is fair for us to pay for cancer causing items being destroyed."

The Judge looks up over me to where the voice emanates, "And who are you?"

"Tiffany Richmond."

"Well, Tiffany Richmond, you're not recognized to speak in this courtroom."

"Everyone recognizes me, Your Honorable," Tiffany informs him. "I was once featured in a Town and Country photo spread."

"Well, we don't read that in this courtroom, so keep your mouth shut."

Tiffany is aghast at the admonishment. "What?"

"You heard me."

"I have something to say, and as a citizen, I have a right to say it."

"What part of *shut up* don't you understand, lady?"

Tiffany puts her finger out and points at the Judge. "Be careful, Judge, or I'm going to give you a very bad review on Yelp."

I turn around. "Tiffany, shut up."

Tiffany is also aghast at me. "What? You're on his side, Mr. Sherlock? That's even worse than giving up."

"Bailiff, escort this woman out of my courtroom."

The bailiff takes Tiffany by the arm. "Come on, Missy. Let's go."

Tiffany's cell phone rings. She pulls her arm away from the bailiff, sees who's calling, and says, "Do you mind? I have to take this call."

"Get her out of here," the judge screams.

The court is silent, except for Tiffany chatting away on her phone, and the bailiff leading her out into the hallway.

Judge Blunt is not a happy camper. "Anything else from the so-called defense?"

"No, Your Honor," I meekly answer.

The gavel comes down. "Decision for the plaintiff. Pay up, Sherlock, and if you ever come into my courtroom again with such a brand of complete idiocy and incompetence, I will put your feet to the fire and keep them there until your knees buckle from the heat."

"I apologize, Judge." I turn away in embarrassed shame and see Fumadoro and his lawyer shaking hands.

I slink away from the bench, but for some reason I stop turn around, and say, "One question, Judge—"

"What now, Sherlock?" he bellows at me.

"Can I ask where the fire took place? We looked everywhere and we couldn't find a report."

Judge Blunt now looks at me like a criminal with three strikes.

"I'm a curious kind of a guy. What can I tell ya, Judge?"

The Judge looks over at the plaintiff, who smiles before answering. "It was actually a series of small fires that took place, not one big one." Their smiles turn into laughs.

"You're kidding?" I can hardly believe my ears.

"Happy now, Sherlock?" the Judge asks me.

"No, but thanks for asking, Judge."

It's over. I can't believe it.

Fumadoro and his lawyer revel in the fact that I know what

it's all about and powerless to do a thing about it. They can't stop laughing. The lawyer says on our way out, "I couldn't believe any insurance company would be stupid enough to write a policy that dumb."

They'll be laughing all the way to the bank.

"Next case."

Bree meets me on my exit out of the courtroom. "He smoked them?"

"Seems to be the case."

Tiffany meets me in the hallway. "Can you believe that judge dissed me in front of all those people?"

I feel dumber than a smelt heading for a net.

Bree asks, "What are we going to do now?"

"Write them a check."

"We're going to pay the guy for smoking his classic cigars?" Bree asks.

"What?" Tiffany pipes up. "He smoked the cigars?"

"Yep."

"Like puff, puff, puff?" Tiffany over-exaggerates puffing on invisible stogies.

"And now we have to pay him," Bree says.

"We can't do that," Tiffany says. "We have to take these guys to court."

"We just did," I explain.

"We'll take 'em again."

"We can't. We already lost."

"My daddy is going to blow his smoke stack when he hears about this."

"Unbelievable," Bree says, walking away in disgust. "And I'll have to be the one to write the payment memo. Jamison sees that and I'll never get back into his loving arms." Bree heads for the elevators.

I stop, lace my fingers together, and put my hands on the top of my head and squeeze.

"Mr. Sherlock, you really blew this one," Tiffany sums it all up.

I'm so low a snail at the bottom of the sea would look like a shooting star to me.

On our trip down in a crowded elevator, Tiffany won't quit. "I told you to do something, Mr. Sherlock, but you wouldn't listen to me. 'No, Tiffany,' you said 'if we argue we're going to end up like Smurfs.' Well, look how we ended up, we're red in the face, not blue. We have to pay a hundred and fifty grand so some guy can puff away on his cancer sticks."

"Enough, Tiffany."

"My dad is going to be as mad as a diva with a bad haircut when he hears about this."

"What do you want me to do, Tiffany?"

"Fix it."

"How?"

"I don't know. Just fix it."

I have to sit down on a metal bench in the first floor lobby to calm down. People pass by on the way to the court or from the court. The latter group is either very happy or very angry.

"I wish I could wash my hands of this whole thing, Mr. Sherlock, but I forgot to bring hand sanitizer," Tiffany informs me.

"Tiffany, why don't you go to your spa, get a massage, and find some way to feel better."

"What are you going to do?"

"Go eat worms."

"I can't believe you, Mr. Sherlock. At a time like this you can only think of food."

***

Lester called but didn't leave a message. Mrs. Chumley called, and did, saying, "The meeting is all set up. Eldin wants to see you, and have a smiley day."

I call Lester. "You get the warrant?"

He pauses after my question. "Sherlock sounds like air deflating from balloon."

"I've had more fun at funerals than I've had so far today, Lester."

"Day will get better as sun rises in sky."

"It's almost noon, Lester. Sun is as high as it's going to go."

"Then I have good news and have bad news, Sherlock, which do you want first?"

"Good news."

"Got warrant. Investigation complete. Sherlock got right prescription on this case."

"What's the bad news?"

213

"When it comes to Medicare, Feds want doctor's appointment, too."

"They want to tag-a-long on our check-up?"

"Insert their own probe."

I feel a little better. "When's the appointment?"

"Soon. Feds like weekends as much as police like weekends."

It costs me twenty-six dollars to get my car out of the lot. If I keep this spending spree going, my thirty-four hundred will soon be only thirty-four. I get on the Kennedy heading north. A million thoughts pass through my brain, the majority of which concern my own stupidity in the Fumadoro case. I have to work hard to get that out of my head and only concentrate on Mr. Mizzi and Loudmouth Lou.

The fact that Lou has pulled the plug on Juan and his mother infuriates me. And for Mr. Mizzi, nothing is as despicable as a cheat, except a cheat who does it for money. I consider Elsa, Arleta, the other kids who were tutored in the tent and where they fit in this whole mess. If the whistle blows loud enough, it could shatter a lot of innocent eardrums. I have to be careful.

I arrive at Ann/Pat halfway through fifth period, and head straight for the cafeteria. The hot lunch and milk lines are empty, kids are digesting their lunches or are already outside. Esther, who looks a little top heavy, is packing up her cash, Winky Torelli is doing her count of today's milk money, and Terrible Teddy lurks in the shadows.

And who do I run into?

"Dad, what are you doing here?"

"Oh, hi, Kelly."

"Are you here to embarrass me again?"

"No."

"Then why are you here?"

"I thought it would be fun to sit in with you on a couple of classes."

"Oh my God."

Out of the corner of my eye, I see Esther enter the storeroom. I bid goodbye to my daughter with, "I got to go."

"Where?"

"I'll meet you in the classroom, Kelly."

"Oh, please no, Dad."

"Save me a seat next to you."

I make my way to the back of the serving area and watch for Esther to come out of the storeroom. It takes her about two minutes to reappear. Next, I wait for the area to clear, and for Teddy to turn his back, so I can sneak into the storeroom without being noticed. Once inside, I don't bother to turn on the light. I stand to the side of the door and softly breathe.

It doesn't take long. The door opens, someone enters in the dark, goes straight for the third shelf, tips up a can of tomato sauce, and grabs what's underneath.

I flip on the light.

He's startled.

"How much did you get today, Teddy?"

Terrible Teddy stands with a ten spot in hand. "Funny meeting you here," he says, trying to regain his composure.

"You don't give up easy, do you? Give me the money, Teddy."

He reluctantly hands it over.

"You're busted."

"Damn."

"Don't swear."

"Darn."

"If I turn you in, Teddy, you'll be thrown out of school, put in juvie, meet other criminals, go downhill from there, and spend the majority of your life in some brand of confinement."

"Come on, it was only ten bucks," he says. "Esther's stealing from the lunch money, so I'm only stealing money that's already been stolen. How about if I confess to only being an accessory to the crime?"

"Sorry, Teddy, but it doesn't work that way."

"You gonna turn me in anyway?"

"No, I want to make you a deal."

"You want to split fifty-fifty?"

"No, I want to take you on a field trip."

"A what?"

"Field trip, just the two of us, next week."

"Where we going?"

"You'll find out next week if you can stay clean until then."

Teddy looks at me in disbelief. "That's all I gotta do and you won't turn me in?"

"Yep." I put out my hand to shake on it.

"Why are you doing this?" he asks as he reluctantly shakes.
"Because you got a problem."
"What, that I'm a criminal?"
"No, that you're a bad criminal, Teddy."

CHAPTER 29

Mrs. Chumley isn't at her desk when I walk into the Principal's office. I go straight to the inner office door and knock. "Eldin, you in there?"

The door opens and I'm shocked. Eldin looks more rested and relieved than if he just returned from a three month summer vacation.

"Sherlock, you're not going to believe what happened," he says, pulling me inside his office.

"Try me."

"The missing money came back. It showed up on the bank statement we got this morning."

I'm not surprised. "Was it deposited a few nights ago?" I ask.

"Yes, how did you know?"

"I went to night school." I pause. "You know who put it back into the account?"

"Yes."

I wonder if Ms. Mossy confessed or got caught.

"It was Mrs. Chumley," Eldin says.

"What?"

"She confessed."

"To what? Taking the money or putting it back?"

"Both."

This doesn't make sense. The only reason I can imagine Mrs. Chumley taking the money is to buy more smiley face stickers. "Are you sure?"

"We're not going to make a big broo-ha-ha out of this. The kids love Mrs. Chumley and telling them she is a thief would be horrible. She's already eligible for retirement, so we'll just give her a party with a cake and let her go."

"Was Ms. Mossy surprised?" I ask.

"Flabbergasted."

"Is she around? I'd like to talk with her."

"She should be in her office." Eldin seems almost giddy with all the happenings of the day. "I called the district, told them about the money, and they're going to delay the Monday meeting."

Something is wrong with this whole picture.

"You're having Mr. Lauder come in during seventh period?" Eldin asks. "If we could make that problem go away, it would be wonderful."

"Yeah, maybe."

"What are you going to do with him?" Eldin asks.

"I'm not sure."

"Mr. Sherlock, I certainly hope you know what you're doing. We just got out from under one rock, I'd hate to have Mr. Lauder bury us under another."

"Me, too."

I excuse myself and walk down the hall to Ms. Mossy's office. I knock on the door before I enter. "Can I have a minute of your time?" I ask.

"Certainly."

The office is neat as a pin. Computers are gone, desk empty, even the milk money file which rested on her cabinets has been put away. "Big day, huh?"

"Certainly has been so far," she says, remaining seated at her desk.

"I never would have suspected Mrs. Chumley as being one to cook the books," I admit.

"Neither did I."

"Let me ask you something, Fern," I say, and wait for her to nod. "To what do you contribute this year's incredible success in getting so many Ann Margaret students into magnet schools?"

"Our teachers, curriculum, and the extra efforts we make for our students the other schools don't."

"Such as?"

"The study program we developed to prepare the students taking the test."

"The one Mr. Mizzi started a few years ago?"

"Yes."

"But he no longer teaches that, does he?"

"No."

"He's taken it to the next level, hasn't he? In his own tutoring business?"

"He's found a need and he's filling it," she tells me. "You can't blame him for doing that."

"Of course not." I pause, give her a slight smile, and ask, "Do you suspect you might have done too well? I understand a lot of other schools are quite jealous of your success."

"There is enormous pressure on this school to perform, Mr. Sherlock. Our parents won't accept anything but success for their children." She pauses. "Isn't that the reason we're meeting with Lou Lauder this afternoon?"

"Yes," I answer. "And no."

"There's another agenda I'm not aware of?"

"When somebody makes a stink, it's sometimes best to make a deal, Ms. Mossy."

"If you can get the Lauder mess swept under the rug, I'm sure it will be appreciated by all, Mr. Sherlock."

"Well, maybe not by all." I walk to the door. "I appreciate you and Mr. Mizzi being there this afternoon."

"No problem."

I need a few minutes to get my thoughts straight, so I walk through the hall and out into the schoolyard where I see Esther Stiffarm out by the garden. "Excuse me," I call out to get her attention.

I approach quickly and when I meet her, she has a handful of radishes in one hand and a load of green onions in the other. "Garden came back pretty well after the big dig, huh?"

"You can't keep a good plant down, Mr. Sherlock."

"I have to hand it to you, Esther, you really know how to play the game when it comes to food."

She answers with a tentative, "Thank you."

"You have the best cafeteria staff in the entire city and there can only be one reason, and that is you, Esther Stiffarm."

She blushes.

"Would you mind joining Principal Puddle, me, and a few others in an informal get-together this afternoon?"

"Me?" she asks. "Why?"

"Because you are a big part of the success of this institution."

"How?"

"An army fights on its stomach, not its arms."

"I don't get it," she says.

"Oh, yes you do," I tell her, "and you should be praised for it." I inform her of the meeting place. "We'll see you in a few minutes."

In need some air to air out my thoughts, I take two laps before the bell ending sixth period goes off. I see the kids coming out of classrooms into the hallways and back into classrooms. Why can't life be as orderly as grammar school? The next bell rings to start seventh period and a bell goes off inside my brain.

It takes a few more synapses, but my stupidity from the morning debacle is eclipsed by a sudden afternoon thunderstorm of understanding. This morning I couldn't believe I could be so dumb and this afternoon I'm a genius.

I get out my cell, dial, and wait for the connection.

"Bree Bisonette, please. Richard Sherlock calling."

Bree doesn't bother with a hello. Instead, she says, "Now what?"

I tell her what I want her to do.

"You're kidding?"

"No, I'm serious."

"You want me to wire the hundred and fifty grand to Fumadoro today?"

"Exactly."

"The least we can do is make him wait ninety days," she says.

Richmond usually makes people wait at least one hundred and fifty days.

"No, I want him to have the money in his account today."

"I don't know if I can get it to him today." Bree is hedging.

"It's local and bank to bank. You can do it, Bree."

"Why am I doing this?"

"I got a way to smoke him out."

CHAPTER 30

Will Rodgers, American commentator, entertainer, and chronicler of American morals and miscues was famous for saying, "I never met a man I didn't like."

But Will Rogers never met Loudmouth Lou Lauder.

"What the heck is this all about?" Lou screams. "You pulled me out of court to come here?"

"It's Friday afternoon, Lou. You know as well as I know that nothing happens in the justice system on Friday afternoon."

He stands defiant. What a jerk.

Since grammar schools don't have conference rooms, Mrs. Chumley, evidently before her demise, set up the meeting in an empty classroom.

"Thank you all for joining me." I walk to the head of the class and take the position of the teacher. "I know it's seventh period, late in the day, but I promise this won't take long. I have to pick up my kids at three too."

Fern Mossy and Larry Mizzi are seated in the front row. Eldin, in the second row, has a tough time seeing over Esther's beehive. Jane Lauder is way off to the left with her husband standing at the edge of the room as if he's about to launch his closing argument. Thankfully, Winky Torelli sits in the back of the room.

Lou shouts out, "Has my daughter been accepted into Butkis Prep?"

"Lou, you're number two on the docket, but first I believe congratulations are in order."

The participants look to one another, wondering who's going to get a smiley face.

"Esther Stiffarm has once again been able to maintain the longest running kitchen staff in the Chicago public school system." I lead the subdued round of applause.

Esther beams in appreciation.

"Esther is able to do so because Esther is smart. She knows how to play the game and work the system to make her kitchen the best in the city." I pause to give my audience time to wonder what the heck I'm talking about.

"Almost every day, Esther does what she believes she has to do to keep her staff in place and in tip-top working order. She pilfers ten or so bucks from the money coming from the hot lunch kids." I pause to let that sink in. "If a sale is eight dollars, Esther rings up three, and palms five, but she has the good sense to write it down, so her accounting matches the register's final accounting of the day. Esther then slips the bills into her hair-do for safe-keeping until the lunch line ends. Way to go, Esther."

Esther's beam dims.

"Next, Esther takes a detour into the storeroom where she places the money under a can of refried beans to be picked up later by one of her workers. She does this a number of times per week, making sure each of her workers gets a few extra bucks. Now, twenty dollars a week might not seem like a lot to you people, but to one of her staff making minimum wage, it's quite a tip, and keeps them around year after year."

Esther's chin rests on her chest.

"Personally, Esther, I don't blame you one bit."

"I only did what I had to do to do my job," Esther says in her defense.

"It's funny," I say, "if it wasn't for Teddy Tulleners, who has a real eye for thievery, I don't think anyone would've ever noticed."

"I hate that kid," Esther says.

"If it is any consolation, Teddy is still smarting from that whupping you gave him."

"Is that what I'm going to get?" Esther asks.

"That's not for me to say," I tell her, and look towards her boss.

"Esther, I'm shocked," Eldin says.

"You shouldn't be, Eldin. Esther's only doing what a lot of people are doing around here."

"What's that?" Eldin asks.

"Doing what they think is the best for all concerned."

Every face in the place sports a look of bewilderment, except Loudmouth Lou. "Can we get on with this?" he interrupts. "I really don't care about ten crummy bucks under some refried beans. All I want to hear is my kid's getting into Butkis Prep."

"Congratulations, Lou."

"She's in?"

"No, but Elsa is, in my humble opinion, one of the smartest kids in the school. She's bright, clever, intelligent, and just like her Dad, knows how to play the game."

"Did she get in Butkis or not?"

"She flunked the test, Lou."

"No, she didn't."

"She got a seventy-nine."

"I don't care."

"You can't get in unless you score ninety or above," I remind him.

"Look at her grades, look what she's done. If she doesn't deserve to get in, nobody does."

"She got a seventy-nine, Lou," I repeat since he didn't listen to me the first time around, which is really no shock to my system.

"I don't care."

"And she got a seventy-nine on purpose."

There is a sudden hush in the room.

"What?"

"Elsa knew not getting a ninety was as good as flunking, so she settled for a seventy-nine. She knew all the answers and she purposely picked the wrong circles to fill in."

"No, no way, not my kid," Lou bellows.

"Elsa wanted to fail because she didn't want to go to Buttkick Prep. She had no interest in the place. They assign too much homework and don't have the activities she likes." I look at his wife. "You knew that, didn't you, Jane?"

The diminutive woman tries her best to melt into the chair and disappear.

"Elsa wants to go to a school with a dance program," I add.

"She does not," Lou argues.

Jane minutely shakes her head in the affirmative.

"Lou, you're so busy getting what you want for your daughter, you neglected to ask Elsa what she wants."

"That's not true."

"Yes, it is," Jane surprisingly says.

Lou's madder than a terrorist in the act, and he's ready to explode.

"Amazing what you can learn when you actually talk to your child, Lou."

"Don't you tell me what to do," Lou screams, pointing his finger at me. "I know what's best for my daughter."

"Elsa's a smart kid, Lou. Certainly smart enough to know how to play you."

"Listen, Sherlock—"

Jane cuts him off, saying, "He's right."

Lou stares down on his wife like she's a lying witness about to be dissected on the stand. "Whose side are you on?" Lou screams at Jane.

"Elsa's."

"She doesn't get into the best high school, she won't get into the best college." Lou speaks down to his wife as if she's the idiot in this picture.

"I'd rather see her happy than in Harvard," Jane answers. She stands, possibly for the first time in their married life, and meets her husband face to face.

"What the hell do you know?" Lou spits out.

"A hell of a lot more than you," Jane spits back.

I quickly move down the aisle and stand between the two before punches are thrown. "Enough."

Lou backs away.

There's a brief pause.

"Lou, I want you to let up on deporting Juan Hernandez." I ask him as nicely as I can, which isn't easy.

"No way."

"It's no fault of his what happened with Elsa," I tell him. "And Juan's mother is only trying to do the best for her child...just like you."

"No. He's a criminal." Lou's anger has shifted to me.

"He's thirteen and the nicest kid you'll ever meet," I try to reason with the man.

"I don't care. He's an illegal alien and doesn't belong in our country."

"It doesn't do you any good to hurt him."

Lou stares me straight in the eye with his now bloodshot eyes. "He'll be on his way back to Tijuana in two weeks."

It's pointless to argue with the man, who has to always win one battle, even after he's lost the war. I give up.

"Ya know, Lou," I say, "you're a real jerk."

Lou grabs his wife by the arm, pulling her toward him. "We're going home."

I move, so the two can depart. "Thanks for stopping by. Hope you enjoy your weekend."

The rest of the peanut gallery has sat in quiet shock, watching the players in the family drama exit stage left. You could cut the tension in the room with a dull butter knife.

"Winky, if you put Lou in the dunk tank in the next school carnival, the PTA will make a fortune."

"Is that why you brought me in here?" Winky asks. "To tell me that?"

"No, I like to give advice, even if nobody ever listens."

I move closer to my 'students' and peer down at Esther, who slumps into her chair like a mound of watery mac n' cheese. "Esther, why don't you go home? You look like you could use some refried beans yourself."

Fern Mossy and Larry start to rise from their desks to follow Esther out the door.

"Wait, you two, I haven't gotten to the real fun stuff yet."

"If Esther stole the money, then we're done here," Fern says.

"Not quite."

Eldin speaks up, "Esther only stole the cafeteria's money."

I finish his thought, "Which wouldn't explain Mrs. Chumley's sticky fingers." Although, Mrs. Chumley's fingers were always sticky from sticking those smiley faces on everybody.

"Esther's money is on a separate accounting," Eldin says.

"Correct," I tell him. "There's a reason why you're the principal, Eldin." I smile down at him.

I take a breath, and continue, "There's all kinds of crazy money floating around this school. The only place there doesn't seem to be any is in the playground, which got obliterated by people looking for crazy money."

I fold my arms across my chest, look down on the participants, get a brief whiff of Stinky's perfume, and say, "The only thing I've been certain about since I got in the middle of this mess is that you people are the absolute best at what you do."

The room is deathly quiet. They all know something is coming, but they're not sure what.

I launch into today's lesson plan. "I don't envy you folks. Dealing with parents like jerk-brained Lou Lauder would be torture on a daily basis. What parents do here is absurd; everybody figures out the system and tries to manipulate to their benefit. If someone doesn't put a stop to parents holding their kids back a year or two, so they can be the biggest and smartest in school, soon you're going to need a parking lot for the eighth graders' cars. And you're going to have three-hundred pounders on the kickball team with girls equal in development to the Dallas Cowboy Cheerleaders on the sideline."

Nobody laughs at my joke.

"You have all these parents demanding so much for their kids, and what do you do? You make every effort to give it to them because you also believe your students deserve the best. You initiate classes to help them with the magnate test, have extra study sessions, provide advanced instruction in certain studies, and I'm sure a lot of other stuff that my daughter would never consider." I pause and stop at the pair in the front row. "Mr. Mizzi recognized the need years ago. He opens up a tutoring business for the parents who can afford the expense, and starts raking in the profits. Ms. Mossy buys the better students laptop computers, which no other school in the district would even dream of having. The parents demand and you answer, all in the belief of what's best for the children. I have to hand it to you people, you delivered. Congratulations are in order."

No one beams, they learned their lesson from Esther's beaming too soon.

I move back to the front of the room and raise one finger before I speak again. "There's only one problem. The school only has so much money per student to work with, and that's where the expert comes in."

Eldin stares at his shoes. He knows what's coming.

"After thirty years as a principal, nobody knows how to finagle the system better than Eldin. He robs Peter to pay Paul, borrows from plumbing to pay for printing, and scrimps on corn chips to pay for computer chips. With Mrs. Chumley's accounting prowess, he's able to mix and match monies each month, and come to a bottom line that always equals out. His creative credits and dubious debits are the work of a master money manipulator."

"I only did it to better the standards in our school," Eldin says.

"And I really can't blame you one bit, but hanging the rap on Mrs. Chumley was a little much."

"She's retiring and moving to Florida," he says.

"Yeah, I pretty much figured that."

"I only did what I did for the benefit of the students," Eldin says.

"And in some manner we all applaud you for it," I say sincerely.

There is a voice from the back of the room. "This really doesn't concern me, I'm leaving," Winky announces, rising from her seat.

"But it will," I tell her. "Sit tight, Ms. Torelli. I promise I'll get to you in a minute. Patience is a virtue."

She's not real thrilled to sit back down.

I clear my throat and start in on the next chapter of the sordid textbook. "But as is the case with many on-going practices of deception, something goes wrong. A fly dive-bombs the ointment, a left hand doesn't know what the right just did, or somebody turned right when everyone else went left." I smile at my analogies, but the audience doesn't seem to appreciate them as much as I do.

"What happens? Money, which isn't there to begin with, is missing from the stolen money. Eldin panics. He doesn't know what to do or where to look. The fact Fern discovered the malfeasance should've stood out like a bad test score but didn't, tells me that Eldin has so much faith in his own people, he'd never suspect anyone on his staff. This is where you come into the picture, Winky."

Her head pops up and her eyes widen. "Me?"

"The only cash flowing through the place on a weekly basis is the milk money, and since it flows through your fingers, you become the logical suspect."

"That's sick."

"Especially to someone who's lactose intolerant."

Again, no one laughs at my joke. I have to work on my delivery.

"To be honest with you folks, I couldn't figure out what was going on. I barked up more trees than a dog with a squirrel complex. I couldn't make heads or tails of Mrs. Chumley's spreadsheets or Fern Mossy's check register. I felt like the kid in the last seat in the last row that's already done third grade twice and is destined for another lap around the same track." I pause. "And to make matters all the more confusing, the school achieves the highest number of students being admitted to magnet schools in its history. Congratulations were in order, but I wasn't sure whom to congratulate. I asked myself, why this year? All that you've been doing under the educational table, you've been doing for years, and all of a sudden you completely blow away the competition. How? Why?"

Larry Mizzi straightens up suddenly.

"I congratulate you all, but I wouldn't be too quick to take too many bows because there were other systems to be figured out, and one person did exactly that. The only difference was in the way he did it. He did it illegally."

Larry slinks back down in his seat.

"Elsa Lauder wasn't the only kid who went into the magnet school exam phenomenally well prepared. There were a lot of kids. They might not have known the answers, but they were well studied in what questions would be asked. Mr. Mizzi, who I'm sure is a very good computer teacher, is also a very good computer hacker. He was able to break into the CPS system and retrieve the questions on the test. All he had to do is use those questions in his Tutor Tent class to guarantee the success of his tutorages."

"That is the most absurd thing I've ever heard," Larry speaks up.

"Say what you want, Larry, it really doesn't make much of a difference anymore."

His ire changes to wonder.

"Don't ask me how I know this, but your tent is coming down this afternoon. Your system is being hacked, a virus is eating away at your computer's innards, and if I were you, you might want to invest in a blackboard."

"What?"

"It's happening as we speak."

"You're lying!"

"No, Larry, I'm told the easiest computer to hack is one that does a lot of hacking. Ironic, isn't it?"

Larry pulls out a new laptop out of nowhere, opens it, and starts to pound away at its keyboard.

I move from the front of the room to where Larry sits. "I'd like everyone to take special notice of the laptop Larry is using. It's one that used to be in your school. Fern Mossy sold the school's unused laptops to her friend, Larry, which I certainly hope for a fair price. And it was a good thing she did because Fern took the proceeds, deposited the money into the school's account, and was pretty much able to turn down the burner on the cooked books. When she told Eldin about her fix to the situation, he wasn't pleased. They had quite a row about it in his office the other morning, but what was done was done. Now, in their minds only one problem remained: The district coming in to audit their books. If that happened there'd be more questions asked than in a third grade sex ed class. They needed a scapegoat not only to placate the district and school board, but to throw suspicion into a netherworld of unresolved issues. They figured they could manipulate the whole shebang into a never-ending muddle of money morass, which they knew they were adept at doing. All they needed was a fall guy or girl. And who was chosen to step up and do what had to be done to protect the children? Hello, Mrs. Chumley."

I watch as Larry Mizzi's face goes from red to crimson to almost purple as he pounds on his computer and sees its screen perform a series of colorful flip-flops.

"This morning, I was relieved of my duties and taken off the case, but I'm one of those guys who, when money is missing, can't stop looking." I shrug my shoulders. "The only difference between me and the prospecting parents is I don't use a shovel."

Except for Larry's eyes, all others are trained on me.

"I know it's not Esther. Her money doesn't cross the bridge into the school's accounts. So, I'm back to you, Winky."

"You have no reason to suspect me," she counters.

"And I didn't until I saw Larry Mizzi make a visit to your home."

Fern Mossy's head snaps toward Larry quicker than a high speed Google search.

"Yeah, I thought Larry was playing around on you, too, Fern, but rest assured, Larry might be a hacker and a cheat, but he's no lousy lothario. He was over at the Torelli's humble abode to collect the money she owed him for Arleta Torelli's tutoring sessions." I turn to the PTA president. "Winky, you must've been having your own cash flow problems, and you decided not to pay, figuring anyone who could get your daughter into Buttkick Prep had to be a crook. No offense to little Arleta."

"I had no idea." Winky keeps up the pretense. "You know I'm a single, working parent and don't have the money to defend myself, so you're picking on me."

"If you could afford a lawyer, I definitely suggest Lou Lauder, but there is really no need. You were only doing what you thought was the best for your child, and I have to give you credit for that." I pause to let the compliment resonate. "But it did dawn on me that it was your signature on the check I received when I won the grand prize at the PTA Casino Night. I don't know how you manipulated the PTA books to free up a little money for the Tutor Tent, but I'm sure it won't take long to figure out. If I ask Mrs. Chumley, I'll bet she'll figure it out in a few minutes."

"You can't prove anything," Winky says.

"You're correct, I can't, nor do I care to even try," I admit.

"You can't prove anything about me, either," Larry adds.

"Correct, again," I agree. "Without Fern admitting she knew about the hacking and the data now unhacked and unattainable, I'd be pretty much dead in the water trying to prove anything.

"But shame on you, Larry, for putting Fern in such a difficult spot. She was betwixt and between trying to balance her love for you with her desire to do what is best for her students. That was cold, Larry."

Fern doesn't speak. I wonder if she's considering putting Larry on hold?

Winky rises first. "I'm leaving. I don't have to sit and listen to these lies and accusations."

"Goodbye."

Larry rises next, shaking his laptop as if trying to get the data to drop out or drop back in. "You can't do this to me."

"I didn't and I have no idea who did," I lie. It's really just a little, white lie, and compared to the ones this group tells, it's whiter than Tide white.

Fern gets up and follows Larry out of the classroom. Sweet couple.

I look at the clock. It's almost the end of seventh period.

Eldin and I are the only ones left.

"I was only trying to do what's best for the children," Eldin says.

"I've heard similar excuses from a few ex-governors of this state, Eldin."

"What am I going to do now?" he asks.

"I'm not sure."

"What would you do?" he asks.

"Nothing."

"Nothing?"

"I personally don't believe kids should be punished for the idiocy of their parents, and I also don't believe they should be punished for the misdeeds of their teachers and school officials no matter how egregious those people may have been." Big word, but I'm sure Eldin knows its meaning.

"But nothing?" he asks again.

"Arleta and the other kids, who don't have the mental chops, will flunk out of Buttkick Prep and be back in the neighborhood schools where they belong in a few months. Larry will go out of business, he just doubled his overhead, and he hardly impresses me as a business dynamo. I'd turn a blind eye to Esther. She's so scared now she'll have to figure out another way to pilfer a few extra bucks, which I promise she will do. If you don't mind, let me handle Terrible Teddy. Winky's PTA term is up. I'd let her go just for the relief of not having to smell her perfume any longer. Get Fern Mossy transferred. She's a liar, but like you, her heart is in the right place with the exception of her choice of men."

Eldin sits, worn out as an out-of-shape marathoner. "This is the first year in my career that I can't wait for summer vacation to begin."

"You don't have long to wait, Eldin."

Eldin sits lost in thought and probably lost in thoughts of disgrace.

I make one last point, "The only one in all this I feel sorry for is Juan Hernandez. It is a shame what's happening to him."

Eldin has only the strength to shake his head to and fro.

The bell rings. Outside in the hallways doors slam open, kids run to their lockers, screams of absolute joy echo through the halls like escaping gulag prisoners; only a couple more weeks to go until summer vacation.

"I got to go pick up my kids. Have a great summer vacation, Eldin."

"You, too."

CHAPTER 31

H"i, Care."
"Hi, Dad."
"Did you learn anything new is school today?"
"No. Can we stop at Arby's on the way home?"
"No."

I proceed in the pick-up line past Tessie the Terminator. "I see you got your car back," she says as I creep by her. "That's a shame."

"You'd miss me and my Toyota if I wasn't around, Tessie."

"No, I wouldn't. Keep moving."

Kelly is, of course, nowhere near the edge of the sidewalk. "Care, do you see your sister anywhere?"

"Who'd want to see her?"

Kelly is talking with some girl fifty yards away. She has her notebook out, scribbling away as she interviews a possible source. I honk my horn. "Beep, beep."

Tessie comes over to whack my back fender. "Keep moving."

I scream, "Kelly, get over here."

My oldest sashays over, at her own pace, and climbs in the back seat. "God, Dad, you're embarrassing me. I was in the middle of asking a possible witness important questions."

"What questions?"

"I had to find out if Tommy Gilmore asked Marcie Bailey out yet."

I finally pull away from the curb and allow the line to start moving again.

"Dad, are you sure we can't stop somewhere on the way home? I'm really hungry."

"Yes, Care, we're going to stop."

"Great! Where?"

"Your mother's house. We have to pick up the clothes you're wearing tomorrow. You did pack, didn't you?"

"Kinda," Care answers.

"What does 'kinda' mean?"

"It was hard to decide," Kelly says. "You didn't tell us if it

233

was a theme wedding or not."

I'm about three blocks from what used to be my house. "I told you to wear the best you have."

"You didn't tell us what color."

"What difference would that make?"

"We don't want to clash with the bride or the maid of honor," Kelly says. "Duh."

"If there is one person you won't clash with, it'll be the maid of honor."

I pull into their driveway. "Get in there, pack up your stuff, and let's go."

The two jump out of the car. I sit. My phone rings three seconds later. It's Lester Oland.

"Doctor's appointment scheduled at four-thirty."

"Today?"

"Prescription ordered. Can't wait to be filled."

"Four-thirty? I don't know if I can make it in time."

"FBI waits for no man, especially on Friday afternoon with Cubs playing a night game."

"Save me a seat, Lester. This one I want to see."

I hang up. This is going to be tight. If I drop off the kids at the apartment and have to fight city streets downtown, I'll never make it. If I take the expressway now, and it's not too jammed, it'll be close, but I certainly don't want my kids in the middle of an FBI raid. I wait a few minutes and try to decide what to do.

Time ticks off my clock. If the kids don't hurry up and get out here, I'll be late no matter what route I take.

I honk the horn in a rendition similar to Tiffany's. I wait. Nobody exits the house. I get out of the car, stand on the front lawn, and yell towards the window of Kelly's bedroom. "Kelly, hurry up and get down here. We have to go. Now!"

The second floor bedroom window opens. "What is your problem, Dad?"

"Hurry up."

"I can't decide what to wear."

"I don't care. We have to go and we have to go now."

"Why?"

I hesitate. Kelly is the last person I'd want to know of my destination.

"Is it something to do with the case?" she asks.

"Yes."

"I'll get Care. We'll be right there."

The window slams shut. Two minutes later, they run from the house, each carrying armloads of clothes.

"You're going to a wedding, not on a six month cruise."

"We'll decide what to wear tomorrow," Kelly says, heading for the car.

"Are we going to go bust somebody now, Dad?" Care asks.

"No."

"Are you going to get all the people in the same room and figure out who did it?" Kelly asks as we all climb into the Toyota.

"No."

"Are we going to set up a sting operation?" Care asks.

"No."

I check the clock in the car. I have an hour at best. There's no way I can drop the kids at the apartment and still make it.

"Then what, Dad?"

I start the car and pull out of the driveway and head toward the Edens. I think quickly and come up with an alternate plan. "Kelly, get Tiffany on the phone for me."

"Is Tiffany going to be in on the collar with us?" Care asks.

"I certainly hope not."

"Hi, Tiffany. It's Kelly. Dad wanted me to call you." There is a pause. "I don't know why. Want me to ask him?" Another pause. Kelly speaks to me, "Tiffany doesn't want to talk to you because she's mad at you."

Oh, jeesh.

"She says you're a no-good quitter, who leaves the kitchen as soon as it gets hot."

How would Tiffany know that? She's never cooked a meal in her life. "Tell her I need a favor."

"Tiffany she says she doesn't do favors for people who don't have the courage of their convection oven."

"Give me the phone," I demand.

"No, Dad," Care says. "You're not supposed to talk on the phone while you're driving."

"It's an emergency!"

"An emergency, cool!" Kelly yells out. "Are you going to turn on the siren?"

"Toyotas don't have sirens."

Care says, "This is really getting exciting."

I get on the Edens. Traffic is thick, but it's moving. "Give me the phone."

Kelly reluctantly hands it over.

"Tiffany, listen. I know you're mad at me, but I'm going to make it up to you. I promise."

She, of course, asks, "How?"

"By proving to you that I'm not a quitter."

"That's a pretty tall order of a martini, Mr. Sherlock."

"Just watch the girls for a couple of hours for me. I'll explain it all to you later."

"When?"

"Later when I can talk."

"You seem to be talking just fine right now, Mr. Sherlock."

"Could you watch the girls for a few hours. Please?"

"Oh, all right," she relents.

"Thank you."

"You know what my problem is, Mr. Sherlock?" she asks.

What would be the point of answering, I have less than an hour. "What, Tiffany?"

"I'm just too nice of a person."

What a horrible cross to have to bear.

"I'll drop off the girls at your building in a half hour. Be downstairs to meet us."

"We have a thing called a doorman at my building, Mr. Sherlock."

"Fine, alert him. I'll be there in a half hour."

I don't know how to hang up Kelly's fancy phone, so I hand it back to her.

"Dad, are you sure this has nothing to do with the case we've been on?" Care asks.

"Positive."

"Are we going to work on the case after the wedding tomorrow?" Care further questions.

"No."

"Why not? We're really getting good at it."

"Who said that?"

"Nobody, Dad," Kelly explains. "We can feel it. It's like a heredity thing. Your DNA generating into our generation."

Traffic creeps along as we head for the Kennedy. "I didn't know there was a detective gene in the pool."

"I'm sure I got one," Care says.

"Have you considered sending me into the Tutor Tent undercover, Dad?" Kelly suggests. "I'm really good at sniffing the truth out of stuff."

"No."

"Why not?"

"That case is over," I surprise them. "They found the missing milk money."

"What?"

"It was all a big mistake. The money showed up in the school's bank account this morning and it was all over. Big misunderstanding."

"You're kidding!"

"As Shakespeare would say 'much ado about nothing.'"

"Oh wow, that's horrible. I was really looking forward to busting somebody in that case," Kelly says.

"Yeah, it would have really been super to see Mr. Mizzi in an orange jumpsuit, behind bars, and mopping down toilet stalls with Big Bubba," Care laments.

"Sorry to disappoint you."

Kelly and Care moan and groan until I pull into Tiffany's lakefront building's circular driveway at a little past four.

"I'll pick you up in a couple of hours," I tell them as the doorman comes out of the lobby of the high-rise building.

"Where are you going, Dad?"

"I have to go meet Detective Oland on the other side of town."

"Why?"

"I have to meet him in front of a restaurant, which serves great Peking Duck." I do my best to not lie and merely evade the truth.

"What are we going to eat?" Care asks.

"I'll bring back a doggie bag."

"You mean a ducky bag?" Care says.

"So to speak. Have Tiffany take you to dinner at one of her fancy restaurants," I suggest.

"Dad," Kelly says, "I'm not buying any of this. Something is going down that you're not telling us."

"Would I ever do that to you, Kelly?"

"Yes."

The doorman opens the passenger's side door. "Hey,

buddy," he says. "Get this piece of junk out of here. We got a service entrance, use it."

"They're guests of Tiffany Richmond," I tell the snobby brat wearing an epilated, ill-fitting, faux-military uniform.

"Sure?"

"Positive." I order the girls. "Out, girls. I'll pick you up in a couple of hours."

"I'm not buying it, Dad. I'm not buying it."

"Good, Kelly. I'm happy to see you've learned frugality."

"What's that?"

**

At 4:29 p.m., I park behind Lester's unmarked. He sits inside. I slide in next to him.

"Medicine almost ready to be administered, Sherlock."

"Looks like a heavy dose."

To the unsuspecting the street is as normal as any Friday, but to the people in the know, like me, the curtain is about to come down. About a hundred yards to my left and to my right are unmarked vans, no doubt filled with agents in SWAT gear. There has to be at least one van parked in the back near the trash cans to release the squad that'll go in the rear door. I see a couple of women, who aren't Asian or looking to buy a set of designer chopsticks, hanging around the street. They each wear billowy blouses to hide the heat they're assuredly packing.

"Where's Anna May?"

"She's inside," Lester says.

"Are they going on her signal?"

"No, going to wait to get last measure of proof, to make pudding sweeter for court consumption."

We sit and wait in silence, our eyes trained on the front door of the Ho Lee Dong One Stop Cancer Clinic. A few minutes go by.

"Oh, Mr. Sherlock."

I must be dreaming, a nightmare of words shakes me to my core.

The car's back doors open. I almost jump out of our skin as Tiffany and my girls climb inside.

"Hi, Dad," Care says.

"I knew something was going down," Kelly says. "You can't

238

fool me, Dad."

"What are you doing here?"

"We told Tiffany what you told us," Care says, "and Tiffany told us about the Ding Dong Cancer Clinic."

"We put two and two together," Kelly says.

"And vi-o-la," Tiffany says.

"Isn't it voi-la?" I ask.

"There's no way we're going to miss this," Kelly says.

"Nothing like taking family along for interesting ride," Lester says.

"How'd you find me?"

"What difference does that make?" Tiffany asks. "This is going to be awesome."

I hate the word *awesome*.

"You can't keep good detectives, like us, down, Dad," Care says.

I'm way past frantic. "You people don't belong here. You could get hurt. A major FBI operation is about to take place."

"And we wouldn't miss it for the world."

The UPS truck pulls up in front of the clinic.

"Time to deliver us some evil," Lester says.

The driver gets out of the truck and heads for the back to open the rear doors. "Hey, what happened to my little, brown buddy?" Tiffany asks.

"He got the day off to spend time with his family," I say as the new guy loads packages onto this dolly cart.

"I'll bet he wears paisley patterns when he's not working," Tiffany says as UPS man makes his way through the front doors.

Thirty seconds come off the clock and all hell breaks loose. FBI agents, dressed in flak jackets and carrying automatic weapons, burst out of the vans like rats from off a flooding sewer, and go through the front door of the clinic like geeks trying to be the first to buy the next series of iPhones. No shots are fired, but there is enough screaming going on inside to rival a theme park's Halloween Horror Night.

"Can we go in too, Dad?"

"No."

Tiffany tries to open the car door, but it's locked.

"He who has key to key, has power to protect," Lester says, smiling my way.

Paddy wagons pull up around us, as do a few ambulances. Their doors open to allow for the future crush of passengers.

The first group to be escorted out the front door are Dr. Ho Lee Dong, his Asian nurse, and four or five other individuals dressed in semi-official medical scrubs. Dr. Dong sports a pair of silver handcuffs on his wrists. These are not the accessories to wear at the start of your weekend.

Next out are a number of the patients who file out in signal file. If anything, this event will probably scare the cancer out of them. They are lined up, and herded into the paddy wagon.

Anna May Wong comes out next, sees Lester's car and hurries over. Her initial question, "Couldn't find a babysitter, Sherlock?"

"I found one, but she's not very good at her job."

The FBI agents come out of the building and are quickly replaced by the evidence techs on their way in. A perimeter is quickly set up with yellow tape, which I believe is a totally absurd method of sealing a crime scene.

Lester gets out of the car, so do I. The girls and Tiffany continue to struggle to unlock the unlockable doors.

"The doc had a great scam going," Anna says.

"The patients never had cancer, did they?" I ask.

"They thought they did because Dong did the diagnosis," Anna says. "Then he was nice enough to order chemo for them but only dripped saline into their arms. Not only was he scamming Medicare, but shipping the real stuff back to China for a hefty profit."

"The FBI should reward you, Sherlock," Anna says.

"An official FBI smiley face on my collar, I can't wait."

CHAPTER 32

I bang on the bedroom door. "Hurry up."
"God, Dad, what is your problem?" is the reply.
"My problem is that we're going to be late."
The door opens. Kelly and Care walk out. I stand in immediate shock. I can't believe what I see. The two look gorgeous. Each is dressed in a print dress, matching shoes, hair perfect, and just enough make-up.
"You have to do something for me," I say.
"What now, Dad?"
"You both have to slow down."
"You just yelled at us to hurry up."
"No, you have to slow down. You're growing up way too fast."

***

The six-hundred bucks Herman shelled out for the Church of the Everlasting Sanctuary of Love and Natural Goodness was money well spent. The apartment looks great. They pushed the furniture around to make an aisle, added a small podium for the altar, and rolled out a red runner on the floor for the bride to walk on. There are flowers, bunting, streamers, and crepe paper strewn everywhere, making the apartment a festooned facility of wedding frivolity. The flute player is off to the side, warming up with a rendition of "Feelings." The minister is wearing an ensemble that would be the envy of the Dalai Lama, topped off with a tied-dyed clerical collar to add religious authenticity to his authority.
Herman is dressed, or cloaked, in a white tuxedo tarp complete with silver buttons, bow tie, and boutonniere.
"Gee, Herman, you look super, like a flowering formal tee-pee."
"Here, Sherlock." He hands me a four-inch ring box.
I open immediately to see a silver band, which looks more like a chain link than a wedding band. "Isn't there supposed to be two of these?" I ask.

"Ludmila's bringing hers. She had to get it sized last night."

"Did she find something blue to wear?"

"I don't know," Herman says, giddy with excitement, "but I can't wait to find out."

There are six or seven other guests in the room, two of which are Herman's size. I don't see anyone wearing a Usanka hat or eating borscht.

"Dad, what are we supposed to do?" Care asks.

I hand her a container of dried leaves. "You and Kelly throw these on the floor in front of Ludmila as she walks up the aisle."

"What is it?"

"Rose petals."

"Funniest looking roses I've ever seen," Kelly says. "Plus, they smell funny."

"They didn't have any dried roses, so I substituted bathroom potpourri that was on sale at Walgreens."

"Oh gross, Dad."

"No, it's not. It's festive."

It's a few minutes past eleven and the expectation in the room increases. The minister waits at this podium rehearsing his speech, the flute player works through "Every Breath You Take," after his sparkling covers of "Proud Mary" and "Old Time Rock and Roll." I can't wait to hear him do the "Hokey Pokey."

Ten minutes go by and we're all still standing around making small talk, waiting for the door to open, and the beautiful bride to enter. It doesn't happen. After another ten minutes and renditions of "Macarena" and "The Chicken Dance," we all find a place to sit. Nobody says much. There's really not much to say, but a heck of a lot to think about.

Finally, at 11:45 there is a commotion on the other side of the entry door. The guest of honor has arrived and everyone gives off a huge sigh of relief, Herman's being the loudest. The flutist launches into "Wedding March" as I run over to open the door to welcome the other half of the wedding party.

No bride.

It's two guys in red and blue shirts balancing the longest cardboard pizza box I've ever seen. "Where do you want us to put it?" the guy in the front asks.

The minister comes from his podium spot and directs the

boys to the table adjacent to the flowing smoothie pyramid, currently not running. "We brought some extra cheesy bread and hot peppers," one of the guys says. "No extra charge."

The other guy says, "That'll be a hundred sixty-seven dollars and thirty-two cents."

Herman pulls out four fifties. "Here, keep the change."

"Thanks, Mister," the kid says. "Congratulations. I really love your suit."

By this time the flute player has exhausted his entire repertoire and starts in again on "Feelings." We all know Ludmila isn't going to show. I have a feeling her and Petrov are in a tattoo parlor getting matching Lenin likenesses on their arms, paid for with money meant for a wedding dress and diamond tiara.

The festivities quickly turn into a funeral with the each guest coming up to Herman and offering his or her condolences.

"I'm so sorry, Herman."

"Better luck next time."

"Next time try Poland. Polish women are more desperate than Russkies."

I feel sorry for my obese friend. No one likes to be left alone, especially at the altar. This is worse than being put on hold.

The three of us are the last to leave.

"Don't say it, Sherlock," he tells me.

"Say what, Herman?"

"I told you so."

"I would never say that, Herman. I'm sorry she left you standing, but 'tis better to have loved and lost than never to have loved at all."

"Easy for you to say, Sherlock."

"Is there anything I can do for you, Herman?"

"Cancel my debit and credit cards."

"You might have to do that yourself, Herman. Anything else I can do?"

"No, I think I'll start in on the pizza and keep eating until I feel better."

"Mind if my girls take a few pieces for the road?"

"As long as they take 'em from the middle," Herman qualifies. "I really love those cheesy crusts."

I signal the girls to load up on the pizza and on the way out, tell them to open the potpourri and leave it on the table. With all the cheese about to be consumed, it will be best to have something to counter a possible gas explosion.

CHAPTER 33

On Monday morning, I call Lester and ask him to do me one more favor. He's not wild about it, but he owes me. His name was in both the Tribune and the Sun Times Sunday editions as the detective who broke up a major Medicare scam going on in Chinatown.

My name, of course, was never mentioned. I don't care. If Lester can help me out here, that'll be thanks enough.

At ten a.m., I arrive at Pat Nixon/Ann Margaret and am saddened not to hear the chipper voice of Mrs. Chumley as I enter the principal's office. No sticker for me today.

Eldin has Terrible Teddy Tulleners waiting for me in his office.

"Where are we going?" Teddy asks as we make our way into my car.

"I want it to be a surprise, Teddy."

"It's a surprise this car still runs," he says.

"Hey, it gets me where I want to go," I tell him. "And more importantly, it gets me back."

"Let's hope."

An hour later, we are both being thoroughly patted down before we make our way into the Metropolitan Correctional Center.

My narration of the tour is pretty spotty. There isn't much audio needed to add to the visuals of prisoners crammed four to a cell, guards carrying big sticks, inmate work crews, and best of all, the solitary confinement ward. Teddy doesn't have a lot of questions, either. Matter of fact, there is little said until I pull up in front of his school a few hours later.

"Hope you enjoyed our little field trip, Teddy."

Looking over at me, his face remains as pale as it was while we were still on the tour.

"And if that wasn't enough of a good time, Teddy, wait 'til you see how the inmates live in Joliet. That place makes the MCC look like a vacation paradise."

Teddy slowly gets out of the car, but before shutting the door behind him, he says, "Thanks, Mr. Sherlock."

"You're welcome, Teddy."
I make sure he's inside the school before pulling away.

**

Lester calls me back after lunch and says we're all set. It is out of his jurisdiction, but he has a good friend in the Sheriff's Office who will be happy to help me out.
"Thanks, Lester."
"No better back to scratch than the scratcher of your own back."
This is not one of the better Lester's Charlie Chanisms, but I get the idea.
I call Tiffany.
"What, Mr. Sherlock?"
"Can you pick me up at three?"
"What for?"
"I want to prove to you that I'm not a quitter."
"And how are you going to do that?"
"You'll have to pick me up to find out."
She gives me one of her Tiffany harrumphs. "Oh, I guess so." She adds another softer harrumph. "I'm just too nice of a girl, that's my problem."
"Yeah, right, Tiffany."
She shows up at three-thirty, which is when I figured she'd show up. I get in her car. "Get on the Kennedy, then take the Stephenson."
"Why?"
"I'm going to prove to you I'm not a quitter."
"Oh yeah, that's gonna happen."
About twenty minutes into the trip, I say, "You know, you shouldn't be so hard on Bree, Tiffany."
"Bree Bitch-o-Nay was trying to come between me and my dad, Mr. Sherlock."
"No, she wasn't because your dad won't let anyone get close enough to him to come between anybody."
Tiffany gives me an odd but knowingly honest look.
"Bree has the same problem as you, Tiffany. She loves a man who doesn't know how to return love. If it's not easy for you, Tiffany, it's even harder for her."
Tiffany doesn't speak. A tear forms in her eye.

"I know it's hard not to have your love returned, but it's not your fault. It is nothing you've ever done. Your father just doesn't know how to love the people who love him."

"I've tried," she says, sniffling.

"I know you have and that's really all you can do. You just have to keep loving him and hoping for the best." I pause. "But while you do that, don't take your frustrations out on someone else. That doesn't do anybody any good."

We travel the rest of the way in silence.

***

Officer Mike Mallory looks like a Cook County Sheriff: tall, crew cut, wearing wrap-around sunglasses. He waits for us in front of the Fumadoro residence.

"What are we doing here, Mr. Sherlock? I thought you already gave up on this case," Tiffany says as we get out of her car.

"It's not over 'til the fat lady sings, Tiffany."

"Aretha Franklin's here?"

Officer Mike gets out of his car to meet us. "I hope you didn't have to wait long." I apologize in advance.

"No."

"You got the paperwork from Lester Oland?"

"Yes. It's at the station."

"Shall we?"

Tiffany has no clue what's going on. We walk up the path to the front door and I push the bell.

"Guantanamera."

"God, I hate that song," Tiffany says.

Don Diego Fumadoro opens the door, puffing on a cigar the size of a pipe bomb. "What the heck are you doing here?"

I smile.

Mike speaks, "Mr. Don Diego Fumadoro?"

"Yes."

"You're under arrest."

"What?"

Tiffany is almost as shocked as Fumadoro.

"You're under arrest. Please put out the cigar. You're coming with me."

"Under arrest for what?"

"Arson."

"Arson?" he blurts out. "What did I burn up?"

"One hundred and fifty grand of classic cigars."

Mike Mallory slaps a pair of cuffs on Mr. Fumadoro, shuts the front door, and leads the man into the rear seat of his squad car. He gives me a smile as his way of saying good-bye.

We wait until the two pull away. "See, Tiffany, it's never over until it's over."

"Or until the smoke clears," she says.

***

As I may have mentioned previously, there is good and bad in every job. One bad aspect of being a Chicago police detective is you have to come in contact with a number of slimy lawyers, who bend the law, find loopholes, and use unbelievably clever and dastardly means to clear their obviously guilty clients in courts of law. One of the good aspects of being a Chicago police detective is you get to know the best slimy lawyers, who are incredibly successful bending the law, finding loopholes, and using clever and dastardly methods to keep their clients out of the jails for crimes they obviously committed. In other words, you know who to call when the need arises.

Robert "Riff" Wrangler, Attorney at Law, has gotten more criminals back on the street than a drug kingpin with a fistful of bribes. Professionally, I consider Riff a despicable and disgusting wart on our society. Personally, he is one of the smartest men I've ever met, honest in a most absurd way, and the man I'd want on my side if I ever needed a defender.

I pay him a visit Tuesday morning.

"What are you doing here, Sherlock? I haven't seen you since I destroyed your testimony in the Randolph case a year or so ago."

"Yes, that was a pleasant, memorable experience for me," I say facetiously.

"You thought I was a real jerk," Riff says.

"Not as bad as some." I sit in one of the two chairs facing his desk.

"What can I do for you?" he asks, lacing his fingers together as if he's about to say grace.

I give him the file and explain the problem as I see it. He

asks a few questions. We talk for maybe fifteen minutes.

"Bottom line, Riff, can you fix it?"

"Sure."

When Riff says he can fix it, Riff can fix it.

"How much?"

"Three grand."

I pull out my checkbook and make out a check for that amount.

"What's the name again?" he asks.

"Juan, Juan Hernandez." I hand him my check. "Address is in the file. I'll let him know you'll be calling."

"I'll get right on it."

I nod.

Riff fingers my check as he stands up to bid me farewell. "Should I ask why you're doing this, Sherlock?"

"No."

We shake hands and I make sure to wipe mine off on my pants as soon as I'm out the door.

I feel a little lighter walking down the hallway to the elevator, no doubt due to my checkbook becoming so much slimmer in the last few minutes.

It was nice being on a roll.

THE END.

A claim was filed in the State of Kentucky in 2012 for damages due to fire for the loss of a multitude of tobacco products. The claim was initially cleared and scheduled for payment, but was rejected later in a court ruling, when the claimant admitted it was a series of small fires.

In 2013 a Corona del Mar, California teacher and in 2014 a Palos Verdes, California tutor were convicted of hacking into national testing organization's computers and retrieving actual SAT and ACT test questions and answers.

In 2013, it was estimated a total of $47 billion in Medicare payments were fraudulent. Phony medical claims, pill dispensaries, phantom treatments, and plagiarized billing, were a few of many deceptive practices used. Unfortunately, Medicare thievery in America has become as common as the common cold.

Thank you very much for reading The Case of the Missing Milk Money. I certainly hope you enjoyed my novel, and if you did, please let others know of your good reading fortune. The easiest way being through cyberspace via social media networks such as Amazon, Facebook, LinkedIn, Goodreads, and Twitter. Please put in a good review to the above and to your friends, contacts, and fellow readers. It will be greatly appreciated.

About Jim Stevens

Jim Stevens was born in the East, grew up in the West, schooled in the Northwest and spent twenty-three winters in the Midwest. Jim Stevens has been writing for over thirty years. Usually without much success, but for some reason he keeps writing. Jim started writing TV series specs in the 1970s and went hungry. He segued into spec movie scripts and starved. He went into the corporate world for a twenty-five year career in broadcasting and advertising, but just couldn't drop his pencil. He found time to write plays in the Chicago theater scene, wrote, produced, and directed numerous short films, videos, and TV commercials, created TV pilots, and even optioned a few movie scripts that never saw the glare of the Klieg lights.

Jim has been writing novels for the past five years. His Richard Sherlock Whodunit series has ranked him in the top 10% of Amazon authors. He is also the author of WHUPPED, a reverse romantic comedy from many different points of view. His most recent novel, Hell No, We Won't Go, A Novel of Peace, Love, War, and Football is his first writing of a 'serious' nature.

If you would like to be the first on your block to get all the up to date news on the detecting of Richard Sherlock and whatever Jim Stevens has to say, please sign up for Jim's email list. All you have to do is drop a line to JimStevensWriter@gmail.com to join a very select and fun-filled group. Don't delay, do it today!